OVER MY
dead
BODY

DENVER ROYALTY

Sheridan Anne
Over My Dead Body - Denver Royalty (Book 2)

Copyright © 2023 Sheridan Anne
All rights reserved
First Published in 2023

Anne, Sheridan
Over My Dead Body - Denver Royalty (Book 2)

Cover Design: Sheridan Anne
Editing: Heather Fox
Formatting: Sheridan Anne

DISCLAIMER

Over My Dead Body was previously published as Carter - Denver Royalty
(Book 2) 2018-2023
The content of Never Gonna Happen remains the same with new edits and
tightening up of each chapter. The story within has not changed. Simply
received a facelift plus new interior formatting, title, and cover.

Chapter One

BRIANNA

A thrill sails through me as I slide my black lace thong back up my legs and over my ass before fixing the waistband into place around my hips. There's nothing quite like Carter Water's ability to get me off at the most inappropriate times.

A hand grips my ass cheek, and I have to jump away, shaking my head at my boyfriend as he tries for round two, but there's only so much action one little bathroom can witness in one night, and my God, we certainly put on a show. "Don't even think about it," I laugh, unable to wipe the smile off my face as I reach for my bridesmaid gown that's haphazardly dumped on the bathroom vanity.

Tonight has been a dream, so much more than I could have

imagined, and I can't wait to see what the rest of it has in store. All I know is that we're only just getting started. And hell, if Carter wants to do that all over again, then consider me down. Only, my hooch needs an hour or two to calm down after that thorough fucking. Carter and I have been together for a while, but he still manages to surprise me, screwing me in ways that would have the kama sutra blushing.

Bracing my hand against Carter's strong shoulder, I step into the champagne-colored gown and shimmy it back up my body before slipping my arms through the holes of the spaghetti straps. Watching my reflection through the bathroom mirror, I make a show of straightening the gown and making sure it's sitting just right before taking a moment to admire the way the soft silk fits over my petite body. I've never felt so glamorous in a dress. I feel incredible. Hell, all of the bridesmaids look incredible tonight.

"God, I love this dress," I murmur to Carter, his heated gaze locked on my body as he goes about tucking himself back inside his suit pants. He straightens his jacket before double checking himself in the mirror and stepping in behind me. His wide chest presses against my back as his fingers brush down my arm and over my waist. Goosebumps begin spreading across my skin, and my knees feel weak from his feather-soft touch. "You and me both," he rumbles, his thick tone right in my ear.

My eyes flutter closed as my hand falls on top of his and as his warm lips drop to my neck, I tilt my head, opening up for him. His lips move across my sensitive skin, and a soft groan sails through my lips as a fiery hot desire blasts through me.

He's too much. So fucking perfect. I'll never get enough.

Carter moves our joined hands down to my thigh, bunching up the silky material, and before I know it, his hand slips between my legs. My fingers lace through his, and I feel the way he rubs me over my lace panties, teasing me just the way he knows I like. "Oh God," I breathe, knowing we need to get out of here, but at the same time, leaving right now would be the worst kind of sin.

He doesn't relent, rubbing my clit through my thong as my knees grow weaker by the second, his tongue moving over the sensitive skin of my neck and sending me into a world full of bliss.

I can't take it anymore.

"That's right, baby," he growls in my ear. "Come for me."

I grind down against him, his words like a trigger, and I come undone as my pussy spasms. I cry out, feeling my body tense with every wave moving through me. My muscles contract as I let out a guttural moan.

"Oh, fuck, Carter."

He sucks a sharp breath through his teeth. "Fuck, what I wouldn't give to taste that sweet, wet cunt."

Good God, the way this man talks to me! Don't get me wrong, I've been with plenty of guys who like to try on the whole dirty talk thing for a little fun, but nobody does it quite like Carter Waters. He has one hell of a filthy mouth, and I am so here for it.

As I come down from my high, Carter stops, and I can feel his arms tense under me, releasing me from his hold as my gown falls back into place. His breathing is ragged, like he's barely holding it together, and he holds my stare through the mirror, seemingly waiting for something.

Soaking in the bliss of my orgasm, I'm ready to give in to whatever he wants from me when his gaze softens. "Come on," Carter whispers. "We better get back out there before someone comes looking for us."

Disappointment floods me, but I know he's right. After all, it's my best friend's wedding and I'm supposed to be the maid of honor. Yet something tells me there's not much *honor* in screwing her brother in the bathroom while she's dancing the night away with her new husband. It's not like she doesn't know. I've been with Carter long enough. I mean, sure. It might have been a sore point at first, but she can see how happy we make each other, and she'd never stand in the way of that.

Sneaking away and having this moment with him was worth it though. Carter Waters is dynamite. I've never met a man who can satisfy me the way he does. Every. Damn. Time. He always rises to the occasion and doesn't dare stop until my legs are shaking and my throat is raw from screaming his name.

Turning in his arms, I press my hands against his chest and look up into those dark eyes that have captured every single part of my soul. "Do we have to?" I murmur, my hand slowly moving up and locking around the back of his neck as I feel his straining erection through his pants, telling me just how badly he wants this too. I rock my thigh against his, watching the way his eyes flutter with need. "The things I wanna do to you—you've got me hungry for more. Wouldn't you rather go upstairs and watch the way I take that thick cock in my mouth? Naked on my knees, my thighs spread apart as my pussy convulses, desperate to feel you stretching me, moving in and out."

Carter groans, his hands braced against my hips as he forces me back a step. His forehead drops to mine, his breathing heavy and full of desire. "You need to stop before I end up fucking you right here over the sink. Again." He pauses, needing a minute to find his cool before finally lifting his head and meeting my needy stare. "You're fucking trouble, Brianna."

A seductive grin stretches across my lips. "You say that as if you never knew, but you and I both know that you get off on my kind of trouble. It was what drew you to me."

I step back into him, closing the gap again, and a shiver runs down my spine, feeling his fingers trailing across the exposed skin of my back. "Don't tempt me, Bri," he murmurs, a plea thick in his tone. "Cassie would kill us if she knew we were in here."

Letting out a sigh, I close my eyes and try to breathe, forcing the desire to simmer down within me. "I know," I groan, hating that he's right.

After giving me a second to find myself, Carter takes my hand and reaches for the door, quickly unlocking it before turning the handle. The door swings wide, and I hastily peer outside, making sure we're not about to be sprung before allowing Carter to lead me out of the bathroom and back to the raging wedding reception.

His excitement pushes him a few steps ahead, but he refuses to release my hand, and I can't help but watch him in front of me. We've been together well over two years, and even still, I find myself so devastatingly attracted to him. The power this man has over me, and in that suit. Crap. He's got me wanting things no woman should ever be bold enough to desire.

Dark hair and even darker eyes with that wickedly sharp jawline covered in just the right amount of stubble. He's ruggedly handsome, but add that sparkle and boyish charm, and good God, he's drop-dead sexy. Hell, all three of the Waters triplets are, but there's something about Carter that gets me every single time. It must be his *I don't give a fuck* attitude that goes along with that cocky alpha confidence that draws me in. Whatever it is, I'm a sucker for it, and I wouldn't have it any other way.

The Waters' family estate is completely decked out and looks absolutely stunning with its tree-lined driveway, landscaped yard filled with fairy lights and decorations, and not to mention the reception hall that's been completely set up to look like a scene from a movie. No other wedding could possibly compare to this. Hell, the reception hall even has a few crystal chandeliers. I'm blown away by how mesmerizing the day has been, but more so, how amazing my best friend looks today. Cassandra Waters is nothing short of stunning. Well, I suppose she's Mrs. Cassandra Payne now.

Every second of today has made me realize I want this with Carter. The past two years have honestly been the best two years of my life. Carter has shown me what it really feels like to have found the love of your life. He's brought me pleasure and peace and an undeniable happiness that I would never be able to find with another, and there's no doubt in my mind that he's the man I'm going to spend the rest of eternity with. He's my man and nothing is ever going to change that. Hell, I can't wait to become his wife and have a million little Carters running around . . . I just need to convince him that he wants it too.

We make our way back to the bridal table where Sean—one of the triplets—is sitting with his wife, Sara, perched happily on his lap. She gives me a beaming smile as Carter takes his seat and promptly pulls me down with him until I'm seated across his lap with my arm slung over his shoulder. I turn to face him, and the overwhelming adoration in his eyes has me leaning in and catching his lips in mine, and the second he kisses me back, I melt.

Every fucking time, I'm putty in his hands.

"I fucking love you," he murmurs against my lips, reaching up and trailing his knuckles down the side of my face as though I were the most precious crystal he's ever seen.

A beaming smile pulls at my lips, threatening to tear my face in two. "I love you, too."

A moment passes between us where he just stares at me, and for just a second, I see our whole life laid out before us. Then just as I go to lean back in, my arm is yanked back by a very beautiful, very energetic bride. Cassie grips my hand and pulls me up off Carter's lap, and he's forced to catch my waist before I sail right into the bridal table.

She dives for Sara next, and I barely get a chance to grab my champagne flute before she's dragging both of us toward the packed dance floor.

"Don't wear her out too much," Carter calls after us, laughter in his rich tone. "Bri needs plenty of energy for what I have planned for her tonight."

Oh God, yes.

Chapter Two

BRIANNA

A thrill sails through my body, sending goosebumps rising over my skin as Cassie looks back at me with such disgust, anyone would think she just stepped in dog shit and was forced to scrape it off her shoe with her teeth.

"I swear, that brother of mine is so gross," Cassie mutters, bracing her hand against my shoulder to lean on me. She reaches down, and I watch with an amused smirk as she grabs her heels and yanks them off one by one before launching them across the room, narrowly missing her new husband's head. I gape at her. This bitch means business. No woman removes her shoes if she's only planning a quick dance. No, we're in it for the long haul.

Straightening back up, I copy her movements and kick off my own shoes. "Where the hell did you disappear to?" Cass asks, watching me as I try to balance without her help. "I've been looking for your bitch-ass for twenty minutes."

Hmm, only twenty minutes? I'm sure we were gone longer than that!

"Where do you think she went?" Sara smirks, a knowing sparkle hitting her bright blue eyes. "Carter was gone too, and when they returned, Bri was more than just flushed."

Cassie's eyes turn on me in horror. "You did not sneak off to have drunk sex with my brother during my wedding."

"I did not," I say outraged, my hand against my heart. Relief flashes in her eyes, but it's short-lived as a wicked smirk stretches across my face. "We snuck off to have mind-blowing, earth-shattering sex, followed by a quick above-panty rub down."

"Ugh," she groans in disgust as I spy Jax, her new husband, walking around the room, collecting the discarded heels, clearly proving he's more than capable of handling his new wife. "Spare me the details."

"You asked," I shrug as the waitress comes around with another tray of champagne flutes. I throw back my current glass and make a quick switch for a new, much fuller one before handing another to Cassie.

"You're going to have to slow down if you intend on catching my bouquet later," Cassie says.

"Please," I scoff. "I could drink a million of these and still be bright and chirpy in the morning."

"I know," she sighs. "It's not fair that you don't get hungover the same way the rest of the world does. I'm gonna be a mess tomorrow."

"But a married mess," I remind her, prompting us each to hold our glasses up and clink them together.

"At least you guys actually get to drink," Sara cuts in as she rubs her hand over her perfect little baby bump while awkwardly swaying to the music. "I would do anything to be able to let loose and have a few glasses of champagne. I can't wait for this baby to come out."

"I bet," I say, looking at her baby bump adoringly. "I can't wait to have a baby. Carter and I would make the cutest babies."

"Jesus, slow down," Cassie scoffs, chugging her champagne. "Do you realize who you're talking about? Carter is not in the market for a baby any time soon. You'd be lucky if you could convince him to buy you a ring."

"Ha," Sara laughs. "That's the understatement of the year."

"I know," I tell them with a heavy sigh, lifting the champagne flute to my lips and taking a much-needed sip. "But a girl can dream."

It's no secret Carter is a reformed playboy, and the thought of knocking up some girl would have him breaking out in hives. He's not ready. Really, we aren't ready as a couple. We're enjoying what we have, and it's been amazing, but I can't help wanting more.

I can picture us being the next couple to walk down the aisle, then a few years after that, we'll start popping out some babies. Either way, I'm thinking about it. I've never been so sure about anything in my life. I can't wait. Just the thought of watching that magnificent man running around with a little boy hanging off his legs makes my ovaries want to explode.

We're in the middle of busting a move when Logan, the third and final of the Waters triplets, comes up and throws his heavy, muscled arms over mine and Sara's shoulders, all but dropping us under his weight. "Have any of you fine ladies seen my woman anywhere?" he asks, his gaze focused out in the crowd, looking for her.

"Nope," I tell him as I finish off my champagne, quickly scanning the crowd for the gorgeous woman who did the impossible and managed to reel in the famous Logan Waters. "But when you find that little hussy, tell her to get her ass on the dance floor. Sara is slowing me down."

"Shut up," Sara laughs. "If I wasn't pregnant, I would have drunk you under the table by now."

"Impossible," I tell her as Logan's brows furrow before glancing across the room toward the open bar his friends have been working their way through. Then without another word, he quickly disappears.

I watch as he goes, but Carter catches my attention at the bridal table, his longing gaze locked firmly on my ass, and giddiness slams through me. I'm overwhelmingly happy that I still have an effect on him. It's no secret that before meeting me, Carter was the biggest playboy in Denver. Hell, he had a nasty reputation for it, and I'm not going to lie, I always worried that I wouldn't be enough for him. But he broke down my walls and proved that I could trust him, that I was all he needed in the world. The second I got over that hurdle, magic took over, and it's been that way ever since. Carter is my world, my rock, and

I wouldn't have it any other way.

As if sensing my stare, his heated gaze travels up my body, lingering on my subtle curves before lifting to meet my heavy stare. Then, unable to resist him a second longer, I hold up my hand and slowly let my finger roll out before indicating for him to join me.

His eyes spark with desire as he gets up from his chair, that heated gaze locked on mine, causing need to bloom deep in my stomach as he slowly strides through the crowd.

Fuck, I love this man.

Carter reaches me in no time, his eyes sparkling as he purposefully holds back, knowing just how much I crave his touch.

I try to keep my cool, but my heart pounds in my chest as I watch him saunter toward me. The way he moves, so confidently and with such purpose, makes my knees weak. I know he's doing this on purpose, teasing me and making me want him even more. And damn it, it's working.

When he finally reaches me, he stands so close that I can feel the heat radiating off his body. I can smell his cologne and feel the roughness of his unshaven face against my skin. It's all I can do to keep from begging him to take me right here and now.

But Carter has never been one to rush things. He enjoys the power he has over me and always takes his time. His warm hands find my waist as he steps in behind me, his chest flush against my back, his body moving so effortlessly with mine, and just when I think his intention is to dance, he leans in and whispers in my ear. "The second I get you alone, I'm gonna taste that sweet cunt, baby girl. I'm going to bend you over and spread those pretty thighs. I want to see you, Brianna. I want to see how your pussy craves me, how fucking wet you are for me. I'm gonna push my fingers inside you, slowly feeling the way your walls contract around them. And only when you're screaming for me, only when you think you can't take it one more fucking second, I'm gonna be right there, tasting you as you come on my tongue."

I'm panting as my knees give out, and Carter is forced to tighten his grip around my waist, keeping me on my feet. "Holy shit," I breathe, suddenly so damn hot.

Carter laughs, his lips dropping to my neck and gently kissing me, but it's all a show. He's only doing it to mask the obvious need and desire in his eyes, needing a moment to find himself before being able to face his little sister.

A moment later, his hand finds mine and he spins me before catching me in his strong arms, my chest pressed right up against his. His arm snakes around my back, holding me to him, right where I should always be. "You're so fucking beautiful," he murmurs as the music slows. He adjusts his hold on me and falls into a slow dance like the world's cheesiest gentleman, but that doesn't stop me from going along with it and falling in love with him that much more.

"And you're a filthy tease."

Carter winks, and I die right there on the spot, knowing I am easily the luckiest girl on the planet.

I watch in awe as the men in the room follow Carter's lead and find their partners. Jax swoops Cass up and pulls her into his chest, kissing her deeply as the onlookers cheer for the newlyweds, while Sean finds

Sara's hand and spins her right into him as she laughs and looks up at her husband in adoration.

The dance floor quickly fills with loved-up couples slow dancing to the music Cassie very carefully picked out. But all I can do is look up at my man and see nothing but love shining back down at me.

Carter pulls me in impossibly tighter, and I rest my head against his chest, listening to the steady rhythm of his beating heart as we move across the dance floor. I bump into Sara and we each balance ourselves against our men and as Sean saves her, I can't help but watch them as they focus on one another, so caught up in their personal love bubble.

"They're so happy," I murmur to Carter.

"Yeah," he says, pride in his tone as his hand slowly trails up and down my back. "They certainly are."

I nod, unable to look away. "They have it all."

"No," he says, pressing a kiss to my head and making my eyes flutter in delight. "*I* have it all."

A soft smile flitters across my lips as my cheeks warm. This man is definitely good with his words. "You don't think they have it all?" I question.

"I guess that depends on what your version of *having it all* means," he tells me. "For me, all I need in this world is you."

"What about the rest of it? Calling me your wife and having our home filled with children," I say, more than aware that I'm getting carried away, but I just can't help it. I'm too caught up in my emotions, and this moment and the atmosphere of the wedding are spurring me on. "I can't wait to have all of that with you."

Carter's body stiffens and his eyes leave mine to look back at Sean and Sara. His brows furrow, and as his body becomes even harder beneath my touch, I realize he's completely freaking out. "Woah," I say, reaching up and gripping his chin before bringing his gaze back to mine. "Stop overthinking this. I don't mean I need to have that right now. I'm talking about the future. I know we're not ready for that. I just . . . that's where I see this going with you."

Carter nods his head and pulls me back into his chest, but the mood has been ruined, and now he's just going along with the motions. I rest my head against him, but his body doesn't fully relax, and the way his heart races is a dead giveaway. The poor guy. I've pushed him too far and completely freaked him out. I know better than that. Carter is like a stray animal that you have to take your time with, slowly creeping toward it and offering treats to gain its trust so it doesn't lash out and attack you. He's probably busy coming up with a million excuses for how to prolong the inevitable.

"Relax," I tell him with a smile as I look up at him, my hand gently moving over his chest. "I didn't mean to freak you out."

"It's okay, babe," he says, his hand squeezing my waist, silently telling me he's alright. "You just caught me off guard. I didn't realize that was something you were thinking about." Then before I get a chance to respond, Carter spins me around, promptly cutting off the rest of our conversation.

At the end of the song, Carter gives me a gentle kiss on the cheek and sends me a wink that has my knees weakening once again, and just like that, he backs away and falls in line with Sean as they make their way back to the bridal table, stopping to refill their glasses. Only now, Carter's looks to be filled with something much stronger than what he usually drinks.

Carter drops down at the table, and suddenly I don't feel like dancing anymore, but I know he needs a moment to sit with his thoughts. Then sensing my gaze, he glances up at me, and I give him a bright smile, hoping like fuck I didn't just destroy something amazing. "I love you," I mouth across the room.

He sends me one of those panty-dropping winks, and as his face lights up once again, I let out a heavy sigh, feeling everything shift back to normal. Then before I can run to the bridal table and convince him to take me upstairs and show him how much I love him, Logan appears and steals the boys away, leaving us girls to do what we do best and keep dancing.

An hour later, Carter and Sean return to the bridal table without Logan, and I make my way over to Carter and collapse in a sweaty heap on his lap. He puts an arm around me, and I sink into his hold, just as we always do, but tonight something is off. "What's wrong?" I question, my head starting to spin from the endless glasses of champagne I've made my way through. "Where did you guys go?"

"Nowhere, babe," he says, his thumb brushing back and forth across my hip. "Don't worry about it."

Carter doesn't meet my stare. He keeps his gaze trained on the door as if waiting for something or someone, and I know without a doubt that something is going down. "Carter?" I prompt, more forcefully until he finally looks up and meets my concerned gaze. "Don't lie to me. What's going on?"

He presses his lips together, and I can practically see him considering whether he's going to speak up or not. Finally, he leans in, his hand dropping to my thigh. "There was a situation with Elle outside, but she's okay now."

"What do you mean *she's okay now?*" I ask, my back stiffening as I search the room for her. "What happened? Did someone try to hurt her?"

"Babe," he mutters, making a point of keeping his tone low. "It's Cassie's wedding. Now's not the time. Can we talk about it later?"

I look at him and take in the seriousness in his gaze before pulling back, my brows furrowed as unease grips hold of my chest and refuses to let go. My fingers trail over the side of his face, desperately searching his eyes. "Are you okay?" I murmur, hating the intense darkness shining through his eyes.

Hearing the fear in my tone, he pulls me in tighter and presses a kiss to my temple, trying to ease my distress. "I'm okay," he finally says as I notice the hand on my thigh is red and raw with grazes and purpling bruises marring his knuckles. "Why don't you go enjoy the rest of your night? There's nothing for you to worry about."

Something cuts straight through my chest and pierces my heart. I can't help but feel as though I've been betrayed somehow, though that doesn't make sense. "You know the bonus of dating countless losers is that I can tell when a man is lying to me," I say, reminding him just how well I know him. "Your hands are bloodied as if you just beat the shit out of someone. What's going on?"

Carter lets out a sigh and looks around to see who's close, and with only Sean close enough, he finally lets it out. "Elle was slipped a date rape drug by some asshole on Jax's team. Logan got there just in time, but she was unconscious and roughed up."

"What?" I breathe, sitting up straight on his lap, my heart pounding erratically in my chest, making me feel as though I'm going to be sick. "Is she . . ."

"Physically, she's going to be fine," Carter tells me, his hand moving in soothing circles on my back as my eyes fill with tears, hating how fucking scared she must have been. Logan even came looking for her over an hour ago, and we all just shrugged it off, too preoccupied with our drinks and dancing to help him look for her, all while she was out there, trying to fend off a fucking rapist. "She just needs to sleep it off. As for everything else . . . I don't know."

"Shit," I breathe, holding onto him a little tighter. "Is there anything I can do?"

"No, babe," he says, his hands still circling my back. "Elle would want you to enjoy the rest of Cassie's wedding. Just please, I know Cass is your best friend and you tell her everything, but just . . . not tonight. Let her enjoy her wedding and remember tonight as the best night of her life."

"I will," I tell him, squeezing his hand. "How's Elle doing? Can I see her?"

"She's upstairs with Logan. The drugs knocked her out, but you'll be able to see her in the morning," he says.

"Okay," I say, sensing he's done talking about it, despite knowing what kind of images and thoughts are streaming through his mind like a dark cloud, poisoning everything in its wake. "Why don't you get yourself another drink and try to relax?"

"That's not such a bad idea," he says before letting out a heavy sigh. He leans in and presses another kiss to my temple before squeezing my leg, indicating for me to hop off him. When I shift to stand, he gets up and heads toward the open bar, and I watch him go with heaviness in my heart.

What happened to Elle tonight is awful, however, Carter isn't the kind of guy to get broken up about it. He gets even. He would have beaten the guy within an inch of his life, made sure Elle was okay, and then called the cops. Don't get me wrong, he feels in a big way, and he would have been devastated to learn that something so horrendous happened on his parents' estate, but he doesn't stew about things that have been dealt with.

Something else is going on, something that's eating him up, which he's refusing to talk about. And for something to have such a profound effect on him, it's big. Really fucking big.

Whatever it is, I just hope he'll come to me when he's ready.

At the end of the night, Carter takes my hand and leads me upstairs to his old bedroom. He loses his suit and lays down on the bed while I put on a show of getting out of my dress and undoing my hair. He's always loved it when I perform for him. He's such a physical being, and I love that about him, and tonight, he's no different. He watches me with an intense desire in his eyes, and all I can think about are those sultry words he uttered in my ear on the dance floor, but as his eyes lift to mine, I realize they're still clouded by something dark, something I don't understand.

I strip out of my underwear and make my way toward him, crawling across the bed and between his legs. Perhaps he needs a release after the massive day we've had. It wouldn't be the first time.

I crawl right up on top of him, straddling his waist, and Carter's hands instantly find my hips, but it seems too robotic, as if he's just going along with the motions. Usually, he gives a squeeze and splays his fingers to feel more skin or pulls me in tighter, but this . . . there's nothing.

Trying not to overthink it, I lower myself to him and press a kiss to his lips. His hand slowly travels up the center of my back and comes to a stop in my hair, prompting me to deepen the kiss, but he's not into it. Instead, he pushes me away, and I sit up with a frown as I try to work him out, heavy rejection tearing through my chest.

"I'm sorry, babe," he murmurs, regret in his dark eyes. I don't reply because quite frankly, I'm fucking confused. Over the past two years, he has never once turned me down, not ever. "Can we just . . . sleep?"

Sleep?

"Um . . . yeah, of course," I say, knowing damn well he hears the hurt in my tone, though I try not to let it show. I climb off him and slide in under the sheets beside him, the same way I do every night, only this time, I've never felt so far away from him.

Carter pulls me into his chest, and his hand strokes up and down my arms as we lay in silence, both of us wide awake, struggling with the demons inside our heads. A single tear falls down my cheek and splashes onto his warm chest, knowing whatever is going on, it's somehow going to tear me apart.

After hours of going through every possible scenario in my head, desperately trying to work out what's got him acting so strange, sleep finally comes. And all I know is, come morning, I wake up to find myself lying alone in an empty, cold bed.

Chapter Three

CARTER

I sit at the breakfast bar of my parents' estate hating myself.

Despite only crashing in the early hours of the morning, I've never endured such a long night in my life. I laid awake, unable to silence the demons tormenting my mind as I held Bri while she slept. What I have to do . . . it makes me sick. I fucking hate myself for having to do this. Just knowing the intense, soul-shattering heartache and pain I'm going to cause has haunted me all night, but it's for the best.

Holding onto this for my own selfish desire is sickening, so no matter how much it's going to destroy me, I have to do it. What other choice do I have?

Hearing someone approach from behind me, I put up all my walls, terrified it might be *her*, terrified this is going to come sooner than I'm ready for. And not having the strength to face what might be coming, I don't even attempt to look up, too fucking ashamed of myself to figure out who stands behind me.

The kitchen cupboards open and close, followed by the sound of someone searching through the fridge, and from the subtle scent of lavender dancing in the air, I can tell it's not my girl.

A glass filled with orange juice clinks against the kitchen counter in front of me. "You look like shit," Sara says, her voice cutting through the tragic thoughts that have tormented me all night. "Spill the beans, Carter. What's going on?"

I shrug my shoulders, not willing to voice anything just yet because the second I do, it becomes too fucking real. "Carter," she demands, her tone low and forceful. "I've known you for fifteen years. I know when something's bothering you. And you know me well enough to know I'm not going anywhere until you tell me what's going on."

I sigh heavily and watch Sara make herself comfortable in the chair beside me, taking extra long to cater to her bump. Then with a deep breath, I face the harsh reality that I've been trying to avoid since the moment I realized what I had to do. "It's Bri," I tell her, keeping my tone low. "I need to end it."

Sara's eyes widen in shock and her jaw falls slack, staring at me as though she doesn't even recognize me. "What?" she breathes, pushing right back off the chair and getting to her feet, immediately beginning to pace in outrage. "Why the hell would you do something so stupid?" she demands. "Bri is your perfect match. She's everything you've ever needed and everyone can see how fucking perfect she is for you. Why would you be so stupid as to break up with her? It's clear to anyone with a pair of eyes that you're both madly in love with one another."

"I know," I sigh, my stomach clenching with the need to be sick. "But she wants more than what I can give her. Kids. Marriage."

"So?" Sara grunts. "What's wrong with that? I'm failing to see how that's a deal breaker. It's the natural course of any relationship, and it's clear you're heading in that direction. I don't see what the problem is. You've been with her for two years now. Don't you want all of that with her?"

My gaze falls to the untouched glass of juice in front of me as I shake my head. "You have no fucking idea how much I wish I did. If I was going to settle down and do the whole marriage and kids thing, it would be Bri a million times over, but it's not what I want. She has this perfect vision of how she wants her life to pan out. She wants the big wedding and all the kids running around, and no matter how much I try to change my own mind, I can't. I'm never going to want those things. I'm content with it being just me and her, but . . ."

"She's not," Sara says with a sigh, finally understanding where I'm coming from. She sits down again, her gaze just as heavy as mine. "You need to talk to her, Carter. Just don't rush into it and end things without offering her a conversation. There might be some kind of middle ground you can find to make this work. She might be okay living without the big wedding and kids."

"And I'll never be okay knowing I'm holding her back from the things she desperately wants in life," I tell her before letting out a sigh. "Of course I'm going to offer her a conversation, but trust me, this isn't something she's going to want to negotiate on. She's either all in or all out. There's no middle ground here. Brianna isn't looking to live only half a life. She wants what she wants, and what's more, she deserves everything, but I just can't give it to her."

I pause, bracing my elbows on the counter and dropping my face into my hands. "She said last night that she wants what you and Sean have. She sees how happy you guys are and she wants that for herself, and fuck, Sara. You have no fucking idea how desperately I wish I could give her the world, and the fact that I can't has me sick to my fucking stomach. It's not fair for me to let this keep going. It's so fucking selfish to hold onto her, knowing I'll never give her what she needs."

Sara presses her lips into a hard line, her eyes welling with tears, feeling the turmoil that has been plaguing me since the moment Bri uttered the word marriage last night. "I'm so sorry," she whispers, placing a hand on my shoulder and giving a comforting squeeze. "The two of you are just . . . you're perfect together, but I understand it, and you're right. If there's no way for you to give her the things in life that are going to make her happy, then you have to end it and allow her the chance to move on with someone who will give her what she needs. God, I hate this. I hate that you're hurting and have to do this. You have no idea how badly I wish I could fix this for you."

Giving her a comforting smile, I reach up and place my hand over hers on my shoulder. "I don't expect you to," I tell her.

"I know," she smiles. "You and Logan are like brothers to me, so when something hurts you, it hurts me too, and I can't help but try to fix it for you, but there's nothing I can do. I just wish I could take away all that pain because the second you talk with her, the second you break her heart, the both of you are going to be devastated, and it's going to be one hell of a long journey trying to heal and find happiness again."

"I know," I say with a sad smile as I put an arm around her shoulder and give her a quick squeeze. "But you know me, I'll find a way to be okay. It's Bri I'm worried about. The idea of her hurting . . . fuck. Promise me you won't lose touch with her. Be there for her. She's going to need you, Cass, and Elle."

"I promise," she says. "You know I'll never push her aside. You might be a brother to me, but she's like a sister to me too. I love her just like I love you. She's going to be alright. It'll take some time, and she might be in a really dark place for a little while, but she'll come around. I'll make sure she's okay."

I nod, feeling everything weaken within me. Knowing I'll break if I allow this to carry on, I swallow my pain and give her a reassuring smile. "How are you doing?" I ask, glancing down at the small bump protruding from her stomach, the very first niece or nephew of what I'm sure will be many.

"I'm doing good," she says. "But I'm hungry, like always hungry. It's ridiculous. I'm worried this pregnancy is turning me into an elephant."

"Don't be ridiculous. You're tiny and fucking gorgeous. If anything, you could use a few extra pounds. Besides, it'll give Sean a little something to grab hold of." Sara gasps, her eyes widening as if horrified, but we both know she's a dirty little minx when it comes to my brother. Besides, did she forget who she was talking to? A laugh rumbles through my chest, and I go easy on her. "Has the morning sickness gone away?"

"Yeah, but my tits hurt," she tells me with a cringe, giving them a rub just to prove her point.

My face scrunches. Sara is like a sister to me. I've known her since we were teenagers, and hearing about her tits really doesn't give me the thrill that hearing about Bri's does. Hell, it's like watching your sister feel herself up. "Yeah, that's too much information."

"You asked," Sara laughs, shrugging her shoulders before getting up and searching the fridge again. She comes back a moment later with a bowl of cereal in hand, her spoon already in her mouth. "Listen, if you're going to . . . end it," she says around the spoon, wincing as she brings up our earlier conversation, knowing how much it kills me to talk about it, "Do it nicely. Bri puts on a tough exterior, but you know just as well as I do that she's a marshmallow inside. This is going to destroy her."

I nod my head, knowing all too fucking well how she is on the inside. Hell, I'm in love with her. I know every little thing that makes up the incredible woman she is. Sara isn't telling me anything I don't already know. "Yeah," I say, unable to find the right words to convey how I'm really feeling.

"Okay. Well, I'm gonna go and check on Elle," she tells me, giving my shoulder another squeeze. "Sean and I are around if you need us."

And with that, she gives me one last broken smile that doesn't reach her eyes before trailing back up the hallway and leaving me here to wallow in my thoughts.

With a sigh, I throw back my orange juice and head upstairs, knowing the longer I put this off, the harder it's going to be.

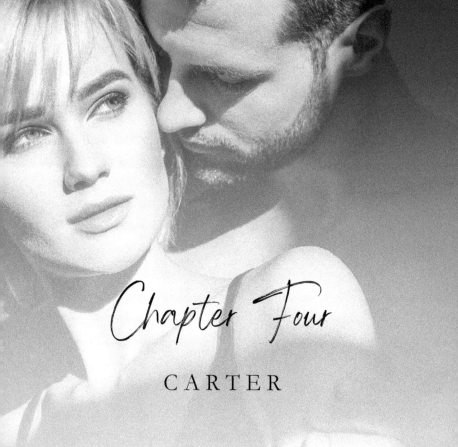

Chapter Four

CARTER

After a night like last night, I know Bri won't be up for another few hours, but if this is the last few hours I'll have to call her mine, then I'm going to soak it up and take my sweet fucking time.

Resisting the urge to climb back in bed and hold her, knowing the second I hold her, I'll change my fucking mind, I take a seat on the couch and watch the steady rise and fall of her chest as she sleeps. She's so goddamn beautiful. Bri is the love of my life, and I hate myself for having to do this to her. I will never find another woman who makes me feel the way she does, who makes me come alive like she does, who makes me so fucking happy I could die.

Leaving her is going to tear her to pieces, but in the long run, it's the best thing to do for her. Her heart will eventually heal, and she'll move on with someone who can give her the life she's always craved and the babies she wants to raise. God, her children are going to be fucking gorgeous with those big green eyes and feisty little personalities. They're gonna be hard work, but she'll love every moment of it.

For me, it's simple. I will never love again. I've already come to this conclusion. It's just a fact, but because I love her, I need to do this. I want to give her the world, and if losing her is how I'm going to do that, then that's what I have to do, no matter how fucking hard it's going to be.

Minutes turn into hours, and the longer I wait, the worse it gets.

A part of me wants to go and shake her awake so I can get this over with, rip it off like a Band-Aid. The other part is screaming at me to continue being the selfish bastard I am and wait it out; to cherish the last few moments I have with her.

When Bri finally stirs, I curse myself for what I'm about to do and seek out every last bit of courage I can find within myself.

Don't fucking back out, you goddamn pussy.

Why can't I just continue being a selfish prick? I'm so fucking happy with her. She'd forever resent me for not popping the question or knocking her up, but at least I'd be happy. I've known this was coming for a while, but seeing her face last night and realizing just how badly she wanted it made me realize how fucking selfish I've been. There was a part of me that hoped she would be content with just me, and I'm not going to lie, it fucking hurts that she's not, but I can't be the person to hold her back from what she truly wants. The idea of this incredible woman resenting me makes me want to hurl.

Bri reaches up and pushes her hair off her face before rubbing her eyes and groaning, not ready to wake up, and I savor the sound, not sure if I'll ever get the chance to hear it again. She stretches out across the bed, clearly searching for me, and when she realizes I'm not there, her head pops up and she squints across the bed.

She sits up and looks around the room. There's no doubt her mind has already gone to the worst scenario after the way I turned her down last night. "I'm here," I murmur into the quiet room, not wanting her to panic.

Her head flicks around at the sound of my voice, and I take her in. If today were any other day, I'd be laughing at the way her mascara has smudged beneath her eyes during the night. Instead, all I can think about is how much worse it's going to get when her tears fall.

My chest aches, and it's impossible to suck in a deep breath, but I deserve the agony and heartache that's about to come.

Bri watches me from the bed, and a curious expression crosses her beautiful face. "What are you doing over there?" she yawns as she sits up in bed and lets the sheet fall around her waist, exposing her perfect tits. And with the morning sun streaming through the window, dancing across her skin and the white sheets, fuck. She's never looked so goddamn beautiful.

I force my gaze to remain on her eyes, knowing just how detrimental one glance at her body could be right now. "Couldn't sleep," I reply with a subtle bounce of my shoulders as if trying to shrug it off as nothing.

"I noticed," Bri murmurs, her tone sad as if already expecting the worst. Her gaze drops from mine, and it cuts me like a knife straight to the heart. She leans down beside the bed and scoops up the shirt I'd worn at the wedding last night.

She gets up and makes her way around the bed, showing off her petite body draped in nothing but my shirt, making what I have to do that much harder. She sits at the end of the bed facing me, and I swear it's as if she can read my mind, or at the very least, sense something isn't right.

There hasn't been one single morning in the two years we've been together where she's woken up and not touched me, and seeing her here, so close and yet keeping her hands so calmly in her lap is killing me. It's wrong. So fucking wrong. It feels as though I'm missing the most important part of my morning. I need to reach out and touch her, but the second I do, I won't have the strength to break her heart.

"Do you know how Elle is doing? Is she alright?" she questions formally, as if she's trying to prolong whatever fears are circling in her mind, the fears I'm about to make reality.

"Yeah," I murmur, finding it difficult to meet her gorgeous green eyes. "I spoke with Logan not long ago. She's fine. Apart from a few cuts and bruises, she came out unscathed. She's a fighter. She's going to do whatever it takes to put that asshole away."

"That's good," she murmurs, also unable to look up and meet my stare, telling me she already knows where this is going. Just that thought alone has my heart sinking and makes me want to fall at her feet and beg for forgiveness.

Brianna focuses those deadly green eyes on her bare thighs, and I watch in agony as a perfectly round tear falls down her cheek and splashes against her creamy thigh. "Why are you doing this?" she whispers, her voice breaking with undeniable pain.

Fuck. I haven't even said a word and this is already killing me.

"Babe," I breathe, my heart on my sleeve. My eyes close as the pain becomes impossible to bear, and the words don't seem to come, so we sit in an excruciating silence, neither of us knowing where to go from here.

I feel her waiting for me to tell her she's wrong, but the longer she waits, the clearer it all becomes. Her tears start to fall as I lean forward in my chair with my head in my hands, trying my hardest not to crumble.

Bri moves her head ever so slightly, and I know she's ready to talk. She takes a deep breath, and I lift my head to meet her eyes, watching as she wipes her tears. "Am I . . . Am I just not enough for you?" she questions.

Fuck. How could she ever think that?

Her self-doubt has me throwing myself out of my chair and crumbling to my knees at her feet. I grab hold of her warm hands, looking up into those sweet green eyes that have completely captured my soul. "Don't say that," I demand, my desperation clear in my broken tone. "Fuck, Brianna. You're everything I've ever wanted and more. I fucking love you so goddamn much."

"Then . . . I don't understand," she says, her tears staining her rosy cheeks. "Why are you doing this to us? We're perfect together. You and me. I love you, Carter. I want to be with you."

"Please, don't cry," I tell her, pulling her off the edge of the bed until she drops right into my lap, her arms and legs circling me as she holds onto me with everything she has, but the moment she buries her face into my neck and I feel her wet tears against my skin, I fucking break.

"I'm sorry," I tell her, my hand in the back of her hair, holding her to me, too fucking terrified to let her go. "Please believe me when I tell you this is the hardest thing I've ever had to do."

"Then don't do it," she begs. "Don't ruin us."

I shake my head, my heart racing as I struggle to catch my breath. "I can't give you what you need," I murmur.

"You can," she says. "Don't you get it? You're everything I need. You're my whole fucking world, Carter. Please, I love you."

I run my hands down her hair, attempting to soothe her, but it's a lost cause. *Rip it off like a Band-Aid,* I remind myself. *Don't drag this shit out.* You're only making it worse for her.

"No, babe. I'm not even close to what you need," I tell her, those very words spoken out loud blacken my shattered heart. She lifts her head from my neck, meeting my broken stare with one of her own. "You want the big white wedding. You want to walk down the aisle and say your vows in front of all of your friends and family. You want to spend nine months nursing your pregnant belly and living in bliss until the day you give birth and finally get to raise a family of your own. You want it all, Bri, and in ten years when you're getting older and you're still not pregnant and are still waiting for me to put a ring on your finger, you're going to resent me."

"What are you saying?" she asks, her bottom lip wobbling. "You don't want to marry me?"

"No, Bri, but it's not because I don't love you. If I could choose anyone in this world to spend the rest of my life with, it would be you. I'd choose you every fucking time. It's just that marriage is not something I've ever envisioned for myself," I explain. "I'm content with it being just you and me, living the way we are. I thought you knew this."

"I did," she says, wiping her eyes on my shirt. "But I thought you were just being an idiot and that would change when you found the right girl. I thought you'd grow up and be ready to settle down, and I had hoped that maybe I would have been enough for you to want those things."

"Fuck, Brianna. You are my everything. You're the love of my fucking life, but I can't give you everything you need."

"I can try," she pleads, the tears falling more ferociously. "I can . . . I don't know. Maybe I don't need the big white wedding. If it's a choice between you and marriage, then I'd pick you every fucking time. We can work around this. It doesn't have to be over."

"No, baby. I'm not going to be the reason that you don't get everything you've ever dreamed of in life. You deserve to get married. You deserve the wedding of a lifetime. I'm not going to hold you back and have you hating me years down the track. I won't."

"No," she sobs. "Don't. Please."

I let out a breath and bring my finger up to her chin, gently raising it until those green eyes lock onto mine, knowing that what I'm about to say is going to be what seals the deal. "What about kids?" I ask her. "I see it in your eyes when you look at Sara's belly. You want a family of your own. You want to be a mom and raise your beautiful babies, so desperately that thought of never getting to meet them tears you apart."

Understanding dawns in her gorgeous green eyes, and she looks at me in horror, seeing this just as clearly as I do. We're not compatible, not anymore. "You don't want them?" she questions, fear shining in her eyes.

I shake my head, knowing just how much I'm breaking her. "No, Bri," I murmur, my fingers brushing over her soft cheek. "I don't."

"Ever?" she asks, her lips trembling as her grip loosens around me.

With a nod, I confirm her worst nightmare. "Ever."

Agony shoots through her eyes, and she looks at me with complete betrayal, her heart in pieces on the ground between us. She pushes up off me and stands in the center of the room looking like only half the woman I know her to be. Bri crosses her arms over her chest, closing herself off from me with furrowed brows, trying to take it all in.

I get to my feet, having no fucking idea what I'm going to say as she remains silent, just staring at me, and fuck, I want nothing more than to run to her and take it all back.

Bri wipes at her red eyes before finally finding her voice. "How could you let us go on for two years knowing that we could never work?" she questions, that broken tone destroying every last shred of goodness within me. "Why would you let me fall in love with you? What kind of monster does that?"

I walk to her, making sure she completely understands what I'm trying to say. "I'm sorry. I was fucking selfish. I thought you knew that I didn't want those things. I thought we were happy and content living as we were. I knew you thought about marriage and children as a possibility, but it wasn't until last night I realized just how important those things were to you. We've never had that conversation."

"Yeah," she scoffs. "Because I was too fucking terrified of scaring you away. I thought you'd get there on your own."

"I want to give you the world, Bri, but this . . . I just can't. You're not going to be happy living in a world where you don't get to be someone's wife or mother."

She looks away, and I step right into her, gripping her chin and forcing her gaze back to mine. "As much as it kills me to say, if it means that you need to be with someone else to get everything you deserve and want out of life, then that's what's got to happen. I need to bow out now and let you have that chance."

Bri stares up at me, and I watch as her walls start locking into place, knowing this might be the last time I ever get to see inside. She's reached her emotional threshold and has taken just about all she can handle. "You're telling me I've spent the last two years falling in love with the wrong man?"

Fuck, that hurt. But yeah, she's right.

I don't respond, but she doesn't need me to, she sees the pain all over me. She's always been so stubborn, always needed to get the last word, and with that, she delivered the final blow, taking me out in one fell swoop.

Bri holds my stare for a moment longer, the silence between us like knives straight through the chest. Then all too soon, she presses her lips into a hard line and nods, finally accepting what will be. And with that, she collects her phone off the bedside table and disappears through the door, leaving me a shallow, broken shell of the man I used to be.

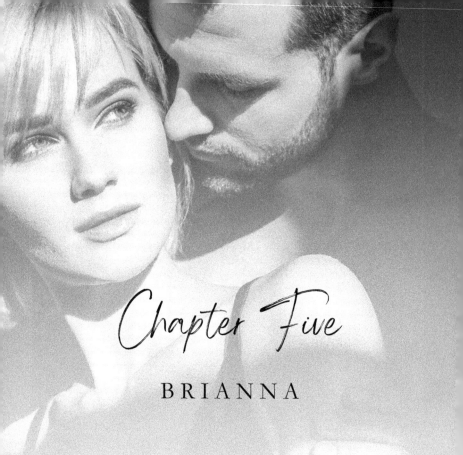

Chapter Five

BRIANNA

After rushing down the stairs in nothing but Carter's dress shirt, I barge my way through every damn door until I find the one person who could possibly give me any sort of comfort right now.

Fuck. Why is this house so damn big?

I need to get out of here. Where the fuck are you, Bobby?

I wipe my sore eyes, but it's useless as another tear streaks down my face. I can hardly breathe, the wretched sobbing now uncontrollable. Fuck, I've never felt so broken, so hollow and empty. How is this happening? Hell, why is it happening? We were so fucking happy. Not even twelve hours ago, he was taking me in the guest bathroom outside his sister's wedding reception. He was supposed to be my forever. Carter Waters is my soulmate, and I know that with every fiber of my being.

I will never, and I mean *never*, find another man who can capture my heart the way he has.

Despite putting on a tough exterior, I know I don't have what it takes to move on from this. My heart is his, every last bit of it belongs to Carter. He took it from me two years ago, claimed it as his own, and refused to give it back, even now. Hell, I don't want it back. I just want him.

Pushing my way through a fourth door, I finally stumble across my twin brother sprawled out across the living room floor. The sound of the door slamming against the wall startles him awake, and he flies up into a sitting position, his eyes wide. "What the fuck?" he grunts in a panic before taking me in. His face scrunches at my attire, but the moment his gaze lifts to my face and sees the heartache in my eyes, he breaks, and I run to him. "What's wr—" he starts to ask, but his words cut off as I slam into his chest, my arms flying around his neck and clinging to him like he's my only lifeline.

The sobs come hard and fast as my brother holds me, his hand awkwardly patting my back. I curl into him, my face firmly against his chest as my tears quickly stain his shirt. His hand comes up to my head and he gently runs his fingers through my hair. "Shhhhh," he soothes as he rocks me the same way Mom would when we were kids.

We sit for ages as he allows my tears to run their course.

"Are you ready to talk about it?" Bobby questions when the heavy sobs slow down.

"No," I murmur, wiping the back of my hand across my face, drying up the last of my tears. "I just want to get out of here."

"Okay," he says without question, reaching across the living room floor and grabbing his phone, wallet, and keys. "Do I need to beat the shit out of him first?"

"No," I sigh, knowing damn well Carter would sit there and take every last punch until there's nothing left of him.

Getting to my feet, I find the closest bathroom and get a good look at myself. I'm a fucking mess.

I do my best to clean myself up, running a hand through my hair and splashing water over my face, but let's be real, nothing is going to take away the puffy, bloodshot eyes and splotchy cheeks. I'm just going to have to deal with the fact that I'll be looking like shit for the foreseeable future. Thank fuck for makeup.

Stepping out of the bathroom, I find Bobby waiting in the hallway, holding up a pair of sweatpants, and I silently take them from him before sliding them up my bare legs. I have to roll them over a few times to keep them up before yanking hard on the drawstrings and tying them off.

"Are you ready to go?" Bobby asks, his gaze shifting around the foyer as if preparing for some kind of threat. Though in reality, I know he's searching for Carter, more than ready to destroy him for hurting his twin sister.

"I should say bye to Cassie first," I tell him. "They're leaving on their honeymoon this afternoon, so I probably won't get a chance to see her before she goes."

"That's not a bad idea," he murmurs before following me through the house, knowing damn well he'd want to take a moment to chat with Jax.

I find myself walking around like a scared little rabbit, constantly searching, praying Carter doesn't come around the next corner. Hell, just one look in his eyes would have me on my knees, begging him to take me back, and I'm almost certain that would kill me.

We make it to Cassie and Jax's door, free of any run-ins, and I gently knock before pushing my way in. The curtains are still drawn and they're both in an alcohol-induced, deep sleep, but I'm not surprised. Neither of them hold their liquor well, not to mention how exhausting yesterday was for them.

Pleased they have a sheet covering what I assume are two very naked bodies, I make my way across the room and bend down beside Cass before gently shaking her shoulder. "Cass," I whisper into the darkened room as Bobby remains by the door, not wanting to wake Jax just to say goodbye when they'll probably talk later.

Cassie moans as she rolls over to face me, peering up at me through squinted, sleepy eyes. "Ughhhh, whadayawant?" she mumbles.

"Nothing," I say with a forced smile. "I just need to get going and wanted to say goodbye in case I don't see you before you leave."

"Mmkay," she sighs as she closes her eyes, unknowingly letting me off the hook so that I don't have to explain the reason for my current state. After all, I want her to enjoy her honeymoon, and if she knew that Carter had just broken up with me, she'd never get on that plane, and I sure as hell don't want her worrying about me. She'll have plenty of time to do that when she gets back. "I'll text you later."

"Alright, have a great honeymoon. Have wicked hot sex, and remember to take lots of photos. I wanna see it all."

"You want photos of the wicked hot sex?" she murmurs.

I can't help but laugh, and the sound seems so foreign on my tongue. "No, you idiot. Just have a great time."

Glancing down at her, I realize she's already fast asleep again, and not wanting to disturb her more, I slip out of the room and head downstairs with Bobby, more than ready to get out of here.

Breaking out through the main door, I race down the stairs in desperation. "Hey," Bobby says, his long legs easily keeping up with my pace as he reaches out and takes my hand, the same way he used to when we were kids. "I love you, and whatever happened back there, you're gonna get past it."

I look up at the guy who has been my rock for so long and give him a tight smile, knowing he couldn't be more wrong. "Love you, too, Bobby. Now, please, take me home."

Home. Now that's something I haven't thought about yet. I've been living with Carter since the day I graduated college. I don't have somewhere to call my own, somewhere to escape the reminders of him.

"Shit," I cry as the realization truly dawns on me. I look up at my brother with wide eyes, horror taking hold of my chest and squeezing until I can't breathe. "I don't have a home."

"You'll always have a home," he tells me, reaching his truck. He stops and pulls the door open for me before helping me up, and the moment I'm settled in my seat, he gives me a comforting smile. "You can stay at my place as long as you want."

I give him a smile, but it doesn't reach my eyes. He knows it and I know it, but there's nothing we can do about it right now other than accept just how utterly broken I am.

We arrive at Bobby's bachelor pad twenty minutes later, and I drag myself out of the truck and into the elevator that takes us up to the penthouse. Stepping into his apartment, I bypass every room and beeline straight for the shower, hoping the hot water will help to wash away some of the raw emotion lingering on my heart.

Carter's shirt drapes over my body, and as I stare at my reflection in the mirror, the tears start all over again. Not being able to handle it, I tear the shirt over my head and lean into the shower, turning on the hot spray of water.

Stepping straight in, I let the hot water wash over me, and I find myself standing there for what could be minutes or hours. I hardly know, but it's not long before my knees give out, and I fall to the ground with my head in my hands, heavy sobs tearing from the back of my throat.

Bobby knocks at the door and I hastily try to wipe my tears before he comes barging in, but it's too late. "Come on," he says as he unfolds the towel that sits on the vanity. He makes a point not to look at me, offering me what little privacy he can while knowing if he didn't barge in here, I would never have gotten out. "You've been in here over an hour."

Shit.

I usually don't condone my twin brother barging in on me in the shower, but today, I couldn't care less. Getting up off the floor, I step out of the shower, and Bobby wraps the towel around me before pulling me into his arms. Despite how awkward it feels, he knows I need this, and he'll grin and bear it until I'm ready because that's just the type of man he is.

After a minute, Bobby leads me to my room, and I find a pair of sweatpants and one of Bobby's oversized hoodies on the bed. "Are you ready to talk about it yet?" he asks as he leans against the door frame.

I sit down on the bed and shake my head, knowing that the moment I open my mouth, the floodgates will break, and I'm not ready to cry again. Hell, the thought of talking about it makes me feel sick, especially when it's Bobby I'd be talking to. I don't like him seeing me like this, but I know he's always got my back. I guess that comes with the territory of being twins.

"Alright," he says with an encouraging smile. "Why don't you put on some of that bullshit reality TV crap you like and have a sleep. It will make you feel better."

God, he knows me well.

"Do you need me to bring in the carton of ice cream and a spoon?" he asks. "I could go and get some trashy magazines and chocolate."

"What?" I grunt.

"I don't know," he says with a shrug of his big shoulders. "Don't you chicks usually like to binge-watch TV and eat shit when you're going through something like this?"

"I don't know," I say. "I've never gone through something like this before."

"Should I call Cass?" he questions.

"No," I sigh, grateful for his help, but I'm not going to burden Cassie with this the day after her wedding. "Let her enjoy her newlywed bliss. I'll see her when she gets back from their honeymoon."

"Alright," he says with another tight smile.

I hop up from the bed and drop my towel before reaching for the sweatpants, not giving two shits about anything. "Ahhh, gross," Bobby grunts, shielding his eyes in disgust. "That's my cue to leave." He does just that and backs out of the room without another word before silently closing the door behind him, leaving me to wallow in self-pity.

Pulling his oversized hoodie on, I slide under the covers before noticing the painkillers, the remote, and the box of tissues already waiting for me on the bedside table. Bobby is going to make one special woman very happy, hopefully someday soon.

Reaching for the remote, I turn on the TV before searching for the latest *Kardashians* season. I relax into my pillow and get halfway through the first episode before my eyes become heavy and I fall into a dreamless sleep.

I startle awake a few hours later when Bobby drops heavily onto the bed beside me. "Wake up," he grunts. "If you keep sleeping you won't be able to sleep tonight."

He couldn't be more wrong. All I want to do is sleep for the rest of time. Maybe I could live the rest of my life unconscious to save myself from the pain of reality.

I groan as I push myself over to use Bobby as a pillow. "I went and got all your stuff from Carter's place," he tells me. "But you'll need to go back eventually. I'm sure I missed some things."

Gratitude pounds through my veins. I don't know how I would have faced having to go over there and get all my stuff. "Thanks," I grumble, but the realization of seeing the pile of bags, filled with my things in the corner of the room just reminds me that it's truly over. "Today would suck so much more if I didn't have you."

"You're my best friend, Bri. My wombmate! I'd do just about anything to see the smile return to your face. I hate that you're hurting, and I hate even more that I can't do anything to help you. I just wish I understood why this happened. Everything seemed so good between you two. I thought this was endgame."

"I know," I mumble into his chest. "Love you."

"Love you, too, sis," he says as he pulls his arms tighter around me.

Letting out a sigh, I grab the remote and turn off the TV before sitting up and making myself comfortable. After everything Bobby has done for me today, he deserves to know what's going on. "He ended it," I say.

"I guessed as much," he tells me, meeting my broken stare. "It just doesn't make sense. I saw the two of you during the wedding. Everything seemed fine. I thought he was madly in love with you."

"He was. *He is,*" I say. "But our lives are heading in different directions. We want different things, and he doesn't want to be the reason I don't get everything I've always wanted. Marriage and children isn't something he's willing to negotiate on. He's never going to want them and I . . ."

"Shit," Bobby sighs, knowing just how important those factors are to me for my future. "He's a fool for not wanting that with you."

I don't respond because, yeah, he is, but how can I blame somebody for being honest about what they want in life? If he doesn't want to have children then I'm not going to be the woman who forces it on him.

"What am I going to do, Bobby? I love him so much," I cry. "These past two years, all I've done is picture our lives together. I wanted to be with him for the rest of my life. He's my soul mate. I'll never find a love like that again."

"You will," Bobby insists, reaching out and squeezing my knee firmly. "It might take some time and a few tries, but you'll get there eventually. You're the most amazing woman I know and men are going to be lined up, dying to give you the world."

"I doubt that," I grumble.

"I know you can't see it just yet, but in time, this pain is going to fade, and you'll find yourself again. You'll go through your hot-girl single era, and Cass is going to hate you because you're having all the fun while she's shacked up with the husband. And then one day, you'll realize that you're okay and ready to open your heart again."

Fuck, I love this big idiot so much.

"I hope so," I tell him.

"I know so. Now get your ass out of bed. I bought you a bottle of wine and Chinese food, and I'm gonna be pissed if it gets cold."

I doubt I could eat right now, but the bottle of wine sounds good, so I let him drag me out of bed and into the kitchen, despite my night of heavy drinking. Bobby serves me up a plate of food and shoves it into my hands, not taking no for an answer, and I try my hardest to eat it, but all I do is push it around the plate.

A list of things I need to do piles up in my mind, and at the very top is finding my own place to live. With wine in my veins and a new determination, I get up and find Bobby's iPad before returning to my spot. I search through all the available listings, and in the space of two seconds, that determination crumbles. There's absolutely nothing.

With a groan, I push the iPad away.

"What are you doing?" he questions, a mouth full of fried rice.

"I need to find somewhere to live," I tell him.

"That you do," he agrees. "But there's no rush. My home is yours until you find the perfect place to call your own."

"Thanks," I say with a tight smile.

It's probably for the best. I love Bobby, and being around him is going to help keep my mind off Carter. The only downfall is that he's in the NHL and plays for a team in New York. He managed to get a few days off for the wedding, but he'll be returning to New York soon, which is when shit is going to get way too hard.

I need to find a way to be strong while he's gone and while I'm waiting for Cassie to return. I don't know how I'm going to get through this, but for now, all I can do is throw back this bottle of wine and hope for the best.

Hearing a text come through on my phone, I groan as I get up and find it laying somewhere in the messy sheets of my bed, and as I go to check it, my blood runs cold. Maybe it's Carter texting to say this was all some sick joke. Maybe he takes it back and wants to give this a try. Maybe we could compromise, start off small, maybe get a dog or a snake. He'll eventually see that we belong together. He has to . . . right?

Unlocking my phone, my hopes plummet as I see it's just a text from Cassie, and letting out a sigh, I click on the notification and watch as her words appear on the screen.

Cassie – Hey, sorry about this morning. I was so exhausted! I had such a great night. I can't believe how magical it was. Hope you're having a great day. We're just about to board the plane for Italy, so I'll check in with you when we get there. Xx

I suck it up as I reply to her text.

Bri – I hope you have a great honeymoon. I love you so much. Your wedding was absolutely beautiful. I'm so proud of you. Make sure you send heaps of photos and have a safe flight. Xxx

Cassie – Thanks, Bri. I love you, too. Tell my idiot brother I love him as well.

Shit. That stung.

Bri – Will do, Cass.

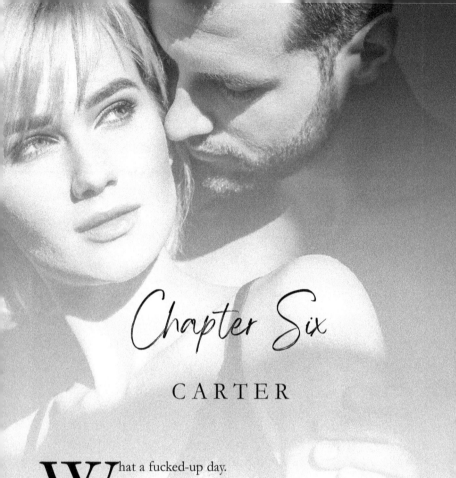

Chapter Six

CARTER

What a fucked-up day.

I let the love of my life walk out the door, after shattering her heart and destroying any hope she held of building a life with me. I'd give anything to want that with her, to be able to give her everything she needs.

She's never going to talk to me again, hell, she won't even be able to look at me. I tore her to shreds. I just wish I would have realized sooner just how deeply she wanted that, and yet, I can't bring myself to regret the two years I spent loving her. But Bri was right. I let her waste two years of her life falling in love with the wrong man.

I'm nothing but a selfish prick.

I sit in my too-empty house, these four walls no longer feeling like a home, as I make my way through a bottle of whiskey, desperately trying to numb the pain. Bobby came to collect all her shit, and it was fucking tragic—the final nail cracking into place and cementing the fact that I let her go. Bobby was two seconds away from beating the living shit out of me, and I didn't even care. In fact, I would have welcomed it.

Those tears killed me. I should have gone after her. I never should have let her walk out the door, and I never should have broken her heart. I should have manned up and given her the life she so desperately craves, despite my feelings on marriage and kids.

The second she left. I knew I'd made the biggest mistake of my life, one I will never be able to make up for. She knows my true colors now, and even if I begged for forgiveness, she'd never come back to me, nor should she. I know I did the right thing. She needs this, but fuck, I hate it.

I pour another drink and throw it back.

Maybe I could try and mend things with her on a friendship level. It would be a long shot, but at least I could have her in my life. I could watch her grow and heal from the hell I've put her through, watch her date a string of men, not a single one of them being good enough for her. But one day, one of those assholes will get down on one knee and give her everything I couldn't, and soon enough, she'll be pregnant and glowing.

Fuck, standing on the sidelines watching that would be torture, but also so rewarding. Bri will be such a fucking gorgeous bride, but pregnant? Shit, she'll be breathtaking. I can just imagine it now, but it would be another man's child within her womb. Never mine.

I pour another.

Watching her leave was the hardest thing I've ever done. I stood at my bedroom window in my parents' estate and watched as Bobby helped her up into his truck, tears streaming down her face. I wanted to scream out to her, tell her it was a sick joke just so I could hold her in my arms just one more time, but then Bobby drove away, and I was left feeling hollow.

How the hell am I going to get through this? She's my rock, my fucking world, and I've torn her to pieces.

I'm a monster.

The bottle of whiskey is just about empty, and I bypass the glass, lifting the bottle right to my lips and finishing the last few drops. The bottle clatters to the ground as my head falls into my hands, the anguish of what I've done eating me alive.

I promised that I would never hurt her.

Fuck, I hate myself.

A text lights up my phone screen, and the moment I see the picture of Bri and me that she set as my wallpaper last year, anger explodes through my body. Reaching for the empty glass tumbler beside me, I launch it across the room, an agonized roar breaking from deep within my chest.

The glass smashes against the wall, shattering into a million pieces, and before I know it, I'm tearing the room to shreds, desperate to find just a sliver of peace.

Sorrow and grief grasp onto me in a devastating chokehold, and I pull the room apart until my breath comes in sharp pants. I collapse onto the bed, the very same bed I shared with her, and stare up at the ceiling.

Night has come, and the thought of sleeping alone in our bed kills me. Before Bri, I had never spent the night with a woman. It was always get in and get out. I had no attachments, but then she came along and changed it all.

I'll never be the fucking same.

Brianna came in like a damn tornado. She turned my world upside down, and I am absolutely nothing without her.

Chapter Seven

BRIANNA

5 MONTHS LATER

My students pack away their art supplies at the end of the day, and the room is suddenly in chaos, each one of them desperate to finish what they're doing before the bell sounds. I can't help but laugh as I watch them. It's the same every day, each one of them busting to get out of class and make the most of their afternoon.

It's been five months since Cassie and Jax's wedding, five long months since I last saw his face, and every day without him has destroyed me. It's simple, Carter Waters is the love of my life, and I need him more than ever, no matter how hard I try not to. He was my light for so long, and without him, I've been scrambling through the dark, never quite able to come up for air.

At first, I thought I would die from the pain, but Bobby promised me that it would get easier with time, and God, I hoped it would. But it never did. So now I live life day by day, barely getting by, so undeniably broken while trying to put on a smile for the people around me. It's the hardest thing I've ever had to do.

It's clear to anyone who knows me that I'm dead inside.

The past few months I've lived on autopilot. I somehow manage to get out of bed, get ready for work, and drive to the school. I sit through six hours of listening to my first graders before finally packing up and heading home, only to sit in my new apartment alone.

The kids finish packing things away just as the bell rings, letting them know it's time to grab their shit and scram, and that's exactly what they do. I love my kids. At the moment, they're the only joy in my day, and despite my broken heart, they manage to keep me from breaking down. Knowing they're depending on me to give them an education gives me something to work toward and keeps my mind off the inevitable.

Some days are better than others, but today . . . well, fuck. Today was about as bad as it gets. I was scrambling through my closet for an old dress and stumbled upon the hiding spot where Cassie stashed all the shit I had from Carter, his suit shirt laying right on top.

I crumbled like a fucking bitch, gripping the shirt with everything I had and sobbing right there on my bedroom floor. His scent had long faded from that night.

I pulled my shit together and tried not to think about it, but the box broke me. After getting myself dressed and ready, I got my ass to the school, but I can't lie, it's been circling my mind all day. But I refused to shed a tear. Maybe I'm getting stronger, or maybe I'm just getting better at pretending I don't miss him.

Letting out a breath, I double check I have everything before locking up my classroom. The only good thing about today is it's Friday, and I can finally let loose and drown myself in a bottle of wine while either doing a deep dive through the box of memories or studiously ignoring it, pretending I never saw it at all.

It's only a twenty-minute drive to my apartment, but just my luck, I get stuck behind a moron who has absolutely no idea how to drive, blissfully unaware that he's keeping me from my new-found drinking addiction. "Get out of my fucking way," I yell at my windshield, the frustration gnawing at me. Though yelling at him is pointless. It's not like the fucker can hear me, but getting it out feels damn good.

Perhaps I need to look into one of those rage room places and spend a few hours tearing the place to shreds. Surely that could help, and I'm sure Cassie would love it too, not that she has anything to rage about.

The douchebag driver finally picks up his pace, but not by much, and I resist the urge to flash my lights at him. I've never really been one for road rage, but I can see the appeal. The traffic lights turn yellow, and I keep up my speed, knowing that I will make it across the intersection safely. But of course, the fucker slams on his brakes.

"FUCK!" I screech, holding the steering wheel in a death grip as I step on my brakes, but it's too late. My car slams into his ass, quickly followed by the few drivers behind me. I fly forward in my seat, but the seat belt catches and locks me in place, my head jolting forward and giving me whiplash.

My chest aches from the seatbelt, and I quickly check myself, making sure I haven't missed any injuries, but mostly, I'm alright—certainly alright enough to give this asshole a piece of my mind. My windshield is shattered, and seeing the moron driver in front getting out of his car, I hastily scramble for the seat belt buckle, seeing nothing but red.

Pushing out of my destroyed car, I storm toward him. The movement causes my neck and chest to hurt, but I'm too fired up to care. "What the fuck is your problem?" I demand, reaching the asshole and watching as he looks at me in surprise. "Do you have any idea how to drive? I mean, fuck! Who the hell gave you a license?"

The guy looks to be a twenty-something idiot with his hat turned to the side and baggy as fuck jeans that are only held up because he stands with his feet about a mile apart. The dickhead's just missing a chain hanging from his pocket and I swear he could have stepped right out of the nineties. Fucking loser.

He looks at me blankly and that only enrages me further. "Answer me, you moron."

"Uh . . ." he grumbles. "I didn't do anything wrong."

"Bullshit," I yell as the drivers from the other cars start gathering around. "I've been following your sorry ass for ten minutes. You were swerving all over the place and you haven't once been able to maintain the correct speed limit. You cut three people off and nearly ran over a pedestrian. And now, you've destroyed not only my car but all of theirs." I wave my hand, pointing toward the other angry drivers who, no doubt, just want to get home like me. "I hope you're up to scratch on your insurance because you're gonna pay for all of this."

"I'm not paying for shit," the nineties wanna-be grunts. "This is all on you."

And . . . that right there is my breaking point.

I run toward him, fists flying, not even having a moment for my jaw to hit the ground. The guy is twice my size, but that doesn't stop me from taking a good swing at him, only before my fist can find home, an arm locks around my waist and I'm hauled backward.

"Stop," a strange man says, his voice too close to my ear.

"Let go of me," I demand, all but clawing at his arm, trying to twist around to get a good look at him.

Hmm, not bad. Tall, dark, and handsome with a jaw sharp enough to cut panties right off women's bodies. There's something dark and exciting in his eyes, like he loves the chase, but I'm not getting those tingly feelings that make me want to slam him up against a wall and have him violate me in every wicked way.

The man ignores me as he hauls me away from the accident and over to the curb. He grips me a little tighter, now at arm's length so he can meet my eyes. "Are you going to try and beat the shit out of that asshole if I let you go?" he questions, his brow arched.

I let out a scoff. "No," I tell him, "But I might beat the living shit out of you if you don't get your hands off me."

The handsome man releases me, and I finally take a second to breathe while hastily backing up a step, putting a little distance between us. Wow, this really is turning into the day from hell.

"Sorry," the dude says, his hands firmly at his side. "I wasn't vibing with that asshole back there and figured he's the type of guy to hit you with assault charges."

I give him a tight smile but don't have it in me to respond. Instead, I glance back at the wreckage, taking in the pileup with a heavy heart. My car is like one of the squished sandwiches I find in my students' lunch boxes when there's too much shit jammed in there.

With a heavy sigh, I drop down to the curb and take it all in. My precious car is ruined, which just adds to the list of things that seem to be fucking up in my life lately. Bobby keeps a car here in Denver that I'll be able to use until my baby can get fixed, but from the look of it, it's a write-off. I might be in the market for a new one.

"Are you okay?" the guy asks as he crouches down to my level.

"No," I grunt, feeling myself teetering closer to the edge, knowing one more thing will have me turning into a sobbing mess in the middle of the road. "I'm just . . . I'm having a really shit day."

"No kidding?" he says, the sarcasm thick in his tone. "Could have fooled me."

I glare at the bastard. After all, he stopped me from getting my sweet revenge on that asshole, and while I'm not the type to physically assault people in the middle of the road, I don't doubt it would have felt good.

Sirens are heard in the distance, and I let out a breath, knowing this will all be over soon. I'll book an Uber, get myself home, and then I'll become well acquainted with the stash of bottles currently residing on my kitchen counter. Hmm, I wonder if the Uber driver would be cool with a quick pit stop at the liquor store. Somehow I'm doubting that I have enough at home. After all, I can't write myself off with just two bottles of Moscato.

The cops show up in record time with two ambulances hot on their tail, and I get up off the curb, more than ready to provide a statement. I make my way over there with the rest of the irritated drivers, and with everyone confirming my story, and somehow forgetting to mention my near assault, I watch with wicked satisfaction as a cop gives the asshole driver a Breathalyzer test and immediately handcuffs him.

I'm forced to be checked over by the paramedic, and after explaining what hurts, he's more than happy to send me on my way.

"Can I give you a lift somewhere?" the handsome stranger asks as I watch a tow truck hauling my car away.

My brows furrow as I glance up at the stranger. "Your car wasn't ruined in the crash?"

"Nope," he says with a slight shake of his head before pointing out a Dodge RAM across the road. "I'm just a witness. I was about to drive by when I saw you going off and figured I'd lend a hand."

"Oh, umm . . . thanks. You didn't need to do that," I say, painfully aware that this guy could have been home nearly an hour ago.

"I did," he grunts. "No one else was barging in to save you. To be honest, I think they were all wanting to see you beat the shit out of that guy."

I scoff. Not doubting him for a second, I look up to meet his stare and give him a tight smile. "Look, I umm . . . thanks for the offer, but I'm not really down with accepting rides from perfect strangers, but thanks though. I'm just gonna order an Uber and get my ass home."

"Alright, your call," he says, putting his hands up to show he won't push this.

He gives me a comforting smile and nods before starting to walk away, and as he goes, I can't help but selfishly wonder just how much sooner I could be home if I didn't have to wait for an Uber.

Shit.

"Wait," I call out, jogging after him. The guy turns back to me, patiently waiting with his brow arched in question. "Are you a serial killer?" I ask with a cringe.

The handsome stranger laughs, and the sound makes me feel somewhat relaxed. "No," he says. "Not today, anyway."

"Ha-ha. Funny," I mutter. "A rapist?"

"Nope."

Dammit. Why do I want to go with him so badly? It's clear this guy is just trying to help, but I have no idea why, and that's the only thing holding me back. I cross my arms over my aching chest and narrow my gaze at him. "What's your deal?" I question.

"Huh?" he grunts, taken aback by my question, but still clearly amused. "What do you mean *what's my deal?* I'm just trying to offer a pretty woman a little help."

I narrow my gaze. "I'm not buying it."

He lets out a sigh. "Okay. Honest truth?" he questions with a cringe.

"Uhh, yeah."

His lips pull into a lopsided grin, and suddenly he's no longer handsome. No, he's ruggedly sexy with boyish charm, and for a fleeting moment, I wonder what it would be like to be his girl. "I saw you a few lights back and thought you were fucking gorgeous, then the crash happened, and I figured I'd shoot my shot while I had the chance. I was going to talk you into a date tomorrow night."

Wow. He really is honest. I mean, he has no chance, but props for trying. If I had never met Carter and he had never destroyed me, I probably would have gone out with the guy just to scratch an itch, but I'm just not ready. Though, what I am ready for is the bottles of Moscato waiting for me on my kitchen counter.

"I'm flattered, thank you. But I'm damaged goods," I tell him, being a little too honest when a straight-up *no thanks* would have sufficed. "If you knew the mess my ex left me in, you'd understand. But I'm kinda hoping that doesn't mean the offer is off the table for a ride home. I'm close by. Only five minutes from here."

He gives me a fond smile, something honest and reassuring in his eyes. "Sure thing," he tells me, laying on the charm that still has no effect on my nether region. He leads me over to his Dodge RAM and helps me in. "I'm Byron, by the way."

"Brianna," I reply.

Byron gets in the driver's seat, and I direct him to the apartment complex next to mine, because, well . . . you never know, and I turn to him with a grateful smile, pleased to find I'm still alive. "Thanks for not killing me," I say, opening the door.

"No problem," he says as I go to make a hasty escape, only he calls out, pulling me up short. "Hey, I know you said you weren't down for anything just yet, but umm . . ." he pauses, reaching into his pocket and pulling out a business card before offering it to me. "Just in case you change your mind."

Not wanting to be rude, I reach in and take the card, knowing it'll be dumped straight in my trash the moment I walk through my door. "Thanks," I say with an awkward smile, and the second I step back from his truck, Byron takes off, finally leaving me be.

Walking to my apartment complex next door, I pull my phone out of my pocket and bring up Cassie's number. Hitting call, I hold the phone to my ear, impatiently listening as it rings. "Hey," she finally answers, way too chirpy for the kind of day I'm having. "What's up?"

"You wanna come over to annihilate a few bottles of wine?"

"Aww, hun. What's going on?" she asks. "Are you having a bad day?"

"The worst," I tell her. "I was in a car accident."

"What?" she shrieks. "A car accident? Shit. Are you okay? What happened?"

"What? Is that Bri?" I hear a familiar, panicked voice in the background, one that makes my heart constrict and agonizing pain flare through my chest. "Is she okay?"

Oh fuck.

Abort. Abort. Abort.

"Shut up," Cassie snaps at her brother as my hands shake with the overwhelming need to disconnect the call. I go to do it, but the thought of hearing his voice makes me feel as though I can breathe properly for the first time in five months.

Since the day Cassie got back from her honeymoon, her relationship with Carter has been strained. While she loves him immensely, she can't find it in herself to forgive him, and that's on my shoulders. She sees how broken I am, and I'm sure that the moment I start healing, she will too.

Cassie continues reaming out Carter. "You forfeited any right to know about her the second you broke her heart."

Oh dear God, please save me.

"Fuck, Cass," Carter growls at his sister. "Just ask if she's alright."

"Clearly she is if she is asking me to come over to drink the night away," Cass says before the background noise fades away, as she clearly walks away from Carter. "Shit, Bri. I'm so sorry, I just answered the call without thinking. I should have walked out of the room first."

"No, don't be sorry," I tell her. "He's your brother. You shouldn't have to feel like you need to mask your conversations in front of him. I just . . . I didn't realize you were with him tonight, otherwise, I would have called later."

"Don't stress," she tells me. "He's a total turd."

"He's not a turd," I murmur, still so defensive of the man who broke my heart. But there's no denying it, my heart still belongs to him. I still crave his touch, still want everything that he is. His only fault was wanting me to have the life I want, one he couldn't give me. Fuck, thinking about it only hurts that much more.

"He is, Bri, and the sooner you accept that the better," she tells me. "Now, what the hell happened with this car accident? Are you alright?"

"It's a long story that starts from seven o'clock this morning," I tell her.

"Right . . . so, two bottles or three?"

"Four or five would be good," I say.

"I'll be there in half an hour," she promises.

True to her word, there's a rap on my door precisely thirty minutes later, and I jump up from the couch and make my way toward the door. Though sitting on the couch was a mistake, my body is starting to feel stiff after the accident. I need to keep moving. Hell, I don't even want to think about how sore I'll be in the morning.

Reaching the door, I take hold of the handle and yank it open, my bottom lip already wobbling. "Hi," I murmur, willing myself not to break down and fall into her arms.

Cass takes one look at me, puts a bunch of grocery bags down on the floor, and throws her arms around me. She holds onto me so tight that I melt into her, soaking up every ounce of her comfort. Cass may be my best friend, but she's also the closest link I have to Carter, and there's just something soothing about being held by someone who shares the exact same eyes. It may be odd, but when she's around, I feel that much closer to Carter.

"Start from the beginning," she orders, releasing me before picking up the bags and striding into my apartment. She walks right into the kitchen, putting three bottles of wine into my fridge before helping herself to the already half-empty bottle of Moscato on the table.

We get comfortable on the couch with blankets and cushions before I get stuck into the bullshit otherwise known as my day.

Cassie has been everything to me over the last five months. After suffering her own devastating breakup with Jax a few years ago, she truly understands my pain. The only difference is, Cassie got her happy ending with Jax, whereas there isn't going to be one for me and Carter. I just have to learn to accept that it's never going to be like how it was.

"You know what?" Cassie says when I finish my recap of my day from hell. "I think you need to take Byron up on his offer to go on a date."

I gape at her. Surely someone slipped her a little something before she came over here because she's clearly not thinking straight. "You're insane," I tell her.

"No, you're insane. I think a hot date is exactly what you need. Shake off those cobwebs growing in your cooch and get back in the saddle," she tells me. "Byron isn't going to be the next great love of your life, but he's a stepping stone, and you're never going to learn to open yourself up for happiness if you don't give it a try. I know you don't feel ready, but I really think this could help you."

"I don't know," I say, my hands starting to shake with nervousness. Before Carter, I would have happily jumped in the sack with anyone, but I was also still in college and living my best life. Now, the idea of being with anyone else makes me feel sick.

"Tough shit," she says as she gets up and swipes his card off my kitchen counter, making me mentally kick myself for not disposing of it like I should have.

"Don't you dare," I demand, flying off the couch and wrestling the card out of her hands, knowing exactly what she intends to do with it. "I'm not dating Byron. He was too . . . I don't know. He was too put together. He couldn't handle this kind of baggage no matter how much he tried."

"Fine," she says, pulling her phone out. "No to Byron. But it is time to reactivate your Tinder account."

Ahhh, shit.

Knowing a losing battle when I see one, I let out a heavy sigh and reach for my Moscato. "Fine,"

After way too many drinks, a shitload of laughing, and swiping, Cass has managed to talk me into a date for tomorrow night. Well, sort of. I agreed knowing damn well I'll be canceling the second she walks out the door, but the only way to get her off my back is to let her think I'm trying. We raided my closet to pick out an outfit, and as it all came together, I realized she was right.

I'm never going to get over Carter. That's just a fact. He's tattooed on my heart, but that doesn't mean I can't try to find the next best thing—not that anyone will ever compare to what Carter and I had together. But to find him, I need to get over the fear of being with someone else.

It's going to hurt. It's going to really fucking hurt, but I need to try. Carter left me for a reason, one I insisted I needed, and if I don't move on and find that one special man who's going to give me the world, then all of this was for nothing. Besides, I can't sit alone in my apartment for the rest of my life, missing the guy who doesn't want to marry me.

With a new determination, I throw back the rest of my drink and collapse in my bed next to an already passed-out Cass, knowing tomorrow is going to be an interesting day.

Chapter Eight

CARTER

The second I overheard Cassie's phone call yesterday, my whole fucking world came to a screeching halt, the words *car accident* on repeat in my head.

Cass ran out the door without telling me a fucking word, and I was a mess. I swear, she did it on purpose. My sister hasn't forgiven me for breaking up with Bri. Hell, I haven't even forgiven myself, and I doubt I ever will, but that's no excuse for running out and not letting me know if my fucking girl was alright.

I didn't get a wink of sleep, and after a massive day of dealing with dickhead clients, it was the last thing I needed. I called her over and over again until she eventually blocked me. All I needed was to know that Brianna was okay. She just had to answer her damn phone and tell me what the fuck went down and that Brianna was doing alright. Is that too much to ask?

What the fuck was I supposed to think? I was close to getting in my truck and heading over there. I just needed to see her, get one glimpse of her, and then I would have left, but I know that wouldn't have gone down well.

Cassie was right. The second I ended it with Bri, I forfeited all right I had to know anything about her life. I broke her heart and let her go. The fact that I'm madly in love with her doesn't matter. The fact that she's all I've thought about since the moment we met holds no meaning either. I let her go, and that's on me.

It's just after five p.m. when Cassie strides through my house with a smug as fuck expression on her face, looking like the self-proclaimed queen of all who dares piss me off.

She barely gets two feet across my living room before I'm out of my seat and crowding her. "Where's your phone?" I demand before she has a chance to say anything.

Cass gives me a wide smile and pulls it straight out of her pocket, holding it up before me. "Right here, assface," she says with attitude.

"Oh, that's interesting," I growl, right on the edge. "You see, I thought you must have lost it."

"Nope."

"Then why the fuck didn't you answer it?" I roar, her need to push my buttons getting at me. I mean, fuck. I adore my little sister, but she's made the past five months hell for me. Doesn't she understand just how much I'm hurting too?

"Calm down," she says. "What's your problem?"

"My problem is that something happened to my woman yesterday and you didn't have the fucking decency to let me know that she was okay."

"Your woman?" Cassie scoffs, her brows so far up they need a different area code. "She's not your woman, Carter. You broke her heart and left me to pick up the pieces. You have no right to know what's going on in her life anymore."

Frustration burns me to the core, and I take a step back, my hands at my temples, desperate for the kind of peace that only Bri can offer me. "Cass," I say with a heavy groan. "Please, for fuck's sake. I get it. I fucked up, okay? Is that what you need to hear? I lost the best fucking thing that ever happened to me, and I hurt the only woman I will ever love, but please, Cass. Put me out of my fucking misery and just tell me that she's alright."

Cass sighs and crosses her arms over her chest, hardly able to meet my eye. "She's fine," she tells me, giving in to my desperation. "She had a shitty day and then got into a car accident on her way home. The asshole in front slammed on the brakes and there was a five-car pileup. Her car is completely totaled."

My eyes widen in horror. The idea of Bri being involved in that makes my heart race right out of my fucking chest. "The fuck, Cass?" I demand, feeling my pockets for my keys and wallet, ready to run out of here as images of Bri in a mangled car torment my mind. "How could you have not told me that?"

"Fucking hell. Let me finish, asshole," Cass demands, stepping in front of me to block my way as I start for the door. "I told you she was okay. You don't need to go racing out of here trying to be her hero. All you're going to do is hurt her more. She has whiplash and a sore chest, and the last thing she needs right now is to have to deal with you. Apart from that, she's absolutely fine. She was too pissed off with the guy who slammed on the brakes that she didn't even have a chance to get shaken up about it."

I let out a breath and have to force myself to sit down, desperately trying to reel in my emotions. "She's really okay?" I ask, looking up at my little sister and letting her see the undeniable devastation that resides in my heart.

Cass watches me a moment before a softness creeps into her eyes, and that chip on her shoulder finally begins to fade away. "Yeah," she finally says. "She's okay."

Relief pulses through me. I don't know what I would have done if something had happened to Bri. It's one thing being apart like this, but if I had lost her from this world and wasn't by her side . . . fuck. I wouldn't be able to handle it.

"I'm sorry," Cass says, taking the seat next to me. "I should have told you as soon as I knew. That wasn't fair, but I'm just so pissed off with you. I can't seem to shake it. Every time I see her hurting, it just . . . it eats me up inside."

"I know it does," I tell her, putting my arm around her and pulling her into my side, hating how much this is affecting her. "You have every right to be angry with me. I hurt your best friend."

"You did, but I forget that you're hurting too."

"Don't worry about me," I tell her. "I knew it was going to destroy me, and I did it anyway. Bri though, she was blindsided."

"You got that right," Cass mutters under her breath, unable to help the attitude that fills her tone. "But I understand why you did it."

We sit in silence, lost in our thoughts, when I finally get the courage to ask the most basic question that's been plaguing me since the day I ended it. "How is she really doing, Cass?" I ask.

I've avoided asking this very question, terrified of just how badly she was still hurting, but it's been five months now, so she's got time on her side. Surely she would have started to heal.

"Do you want an honest answer or the one that's going to make you feel better about yourself?" she questions.

Shit. I suddenly don't know if I want to hear this. "Don't hold back, Cass."

"She's broken, Carter. I've never seen someone in so much pain, not even me when I was in New York and away from Jax. You broke her to pieces, and she hasn't been able to put herself back together. She's lost," she tells me. "She misses you, and it kills her that she can't have the life she always wanted with you."

My head drops into my hands, my whole fucking world rocked by Cassie's words.

Hearing that Bri is barely surviving is tearing me to shreds. I hate that I've done that to her. But on the other hand, hearing how she still needs me . . . fuck. It makes me feel alive for the first time in five long months.

God, I must be the most selfish motherfucker who ever walked the planet.

Cass sits up straighter, and I sense her debating whether to continue, and I lift my head to meet her stare. She cringes before finally letting it out. "I convinced her to go on a date tonight."

What the actual fuck?

It's like a knife right through the chest. I knew this day would come, but fuck, I wasn't ready.

"What the hell, Cass?" I demand as thoughts of random guys with my girl start clouding my mind, the rabid jealousy already putting me on edge. This is exactly what I asked for, so I have no right to complain about it now that it's here. What if this guy doesn't have her best interests at heart? What if he hurts her?

"What do you mean, *What the hell?* She needs to move on, and she won't do that while she's sitting at home every night, unable to forget about the man she wanted to spend the rest of her life with," she says. "She needs to get out there again, needs to put you aside in a little box and forget about you so she can find the one guy who is actually going to give her the world. This is what you asked for, Carter. Isn't that what you wanted?"

"Yes . . . no. I don't fucking know. I want her to find someone who can give her everything she wants in life," I tell her, but I'm not convinced by my own words. Maybe I don't want her to find someone. I know it's what's best for her, but despite what we want for our futures, she's still my girl, still the woman I love. Always will be.

"I hate to break the bad news, brother, but she can't find that if she doesn't start dating. Her knight in shining armor isn't just going to magically fall from the sky one day. She needs to go out there and find him."

"I know," I sigh, hating myself that much more.

"You still wish you could give her that?"

"Every fucking moment of every day," I tell her. "I wish I could be like you and Sean and see myself being married with kids, but I just can't. That shit isn't in the cards for me."

"I know. You don't need to apologize for who you are."

"I do," I insist. "I hurt the woman I love because of who I am."

"I don't know how to help you, Carter," Cassie admits, throwing her arms around me. "I want you two to be together so bad. I know it's what you both want, and I keep wishing you could be that guy for her. You know, the one who takes her on crazy adventures and marries her in a fucking hot air balloon, but I know it's not going to happen."

"I know," I say as I hold her tight, picturing that hot air balloon so damn clearly and willing myself to want it. "Maybe one day I might be that guy."

"That could take forever," she says.

"And forever could be too late."

I sit in the darkest corner of the bar, nursing my drink as I keep my eyes locked on the door, just waiting for her to walk through it. There are at least four men here sitting alone at tables, all of who look like the kind of guys Bri might date, and I want to knock every last one of them out.

This is fucked. I can't believe I'm doing this like some jilted ex who can't possibly let go. But I suppose that's exactly what I am. I've turned into the worst version of myself, but I need to make sure she's alright. What the fuck was Cass thinking setting her up with some stranger off Tinder? I don't know anything about this guy Bri's meeting, but if he turns out to be some asshole who's gonna hurt her, then you bet I'm gonna be fucking ready.

I haven't seen her since the day I broke her, and I'm a mess of nerves. I never get like this, but there's just something about her that drives me crazy.

Hands down, this is going to be the hardest night of my life. I must be fucking crazy to put myself through this type of torture. I can just see it now; Bri is going to walk through that door looking like a fucking dream, and it's going to bring me to my knees. She'll smile at her date, and if he's any kind of gentleman, he'll stand, offer her his hand, and kiss her on the cheek, which is right about when my patience will snap and I'll kill the fucker.

Shit.

I've got to get a hold of myself, or better yet, get the fuck out of here before it's too late, but we all know that isn't going to happen.

As the minutes tick by, the condensation drips down the side of my glass, and I remain seated, pleased the bar is full enough to keep me concealed. But that goes both ways. I might be concealed from her, but with the bodies filling every corner of this bar, she'll be concealed from me too.

When the fuck did I sink so low as to stalk my ex-girlfriend?

The door opens, and my gaze snaps toward it with pure desperation, just as it has every other time, and fuck. There she is—a radiant fucking angel.

My breath catches in my throat, and I have to remind myself to breathe. She looks fucking stunning. Black thigh-high boots, a short black skirt, and an oversized sweater that falls off her creamy shoulder—the very shoulder I used to bite when she came.

Her long brunette hair flows out with the breeze of the open door, and as it falls closed behind her and she starts looking around the bar, I turn my back, not wanting her to see me. Movement to my right catches my eye, and a guy who looks and dresses just like me stands and gives her a beaming smile, his eyes lighting up with appreciation.

Bri smiles back, but after two years of learning her inside and out, I can tell she's nervous and really doesn't want to be here. She's determined though, and she's going to see it through, even if it's just to get my sister off her back.

Bri approaches the guy, and as she gets closer, I notice her perfect body has changed. She's a lot smaller than she used to be. She's fucking skin and bone, and it does nothing but piss me off. Don't get me wrong, she's still fucking gorgeous, but she doesn't look healthy. Her skin used to hold a beaming glow, and now . . . she looks flat. Like she's struggling to survive.

She reaches her date, and just as I thought, he leans in and places a soft kiss on her cheek—a hollowed-out cheek that used to be plump.

Guilt rests heavy in my gut, and I know I should leave, but I can't look away as they start their introductions.

The date pulls her chair out, and she hastily takes her seat at the table. From here, I can see her perfectly. She smiles and laughs with him, and while I recognize it to be fake, he's eating it up like he's already scored for the night.

The longer I watch them, the harder it gets to withstand, and I find my hand clutching my glass so hard, I fear it might shatter under the intense pressure.

This is fucking torture. I can't endure another second.

Common sense returns to me, and I get up to leave, but Bri's eye catches my movement. I suck in a breath, motionless as I watch her gaze shift to me, those gorgeous green eyes landing on mine for the first time in five long months.

The world fades around us, and as she looks at me, her face pales, undeniable pain rocking through her stare. The longer I stand here, the harder it gets, and not wanting to make this worse than it needs to be, I take my chance to get out of here.

I swallow hard over the lump in my throat, finding it fucking impossible to breathe as I sail through the back exit, my whole world knocked off balance. I beeline straight for my truck, feeling like a fool for showing up here tonight. I should have left her alone. Should have allowed her peace to figure out her next steps.

I'm halfway to my truck when I hear the broken voice of an angel calling out from across the lot. "Carter," Bri says, a whimper in her tone that has me coming to a stop, unable to fucking move.

I don't want to turn around. I know I shouldn't. It's only going to make it that much harder, but her broken tone has me turning and walking straight for her. There's nothing I can do to make this better, but at the very least, I owe her an explanation.

Bri meets me in the middle of the parking lot, barely a breath between us. She crosses her arms over her chest as if trying to protect herself, and a moment passes, neither of us knowing where to go from here.

Unshed tears linger in her eyes, and when she finally looks up at me, I have to ball my hands into fists to keep from reaching out and pulling her into my chest. "What are you doing here?" she finally asks, working hard to control the emotion in her voice, but I hear it loud and clear.

I let her see the raw honesty in my eyes, not daring to give her some bullshit excuse about this being a coincidence. "What do you think I'm doing here?"

Bri shakes her head, those tears finally falling and streaking down her face. "That's not fair," she says, her voice wavering with pain. "You can't do this."

"I know," I admit. "I'm leaving. I'm sorry, I shouldn't have . . ."

She nods but doesn't respond. Just stands there as we both wait, not wanting this stolen moment to come to an end. I creep in closer, the soft breeze picking up her subtle perfume. "Don't go back in there," I beg. "Let me take you home. You don't want to be here."

Bri looks up at me with those beautiful eyes that I love so much, and I reach out, wanting to touch her, but I pull back. The touch would be like the sweetest heaven, and I'll be sucked in, ruining us both. I can't risk it. "Have you changed your mind?" she questions, her voice so small and hesitant, yet so full of hope.

"No," I tell her, the single word shattering my heart all over again.

Bri wipes the tears off her cheeks before standing tall and plastering a fake smile across her face. "Then I'm going back in," she says with determination before turning on her heel and disappearing back inside the bar, taking my heart right along with her.

Chapter Nine

BRIANNA

What the hell was he thinking showing up here like that? Five months of struggling, five months of agony, and while I haven't come very far at all, just seeing him like that has undone any kind of progress I've made. Why can't he just leave me alone? Is that too much to ask?

The way he looked at me, the way he smelled. It all came rushing back. I wanted nothing more than to fall into his arms and let him hold me just like he used to, beg him to take away the pain and love me like I know he desperately wants to. Fuck, the pain in his eyes was almost enough to bring me to my knees. I still don't know how I managed to survive.

God, I miss him.

He wanted to touch me. I could see the way his hands balled into fists, how he tried to reach for me before thinking better of it. Had he touched me . . . had he given in to his most basic urges and stepped into me, folding me into his warm, strong arms, I would have dove straight in and refused to let go.

There's no doubt in my mind—Carter Waters is still deeply in love with me, and seeing me tonight wasn't easy for him. He's hurting just as much as I am, and I don't doubt that the ghosts of our relationship haunt him, but he shouldn't have come. He had no right to do that, to show up the way he did. What the hell was he planning on doing? Was he gonna knock out my date and put on some heroic show to defend my innocence? Because he knows better than anyone that there's nothing innocent about me. There's nothing here worth saving, not anymore.

Realizing my date has been in there alone for way too long, I take a deep breath and try to find the courage to keep going. Turning on my heel, I head back into the bar, desperately trying to mask the unease that rocks through me, but fuck it's hard. Seeing Carter like that was the hardest thing I've ever had to endure. My heart shattered all over again.

My date smiles as I sit back down, and as he launches into another bullshit story about his work, I try to force a smile. Being here feels wrong. The guy is nice enough, but I can't for the life of me remember his name. The second I saw him, all I could think about was Carter.

The guy looks so similar in his style, body shape, hair, and mannerisms.

This is only going to end badly for me.

This was a mistake.

Feeling the familiar sting in my eyes, I realize I'm seconds from breaking. I thought I could walk back in here and handle it, but as the tears begin to well, it becomes too much. A panic starts drumming through me, and I cut off his story to hastily excuse myself for the bathroom. I all but race across the bar before slamming through the door of the ladies' room, hyperventilating as I grip the sink and try not to be sick.

The tears spill down my face, staining my sweater. Just the thought that Carter saw me here meeting another man is gut wrenching. That must have stung for him. The need to splash water on my face comes over me, but seeing as though I'm wearing mascara and am supposed to be on a date, that probably isn't such a great idea. What I do need though is to get the hell out of here.

Do I escape out the back door or tell the guy it isn't going to work and leave like a normal human being? Shit, ghosting him sounds really good right about now. I've already run out on him twice, surely he couldn't think the date was going well anyway.

Yep. It's a shit move, but ghosting him it is.

Wiping the tears off my face, I let out a shaky breath before moving across the bathroom and peeking out the door. My date is busy ordering himself another drink, and it doesn't go unnoticed that he's only buying one for himself. Clearly he's not feeling this either, so I make it easy for the both of us and slip straight out of the bathroom and dash for the same back exit I'd followed Carter out only a few minutes ago.

I stand outside the open back door and sit down on a stool I can only assume is for the bouncer, coming to the conclusion that the whole dating thing simply isn't for me. Pulling out my phone, I search through my recent contacts and find Bobby's name before hitting call.

It rings twice before my twin's voice sounds through the phone. "What's up?" Bobby calls over the background noise, skipping straight over the hellos.

After the car accident yesterday, Bobby must have called at least twenty times just to check up on me like a good twin brother should, but I quickly realized that perhaps I should have kept it to myself. I shouldn't have worried him like that. That was selfish of me.

"I'm on a date," I tell him with a cringe, my unease coming through loud and clear.

"Uhhh . . . cool," he grunts. "That's good. I suppose, but if you're on a date, why the hell are you calling me?"

I let out a heavy sigh and glance back through the open back exit, seeing my date inside and noticing how he doesn't even bother looking around for me. "Because I'm standing at the back door wondering if I should high-tail it out of here," I tell him.

"Ahhhh, so the guy is a dud, huh?" he laughs. "But I don't know if I can really help you. I'm a fucking stud. I've never had a chick run out on me. Maybe give Cass a call. Isn't this what girlfriends are for anyway?"

"Yeah, but I want to talk to you."

"Alright, alright. Hold up," he says. A moment passes and I listen as the background noise fades to a dull hum. "What's going on, Bri? You good?"

"Where are you?"

"Some run-down bar," he tells me. A pang of jealousy cuts through me. I miss Bobby. I hate that he's so far away in New York, but that's where he needs to be for his career, and now all these new people get to spend time with him and soak up his awesomeness while I'm stuck over here, trying to figure out how to get by. "A few of the guys wanted to let off some steam, so here we are. But we're not talking about me. What's going on, Bri? Do I need to come home?"

"No, no," I rush out. "It's just . . . Carter kinda crashed my date."

"The fuck?" he spits. "What's this guy's deal? You might not be ready, but you needed this. You need to try, otherwise, you're going to continue being this half version of yourself. Carter isn't the be-all and end-all. He's just a guy. You'll find someone special eventually, but to do that you need to at least try to find him. I love you, Bri, but I love you more when you're happy. Do it for me."

"Maybe I should just switch teams," I sigh.

"No, chicks are fucking crazy. You couldn't handle that shit. Besides, the poor guy went to the effort to come out and meet you. Even if he's a dud, the least you could do is give him a chance and try to enjoy your night. He might not be the next big love of your life, but he might be able to make you laugh."

"He looks and dresses just like Carter."

"Hmm," he murmurs, seeing my issue. "Is he paying for your

dinner and drinks?"

I peer back inside the door, noticing my date now starting to look around a little in concern. "I think so. Maybe. I don't know."

"In that case, make the most of it and get a free meal. It's only fair, right? The number of random chicks who have scored a free meal out of me is ridiculous."

I scoff. "You're in the NHL, making millions. I doubt the occasional free meal is going to break the bank. Besides, I thought you were too much of a stud to have chicks bailing on you."

I can practically hear Bobby rolling his eyes. "Weren't we talking about your problems, not mine?" he questions before taking a heavy breath. "Look, you've made a big step just going out tonight. So make the most of it. Go back in there and try to enjoy this guy's company. Have fun, have a few drinks, and at the end of the night, when Cass asks you how it went, you can at least be honest and tell her you tried."

Fuck, I hate when he's right. "Fine," I groan, giving up. "I'll go back in."

"That's the spirit," he says. "Can I go now?"

"Yeah," I say, desperately wishing we could have had this conversation face-to-face instead of on the phone, miles away from each other. "Love you."

"Love you, assface," he says before ending the call.

With a smile, I get up off the little stool feeling a heaviness in my veins, and I go to walk back inside the bar when I find myself pausing and pulling out my phone once again, madly hashing out a text.

Brianna – Did you happen to tell Carter about my date? I think he's got his wires crossed because the assbag seemed to think it was an invitation and crashed.

Cass responds instantly.

Cassie – HE DID WHAT? FUCKING HELL!!!!!!!! I'm gonna kill him. I'm so sorry, Bri. We were having a talk this morning and he was checking up on you after the accident last night. He's still hurting, just like you, so I mentioned you were going on a date to ease him into it, so he wasn't blindsided. I never thought he'd show up like that. Fuck, he makes me so angry. I'll talk to him, make sure he knows where the boundaries lie. Are you okay?

Brianna – No, not really, but I'll be fine. What's my date's name again?

Cassie – Only you would forget your date's name while you were in the middle of the date! It's Xavier.

Brianna – Thanks. xx

Cassie – Remember, you don't have to suck his dick on the first date, but if you smile and pretend that you will, he's more likely to buy you extra drinks.

Ugh, it's just like her to offer a little support, but I don't think I need it right now, no dicks will be sucked tonight. The poor guy is lucky I'm going back in at all.

Without responding, I tuck my phone away and stride back into the bar, holding my head high, determined to try and enjoy this. Xavier sits at the table and I walk up with a smile before dropping back down into my chair.

"Is everything okay?" he questions, an understandable hesitation in his tone.

"Honestly, no," I tell him. "It's been a rough few months and an even rougher night for me, but if you're willing to give me a second chance, I'd like to see if we could start this date over."

"Sure thing," he says as he stands and holds out his hand like a perfect gentleman. "I'm Xavier, it's a pleasure to meet you, Brianna."

W hat the hell was I thinking dating this guy?

The first date was nice, it ended on a high and I allowed him to kiss me on the cheek. He opened doors for me, paid the bill, and was a perfect gentleman, so I agreed to go on a second.

Big fucking mistake.

Xavier is a grade-five clinger.

Our second date consisted of dinner at my place followed by the teensiest amount of fooling around. My bits never got touched, and I sure as hell wasn't ready to fondle him, but honestly, after the mess of saliva he left across my face, I'm assuming he wouldn't know what to do with my lady bits anyway.

He left super late after I "cooked" a nice dinner. We hung out and watched a movie on the couch while I ate ice cream straight from the carton. But when he attempted to hold my hand, shit got weird. I've never been a big hand-holder. Carter was the only man I've ever done it with, and that was purely because I couldn't get enough of him and needed to be touching him as much as I physically could. Before him, never.

After our first date, my walls were down, so I gave Xavier my number, which is where I went wrong because he won't fucking leave me alone. He texts me while I'm working, while I'm grocery shopping, while I'm driving, while I'm sleeping in the middle of the fucking night, and when I don't respond, the calls start. I mean, shit. My phone doesn't have enough data to deal with this kind of insanity.

Like I said. Grade-five clinger. He's starting to give me serial killer vibes.

Don't get me wrong, he's super nice and fun to look at. I'm even considering jumping in the sack with him just to see if he's got what it takes to get me off. Then I can get rid of him. I'm just worried there'll be tears when I do . . . and not from me.

So maybe it's been nice to have someone who cares, but it's not going to go anywhere romantic. I'm already unable to stand the guy. I'll give it a few more days of fun and then it's over. My time with him is turning into my drug to block the thoughts of Carter. It's good, but only lasts a little while, and lately, it's not working at all.

I've come to the realization that Carter has ruined me for other men. Not that I've truly tried yet, but I just don't feel that tingling sensation when I'm around sexy men like I used to. I mean, I'm happy to look, but when it comes to getting down and dirty . . . there's only one big dick I want in and around my business.

And fuck. I miss that dick. It was a good dick. If there's one thing Carter Waters knew how to do just right—it's a good fuck. He could get me off in ways no one ever could. Hell, not even I could get myself off like he did.

Maybe I just need to have fun and not think about my future, maybe see how things play out. It's not like I'm going to jump straight back into another relationship. I just want someone there to distract me. Someone to keep me busy.

It's been a week since that first date with Xavier and that awful run-in with Carter. Xavier has since gotten used to just showing up at my apartment. At first, I thought it was a bit much and super intrusive, but he bought a bottle of wine and dinner, so I let him in.

Since then, the clinger barely leaves.

A knock sounds at my door, and I let out a heavy sigh, really not in the mood to do that again tonight, but if I don't, I'm going to fall down the rabbit hole, and that's never pretty. Getting up off my couch, I hit pause on the latest episode of *The Kardashians* and make my way across my small apartment. I open the door and, surprise, surprise, it's Xavier standing out in the hallway. I groan to myself. It would be nice to just have a night to myself, but then I know that if he wasn't here, I'd start missing someone else.

Why does heartbreak have to be so damn hard?

Xavier comes in and makes himself at home. He dumps a bag of food on the counter knowing that the only thing in my fridge is alcoholic and comes in a very pretty bottle, which honestly, can afford to be a little bigger.

"How was your day?" he asks as he finds my plates and starts dishing up the food.

"Ehh," I tell him with a shrug, the aroma of Thai food making my stomach grumble. "The kids were a bit much. I had to use my cranky voice like . . . four times."

"Shit, I'm sorry. That sucks."

"Yeah, it's fine. They usually get a bit rough by the end of the week, it's nothing I'm not used to," I tell him, walking around the kitchen to find a couple of wine glasses. "They'll be their usual perfect selves come Monday, and if they're not, I'll just give them a little quiet reading and then they generally settle down."

"Seems like you know all the tricks of the trade," he says as if he truly knows me.

I give him a forced smile as I get cozy on my couch and pull a blanket over my legs. Xavier comes and hands me a plate before taking the spot beside me, thankfully not trying to share my blanket. "Hope you like Thai," he says.

"Who doesn't?" I reply as I dive straight into my dinner, not having realized just how hungry I was.

Hitting play on *The Kardashians,* I quickly pick up where I left off, feeling slightly awkward with Xavier so close beside me. But when he starts talking in the middle of my show, that awkwardness quickly morphs into a blatant irritation, especially considering my need to be polite and answer all of his questions.

I give up and let the show play, promising myself that I'll re-watch it when he eventually leaves, but if this week has taught me anything, he's in for the long haul. I mean, I could probably kick the guy out, but he brought dinner and that just seems rude.

I wonder if Byron from the car accident is the type to linger. I bet he's a bit of a clinger too, but nobody could be as bad as Xavier.

After a long week and a whole bottle of wine, it's not long before the yawns start to kick in and I find myself falling asleep on the couch.

The noise coming from the TV begins fading into my unconsciousness, and there's no telling how much time has passed before I feel a pair of strong arms slipping around my body. I'm jostled on the couch and scooted across before a body moves in behind me, and I realize Xavier is trying to force a cuddle, but my sleep deepens, and not a moment later, the world falls away.

Chapter Ten

CARTER

"**C**ome on, buddy," I beg with desperation as I look down at my limp dick, willing him to play along just for tonight. "You can do it."

This shit doesn't happen to me. But here I am, standing in my date's bathroom, hating myself for being such a fucking loser.

I've never once had a problem performing, until now. I have a very willing woman in the next room, offering to suck my dick and allow me to fuck her until she passes out, but my dick doesn't want a bar of it, and honestly, neither do I.

I can only imagine the shit Logan is going to say about this after the hard time I gave him when he broke his dick playing hockey earlier this year. Fuck, I went hard on him, unlike how my dick isn't going hard on me right now.

After last week, seeing Bri starting to date again, it flicked a switch inside of me. If she's trying to move on, then why shouldn't I? It's that very thinking that got me caught up in this situation in the first place—standing in a random woman's bathroom, talking to my dick, and thinking about my ex.

Just fucking great.

I haven't had sex since Cassie and Jax's wedding with Bri in the guest bathroom, and believe me, I want to, but the thought of sleeping with another woman makes me feel nauseous. However, remembering that last time with Bri kind of helps my situation, picturing the way she was bent over at the hips and I slammed into her from behind. She grasped onto the wall to avoid hitting her head and used it to push back into me.

Fuck yeah. It was nothing short of magical. It always was with her. I grasp my dick as I picture that moment clear as day in my head, and just as I knew it would, my dick grows hard.

I go to step out of the bathroom, but realization hits me like a fucking wrecking ball. I'm about to fuck some strange woman while thinking about Bri. Before I met her, I never would have had a problem with something like that, never would have thought twice, but now it just seems so . . . wrong.

Fuck.

"Carter?" I hear from the other side of the door. "Is everything alright in there?"

Ugh. The sound of her needy voice has my cock deflating like a fucking balloon. Great, another night where I'll go without having sex. What has my life come to? I guess I'll be heading home to take care of business myself, just as I've been doing for the past five months. At this point, I'm gonna get calluses on my palms from how often I've been needing to rub one out, each time with Bri's flawless body stuck in my head.

"Carter?" the woman questions again.

Damn it. How am I going to get out of here? If I go out there, that woman is going to maul me again, and I just can't take it. Her hot breath on my mouth was putrid, and having her hands all over me made me feel desperate for a shower.

I mean no disrespect to the lady, I'm sure she's a really nice woman when she isn't trying to maul random men, but I just can't do it. I'm clearly not ready.

Looking around the bathroom, I take in the small window above the toilet. The idea hits me like a freight train, but I'm going to have to be smart about this. It's a small window and my clothes are in the bedroom. This isn't gonna be pretty.

Eyeing the towel hanging over the shower, I consider using that and making a break for it, but then an image of me running up the street in nothing but a towel comes to mind, and I just can't risk it.

I definitely would have done something like that in college, but I'm the CEO of a multi-million dollar construction company with my family name plastered all over it. Doing something so reckless is likely going to get me splashed all over the internet. I can't put my company and my family through that kind of embarrassment. Not to mention, it's not something I want Brianna to hear about.

Shit. I'm going to have to get my clothes and somehow walk out of this place with my dignity intact. Though considering my limp dick, I think I've already lost that dignity.

Not wanting this to go on another minute longer, I avoid my reflection in the mirror, too ashamed to even look at myself before creeping toward the bathroom door.

"Hey, uhh . . . love?" I call through the door, having no fucking clue what this woman's name is.

I hear her move across her room and put herself right on the opposite side of the bathroom door. "Yes?" she asks far too eagerly.

"Could you grab me a glass of water? I'm not feeling so hot," I lie.

"Oh, um sure," she says, a slight hesitation in her tone. "Do you need some painkillers or anything like that?"

Hmm, good idea. That would buy me an extra minute or two. "That'd be great."

"Okay," she says, and I listen carefully through the door, hearing as she walks back across her room and through the door. There's a soft thumping as she makes her way back up the hallway to her kitchen and, realizing this could be my only chance, I make my move.

Darting out of the bathroom, I scurry around the woman's bedroom, collecting all of my clothes and making sure I still have my phone, keys, and wallet as the woman hums to herself in the kitchen. Having everything I need, I hurry back into the bathroom, closing the door behind me before hastily pulling my clothes back on.

I'm just about done when I hear a creak in the floorboards and panic sails through my chest. Shit, she's on her way back.

Reaching up for the latch of the window, I quickly flick it before shimmying the old window up, and from the way it squeals in the silence, it's clear this window hasn't been opened for a while. Not having time to pull my shirt on, I shove it in my mouth and bite down before stepping up onto the toilet and hoisting myself up.

I hear her voice on the other side of the closed door as I slide through the small window, scratching up my waist in the process. When I hit the ground, I accidentally squish her poorly cared for garden. Thank fuck this is a one-story home.

"Carter?" the woman calls, her voice sailing through the open window. "Babe, can you open the door?"

Not likely.

"Carter?" she calls again.

Yeah, it's time to run.

My feet pound against the pavement, feeling like a fucking teenager again. I can't remember the last time I snuck out of a woman's window to avoid fucking her, but hell, I'm ashamed to say that definitely wasn't the first time. I suppose as a teenager, it was probably excusable . . . kind of. But as a grown-ass man. Fuck. There were definitely better ways to have done that.

After getting halfway down the street, I stop and pull my shirt on before finding my phone and searching through the endless apps to book an Uber. As I do, I see a bunch of missed calls from Sean.

Stopping in my tracks, I quickly book my Uber and call him back before bringing the phone to my ear. The call connects and the sound of someone screaming in agony fills the speaker before Sean's voice comes over the noise. "Hey," he calls. "About time you called me back."

"What the fuck's going on?" I ask. "It sounds like someone is being murdered in there."

"Sara's in labor," he tells me, elation in his tone. "We're having a fucking baby, bro. We're at the hospital now."

"No shit," I boom. People on the street stop to stare at me as I look around, trying to figure out the fastest way there. "How's it going? Do I need to get down there?" Excitement takes over every thought in my mind. My brother is about to have a fucking baby. How great is this? In the next few hours, I could have a little niece or nephew to corrupt.

"Nah," he says with a smile in his voice. "It's still early. We've got time. Give it a few hours then start heading down."

"Okay," I say, finally starting to calm down. "How's Sara doing? Is she alright?"

"Do I fucking sound alright?" I hear Sara screeching in the background, and I realize I must be on speakerphone.

My eyes widen, and I've suddenly never been so scared to speak in my life. "You sound great, Sara," I say encouragingly, hoping like fuck that was the right thing to say.

"You're full of shit," she grunts just before a blood-curdling wail tears out of her. "I hate this. You assholes better have a big fucking push present for me after this," she demands.

Push present? What the fuck is a push present? "Of course we got you . . . one of those," I tell her, hoping like fuck Sean is on the ball with this, otherwise the motherfucker is quickly running out of time. Though I don't doubt that after pushing out a baby, Sean is going to get Sara anything and everything she could ever want. Not that he doesn't already give her the world.

Sara whimpers, the pain clear in her tone, and I can't for the life of me understand why Bri would want to put herself through that so badly. "Alright," Sean says, cutting in. "I've got to go. I'll give you a call when it's time to head down here."

"Sure thing, man. Let me know if you need anything," I say as I hear Sara in the background demanding the *good shit*, and fuck, I'm glad I'm not Sean right now. I can't imagine anything worse than watching the woman you love physically tear her body apart as she pushes a watermelon out of such a small hole. I'd be traumatized.

Sean ends the call, and I'm left waiting for only a few minutes before the Uber arrives. The moment I drop into the car, I tell him to step on it, far too excited to take my time.

From what I've heard, pushing out a baby can take a really long time. Not the pushing part, but the bit before . . . shit. What the hell would I know about any of this? The only knowledge I have on this shit is what I was taught during those awkward high school sex-ed classes. But, Sean said I have a few hours, and that's all I need to know. Hell, I could have a shower, get the woman's stench off me, and maybe even spare some time for a nap. Fuck, that makes me sound old.

By the time I get home, the excitement has sobered me up—

not that I was wasted before, but the few drinks from the dive bar were definitely felt. After hurrying up the stairs, I jump straight in the shower before getting dressed and heading back down to my living room. I check the time, more than ready to go, and realize that it's only been ten minutes.

Shit.

It's gonna be a long wait.

Dropping onto the couch, I turn on ESPN and grin as a repeat of Logan's last game appears on the screen. It was a home game, and I made a point of being there to support him, yet I can't find it within me to turn it off. There's no doubt about it, Logan is the fucking best player in the NHL. Sorry, Jax, but it's true!

The minutes tick by, and the longer I wait, the worse my patience becomes. Shit. I'm not going to be able to wait for Sean's call. Hell, with everything going on right now, there's no guarantee that he'll remember to call. It wouldn't be the first time Sean's forgotten the basics, but who could blame him?

I've barely been home an hour when my patience wears thin, and I grab my phone, keys, and wallet off the coffee table before storming right back through my door. Within seconds, I'm firing up my truck and pulling out of my long-ass drive, more than ready to meet my new little niece or nephew.

Chapter Eleven

CARTER

After parking my truck at the hospital, I hurry straight to the reception desk and try to figure out where the hell the maternity ward is. I've been to this hospital more times than I can count. Hell, between me and my brothers growing up, we should be on some kind of frequent flyer reward program. I know all the ins and outs this hospital has to offer, but the maternity ward . . . that's somewhere I've never wanted to be before.

The nurse at reception gives me instructions, and I follow them religiously until the elevator doors open on the maternity ward. The first thing I see is my family sprawled through the waiting room, slumped over their chairs as they wait for news. A wide grin stretches across my face, and I step out of the elevator, more than happy to see them all.

Jax is the first to look up and notice me smirking at them. "You couldn't wait either?" he questions, a knowing sparkle in his eyes as the others look up.

"Tried . . . failed," I tell them as I take a seat beside Cassie, who shuffles around in her chair, lays down, and uses Jax's lap as a pillow and mine as a footrest. Usually I'd push her off, but today is special. If she wants to use me as her personal pillow, then that's fine. And to be honest, after my casual stalking of her best friend on her date, it would pay to give Cassie anything she wanted right now. I don't think I've ever seen her so mad.

The minutes tick by painfully slow, and I do what any other brother would do to pass the time—I very carefully and discreetly tie Cassie's shoelaces together because why the fuck not? A stupid grin settles over my face, and I glance up to find Logan watching me with a glimmer of amusement in his eyes. I hold my breath waiting for him to bitch me out, but the fucker doesn't say a damn word, just shakes his head, pretending as though he's above the idiocy. Just putting it out there—he's not.

Cass eventually falls asleep, lightly snoring on Jax's lap as he runs his fingers through her hair, while Logan has his arm thrown over Elle's shoulder, holding her close to his side, each of them looking as though they just came straight from a game. To say they look exhausted is an understatement. It's getting very close to the end of the NHL season, and Logan has been working his ass off, which is only expected as he's the captain of the damn team.

It's been two long hours of torture when a familiar voice sounds at the top of the hallway. "What the fuck are you all doing here?" Sean demands. "I said I'd call when it's time to come."

"Like that was ever going to happen," Cassie scoffs, her eyes still closed before groaning and sitting up.

Sean rolls his eyes and makes his way toward us. "I should have known," he mutters, shaking his head in exasperation before collapsing down onto one of the chairs, looking more exhausted than Logan. Though I can't imagine how exhausted Sara must be.

"What's going on?" I ask. "How's Sara doing?"

"Amazing so far," he says, bringing his hand up to cover his mouth as an almighty yawn comes tearing out of him. "She's only about halfway dilated, so it'll still be a little while."

"So, what are you doing out here then?" Logan grunts. "Shouldn't you be in there catering to her every need?"

"Yeah, she sent me for ice chips, but honestly, I think she just kicked me out so she could talk shit about me to the midwives," he says, amusement in his eyes. "Either way, I'm hungry and my hand needs a break." With that, he holds his hand up to show us the claw marks carved into his skin. "She likes to squeeze. It helps her deal with the contractions."

"That's fair enough," Elle smiles. "Obviously I've never experienced it before, but my friend Jaz and I watched a birthing video once, and I've never been the same since. It was horrifying.

Best birth control I've ever seen."

Cass laughs. "I wonder if it's the same video my dad made me watch when he found out that Jax and I were dating. I still have the mental scars. I cross my legs every time I think about it."

Elle laughs as she relaxes back into Logan's side, her lips pressing into a firm line. "Sara must be in so much pain," she muses. "Just the thought of it scares me."

Cass sighs in agreement before glancing up at Sean. "How far apart are the contractions?"

"Every few minutes," he says.

"Shit, she doesn't even get a chance to catch her breath, and you're out here thinking about your stomach and how much your hand hurts. Fucking hell, Sean. You don't have time to eat. Get your ass back in there for her next contraction. I swear, if you miss even one, she'll hold it over you for the rest of your lives."

Sean's eyes widen, realizing just how right Cass is. "Oh fuck. You're right," he says, shooting back to his feet. "I better go find the ice chips and get back in there."

"Quit stressing," Cassie says as she goes about getting to her feet. "There's a vending machine down the other end of the waiting room. I'll grab you something to eat and Jax can find the ice chips. You go be with Sara and we'll bring everything to the door."

Relief flashes in Sean's eyes as Cassie goes to step forward, but her tied shoelaces have her tumbling forward. "Fuck," she screeches as both Jax and Sean dart toward her, catching her by the arms before she falls.

A grin tears over my face, and I try my best to smother it, but it's too hard, and the wicked snickers burst out of me. The moment Cassie rights herself, she spins on me, fire burning in her eyes as Sean disappears back down the hallway. "You're going to regret that, Carter Waters," she declares.

My wide grin morphs into a wicked smirk, and I lean forward with her challenge. "Bring it on, little sister."

She steps out of her shoes, kicking them into my shins, and before I know it, she's flying at me, her arms and legs going wild. She crashes into me, her knee way too close to smacking into my junk, and I do my best not to drop her while she does her best to beat the ever-loving shit out of me for sweet revenge. And while she's not a kid anymore, she's still only five-foot-nothing and incapable of causing any real damage.

Laughing, I grab her hands and hold them behind her back, rendering her useless. "Yo, Jax. Come and get your wife."

"Nah," he mutters, burying his hands in his pockets. "She's your problem now. I gotta find ice chips."

Cass lets out a groan before turning her narrowed gaze on me. "Let me go, you big bastard," she demands.

"Only if you admit that I'm your favorite," I tell her.

"Oooh," she laughs. "Seems someone is still a little hurt that I let Logan walk me down the aisle. What's the matter, Carter? Jealous? We all know Sean was my second choice. Tell me, where does that put you?"

"Wrong answer," I grin.

"Quit fucking around," Logan scolds as he gets out of his seat and rescues Cass, knowing damn well this could go on for hours. He fixes Cass with a hard stare. "You promised Sean you'd get him something to eat and you know Jax is gonna get lost finding his way back here."

"Shit," she breathes, realizing Logan's right. Cassie quickly drops down beside me, all fun and games over as she hastily pulls her shoes back on before holding her hand out to me. "Cough it up," she tells me. "The vending machine isn't gonna start spitting out food because I'm pretty."

Rolling my eyes, I reach into my pocket and pull out my wallet, handing her all the cash I have. It's way too much for a vending machine, but if anyone can rise to the challenge, it's Cass. Besides, there's no way she isn't going to return here without all the snacks in the world. The problem is that she'll scarf down all the good ones before she gets back.

Both Cass and Jax return twenty minutes later, both their arms loaded up with snacks, and as my stomach starts to grumble, we all dive in, annihilating them in no time. Hell, after Logan's game tonight, the snacks aren't even close to enough, and he orders UberEats for every sorry bastard in the waiting room.

Hours pass and my ass starts to get very uncomfortable. Elle passed out on Logan's lap two hours ago, and Cass has been snoring since the second she finished her meal. I've tried to sleep but can't bring myself to close my eyes.

It's nearing four in the morning, and I start getting a little nervous.

This is taking a really long time. I know this shit is supposed to take forever, but judging by the updates we got from Sean earlier, it should have happened by now.

Commotion down the hallway has both the girls waking, and we all look around, meeting each other's stare, certain this is it. Excitement burns through my veins, and I get ready to take all these assholes' money. After all, with only four walls to stare at, it wasn't long before we started making bets on the baby's gender, and I feel it in my bones. It's definitely a little boy.

We peer down the long hallway, all of us jumping to our feet. Cass and I are unable to control ourselves and both of us start creeping forward. We look down the hall, and my hand shoots out, gripping Cassie's arm to bring her to a stop. Something doesn't feel right about this. The commotion gets louder, and Sean comes into view as he's pushed out of the doorway to make room for Sara's bed. Nurses and doctors flood out behind them as they rush down the hall.

What the fuck?

They burst past us, and the look of panic on Sara's flushed face has us all falling behind them with desperation. "What's going on?" Logan and I ask at the same time.

Sean latches onto his wife's hand, holding on for dear life as they rush down the hallway, and the sound of her pained cry is something I know will stay with me for the rest of my life. "She has to have an emergency C-section," Sean calls over the noise. "The baby is stuck, and Sara's blood pressure is too high. They're both going into distress."

"Fuck," I curse. That can't be good.

"Sean," Sara says, looking up at him with fear in her eyes. "It hurts so bad, I think I'm going to be sick."

He kisses her hand as they continue rushing. "It's going to be okay," he soothes her. "The doctors know what they're doing. You're both going to be okay. *The baby is going to be okay.*"

Sara nods, but the fear doesn't fade from her eyes.

Jesus. Reason number one why I shouldn't be having kids. I can't handle this shit.

They go through a set of large double doors at the end of the long hallway, and we're all stopped from following. Sean disappears, clutching Sara with everything he has. I want nothing more than to be in there for them, letting them know everything is going to be alright, but this is on Sean's shoulders now. He's got this. If anybody can keep her calm and help her through it, it's Sean.

We stand outside the double doors, not wanting to go back down the hallway to the waiting area. They're nearly at the finish line. Any minute they could have a baby. The first Waters baby. Fuck. I'm excited. We just need to get over this last hurdle, and then the second Sara gets to hold her baby, she'll forget about the pain and be flooded with happiness. At least, that's what Cass keeps telling me. Personally, I don't think any woman is gonna forget that kind of trauma. Hell, Cass still hasn't forgiven me for accidentally breaking her finger when she was six.

An eerie silence comes over us as we wait.

It feels odd to be waiting right outside the doors like this, but

I couldn't care less. Sean is going to come out of these doors any minute now and let us know that he's had a baby, and when he does, I want to be right here for him. He's going to be proud as fuck, and I couldn't be happier.

When five minutes turns into ten, I become fidgety again. We all do. Logan leans against the wall, trying to play it cool while both Cass and Elle pace in front of the door.

Then finally, my phone rings in my pocket and I scoop it out, finding a video call from Sean. I answer it as fast as humanly possible and his beaming face quickly appears on my screen as everyone crowds around. "It's a girl," he announces proudly, the small crib in the background.

"Fuck, yeah," I cheer as Cassie throws herself into Jax's arms in a bruising hug, her excitement having her squeezing him until he can't fucking breathe. "When can I meet her?" Cassie calls out, leaning in toward the screen.

"Give Sara a chance to get stitched up and meet her daughter and the second we're back in the ward, she's all yours," Sean says, glancing back and forth between the crib, his wife, and the screen. "I better go, but I'll call when we're ready."

We let him go, and the second the screen goes dark, Logan fixes me with a smug as fuck grin. "Told you it was a girl," he says, his brows bouncing. "You owe me five hundred bucks."

Shit. I was so fucking sure too.

I let out a heavy sigh, still wanting to deny that I was wrong, when a blaring alarm echoes through the hallway. My eyes widen, and not a second later, the hallway fills with nurses and doctors flying toward us. We all plaster ourselves against the wall, letting them pass through the double doors, and I hold it open for them as they go, but as they stop at Sara's door and barge through, it sends nothing but sheer panic and fear through each of us. I find myself holding onto the open door, more than ready to race in there after them.

"What the fuck's going on?" Logan calls out to the passing nurses, but every single one of them ignores us, and honestly, as much as it kills me not knowing what's happening in there, I'm glad they're not wasting precious seconds by stopping to fill us in.

The doors open and close, and my beautiful niece is rushed out of the room by a midwife and sent down the hall right before Sean is shoved out by an angry nurse, the door quickly closing in his face. Whatever is going on in there has everything to do with Sara.

Sean tries to fight his way back into the room, and Logan and I have no choice but to hurry through the double doors. We race down the hallway to step in and grab him, forcing him back from the door. Whatever is going down in there, the doctors need room to move, and while Sean desperately needs to be at his wife's side, he can't help her right now. He's only going to be in the way.

"What's going on?" I demand, desperately trying to pull his attention to me and calm down enough to stop fighting us.

"She's hemorrhaging," Sean says through a clenched jaw, undeniable fear and desperation shining in his wet eyes as he tries to push us off, determined to get back to his wife. "They can't stop the bleeding."

"Fuck," Logan says as Cassie falls into Jax's arms, her whole body shaking with fear as the whole family now hovers outside Sara's door.

Tears fall from Sean's eyes, and I can't help but feel empty inside. The helplessness in his eyes fucking kills me, and suddenly I'm right back where I was years ago, standing at my father's side as he could do nothing but watch as my mother lost her fight to breast cancer. "She was losing too much blood," he tells us. "Something must have gone wrong."

"Hey," I say, trying to break him out of the panic, but I know it's useless until he can get back in that room and physically see that she's alright. "She's going to be alright. The doctors know what they're doing," I tell him, repeating the very words he'd used to soothe Sara earlier.

With that, Sean loses the fight and gives in to the fear. He stops trying to push us away and breaks down, falling against the wall and sliding to the ground, his head buried in his hands. Cass sits next to him and takes his hand in hers, gently squeezing and desperately trying to soothe his fear, but nothing can save him now, not until the doctor comes out of the room and physically tells him that she's okay.

Jax leans against the wall as I pace up and down the hallway, my hands shaking at my sides. Logan holds Elle, who's silently crying in his arms, and I'm sure this is all bringing back memories of her past when she knelt over her little sister and watched her bleed out, unable to save her.

Each passing second feels like a lifetime, and it's ten long minutes before a doctor drenched in blood comes striding out of the room, looking completely defeated.

My stomach sinks as Sean flies to his feet, a heaviness weighing down on my chest. Sean's eyes are wide as the doctor steps up to him, and I watch in horror as he raises a hand and places it on Sean's shoulder, regret heavy in his eyes. "I'm sorry," he says, undeniable pain resting in his haunted stare. "Your wife didn't make it."

No.

No, this isn't happening. He's wrong. *He has to be wrong.*

Beautiful Sara. She was happy and healthy. I saw her just a few minutes ago, she can't just be gone.

Sean shakes his head in disbelief as my heart crumbles. Tears well in Sean's eyes, and I've never seen such a broken man. The doctor welcomes Sean back into the room to say goodbye, and he pushes past the doctor, blocking out whatever it is he's saying while the rest of us crowd around the open door, not able to believe it for one fucking second.

The sight before me tears me to shreds.

Sara lays on the operating table with pools of blood on the floor around her and we watch as one of the many midwives drapes a white sheet over her motionless body. Cass whimpers beside me, but all that matters right now is the way Sara lays so still, her eyes closed, and for a moment, I can imagine she's just sleeping, but I know that's not right.

There's no movement in her chest, no sign of breathing. No fingers twitching. No heartbeat on the monitor . . . just a flat line.

Sean stumbles toward her, standing at her side as he brushes his fingers over her face, and then he fucking breaks. Sean falls onto her, throwing his arms around her lifeless body and clutching onto her with everything he has, screaming in agony—the sound one that will haunt me until my dying days. "No," he sobs, so fucking broken. "No. Come back to me, baby. I can't fucking do this without you."

Unable to handle the devastation, I stumble back into the hallway and fall against the wall, barely able to catch my breath as I drop my head into my hands. I hear Cassie's sob, now deep within the room and soon enough both Elle and Logan are by my side, wanting to give Sean the privacy he needs.

Cassie and Jax follow suit not a second later and all we hear from is the sound of Sean's overwhelming grief drowning out the flat line of the heart rate monitor.

A voice sounds at my side and my head whips around, not having noticed anyone approaching. "Excuse me," a woman says. We turn around to find a young nurse pushing a bassinet with the most beautiful baby inside. "I'm incredibly sorry for your loss. I know there are no words that could possibly take away your pain, and I am so sorry for having to pull one of you away from this. However, hospital policy requires a family member to remain with the baby as we weigh and measure her. She will also need to be fed so if you have any input there on the dad's wishes, that would be great."

I step up to the bassinet and look down at the tiny baby—a beautiful innocent creature who's going to grow up without her mommy. I reach into the bassinet and run my finger over the soft skin of the baby's hand, tears brimming in my eyes.

Cassie moves in beside me and gives the nurse a forced smile, always doing what she can to be polite, even in the devastating face of grief. "I'll stay with her," Cass tells the nurse while giving my hand a squeeze.

The nurse nods and leads Cassie down the hall, pushing the bassinet along with her. Jax trails after them, his head hung low and his hands buried deep in his pockets, but I'm sure when Cassie needs him, he'll be able to pull himself together and be her rock, just as he's always done.

The rest of us remain out in the hallway, allowing Sean these last few moments with his wife, and the second the heart rate monitor is turned off and the room within falls into silence, it becomes too fucking much. I fall to my knees, my head buried in my hands as I sob for the girl I've known since I was a teenager, the girl who was as close to me as my own sister, the mother of my beautiful niece, and the woman who always told me, especially over the past five months, that despite all the pain and hurt that I'd caused, that I was still a good man who was deserving of love.

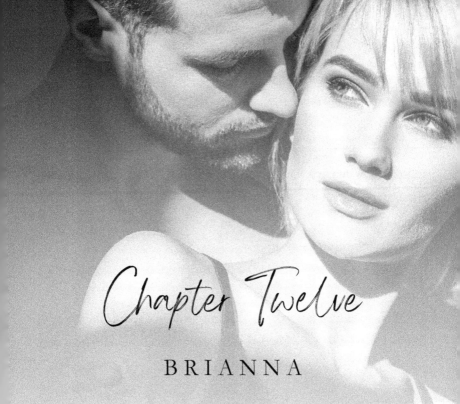

Chapter Twelve

BRIANNA

A loud banging at my front door startles me awake, and I fly out of bed, my arm whipping around and catching on the charging cable for my phone and sending it flying halfway across my bedroom. "Fuck, fuck, fuck," I mutter, scrambling after it, knocking into walls as I desperately try to wake myself up.

The pounding on the door continues, and I curse and grunt to myself, not one to handle early mornings very well. This is definitely not what I planned for my Saturday morning.

Finding my phone halfway under my bed, I consider leaving it and getting it later, but there's no telling who's at my door. I want to have it in my feisty little hand in case I need to call 911 or hit some asshole over the head with it. But fuck, if I were to break my screen on someone's head, I'd be pissed.

Getting on my hands and knees, I reach under my bed, pushing my monster cock out of the way before curling my hand around the phone and yanking it. Then using the edge of the bed, I haul myself up to my feet and am just about to trudge to the door when I catch sight of the time. Shit, it's 6:30 in the morning on a Saturday.

What the absolute fuck?

Who in their right mind would be banging on my door this early?

Fucking Xavier. That's who.

I was able to deal with the barging in for constant dinners and the overwhelming need for attention, even during the middle of my shows. But a Saturday morning wake-up call is where I draw the line.

The rapid pounding on the door gets louder, and I groan as I hastily hurry to my closet to grab a robe, more than aware of how the banging is going to piss off my neighbors. I mean, shit. I still consider myself to be the new girl in my apartment complex, and the last thing I need is the neighbors hating me for stupid shit like this.

Whipping around to scurry out of my room, I come to a startled stop, finding a body in my fucking bed—a body that was there without my fucking consent. Fucking Xavier. He just signed his death certificate. Rage burns through me, and I grip the edge of the covers, yanking them right back, needing to double check the asshole still has his fucking clothes on.

I go to give him a piece of my mind and throw his bitch-ass out of here when the pounding at the door gets that much worse.

"Fucking hell." I grit my teeth, storming out of my room. I swear if this is Bobby carrying on like this, I'm going to whoop his ass, and trust me, after finding Xavier in my bed, I'm gonna be a force to be reckoned with. Though on the bright side, at least Bobby would be able to help me get this asshole out of my apartment.

Finally making it to the door, I grip the handle and go to yank it open when it occurs to me that it might not be Bobby at all. He has a game tonight and needs to be in New York. There's no way he'd risk missing that to be here in Denver.

My brows furrow as I step closer to the door, trying to listen through it for any hint of who it might be, when the banging sounds again. Anger blasts through me, and suddenly I don't give a shit who's on the other side. I tear it open, rage burning through my veins. "Who the fuck do . . ."

Shit.

Carter.

I suck in a gasp, my jaw dropping in shock as I take in the man standing before me. My lack of sleep and rage about Xavier only sends me over the edge. "What are you . . ."

Wait. Something's wrong.

Those eyes I love so much are red-rimmed, and that liveliness I could always count on is non-existent. Even at the bar last week, he seemed broken, but this right here—this is an empty, shattered man.

I wrack my brain for what could possibly be going on, but all I know is that for Carter to be standing here at my door after everything we've been through, it must be bad. "What is it?" I breathe, terror gripping hold of my chest and refusing to release me as I search his broken stare. "What happened?"

His brows furrow, the pain only getting stronger as if having to say whatever it is out loud makes everything worse. Carter creeps toward me, his hands flinching at his sides, desperate to reach out and draw me into his strong arms, but he won't, even now. "It's . . ." he starts, and I feel myself already hanging off his every word, but he cuts himself off, his gaze lifting over my shoulder as I feel an arm snake around my waist.

I flinch away from Xavier's touch, thoroughly disgusted by the man beside me, and glare up at him, but he doesn't notice as Carter's ferocious stare holds him captive. "What's going on, babe?" Xavier asks me, a challenge in his tone as he fails to read the fucking room, his grip tightening around my waist.

Fury blasts through me, and I shove his hand off my waist before stepping closer to Carter, and even after five long months apart, Carter still knows me well enough to see that whatever the fuck is going on in here isn't my doing. "Get the fuck out," Carter growls, stepping into my apartment and discreetly putting himself in front of me.

"Excuse me?" Xavier scoffs, looking at Carter as though he's the one intruding. "Who do you think you are?"

Carter doesn't respond, just stands there, intimidating and imposing in the doorway, and all I can do is lift my hand to his back, unable to keep from touching him. Heat spreads through my touch, and for just a second, something eases within me. Carter leans into my touch, not daring to take his sharp glare off Xavier, and I watch as Xavier looks at me, his brows furrowed, clearly wondering why I haven't stepped in and told Carter to fuck off. But if that's what he's waiting for, he'll be waiting a long fucking time.

Xavier holds Carter's stare like some kind of pissing contest before finally glancing back at me. I let out a frustrated sigh, knowing I'm going to have to intervene before Carter physically removes him from my apartment. "You need to leave."

"What?" Xavier grunts, taken back. "I thought we had something going here."

"Fuck no," I say, not leaving any room for argument. "You've suffocated me all week, showing up here uninvited and blowing up my phone. It's insanity. The only reason I didn't kick you out is because I'm too fucking polite for that, but last night you crossed a line. Sleeping in my fucking bed? What the hell? When a woman falls asleep on the couch, that's your cue to get your shit and leave. You don't fucking take her to bed and climb in."

Carter sees red and all fucking sense of control goes flying right out the fucking door. In the blink of an eye, he slams Xavier up against my wall, his hand braced around his throat. "What the fuck?" Xavier grunts, his eyes wide with fear as he tries to push Carter off him.

Undiluted rage burns through Carter's eyes like molten lava, and I realize that despite everything Xavier's done, he's in a lot of trouble here. Rushing in, I force myself between the two men and grip Carter's arms, knowing he feels the effects of my touch, just as I feel his. Reaching up with my other hand, I cup the side of his face, ignoring the way the feel of his skin on mine lights me up for the first time in five months.

"Carter," I breathe, trying to gain his attention as I step right into him, his chest pressing against mine. My hand pushes around the back of his neck, and I pull, forcing his gaze to fall to mine. The moment I do, I feel his body finally begin to relax. "You need to let him go."

Carter looks torn but finally sees sense and releases his manic hold on Xavier, and the second he does, Xavier hightails it for the door. "I didn't sign up for this bullshit," he says, grabbing his keys off the table and disappearing.

Thank fuck.

I hastily take a step back from Carter, looking up at him in concern. "What the hell has gotten into you?" I ask, not trying to sound mean, but my tone isn't helping my case. "You can't come in here and try to dictate my life. Hell, I don't even recall inviting you through my door either."

Carter scoffs, reaching back and yanking the door shut with a hard thud. "What does it even matter? You don't even like that asshole a little bit."

"So?" I grunt, crossing my arms over my chest, desperately wishing I could head back to bed for a few hours. "That doesn't give you the right to kick him out of my apartment."

"The fucker got into bed with you without your fucking consent, Bri. What was I supposed to do? Leave him be and hope like fuck he doesn't try something tomorrow night?"

Fuck. I know he has a damn good point, but the last thing I want to do is admit it. So instead, I just glare at him, waiting to hear what he has to say for himself.

"Bri, please," he sighs as he leans back against the closed door and drags his hands down his face, looking more exhausted than I think I've ever seen him. "I'm not here to start a fight."

"It's a bit late for that," I say under my breath, trying like fuck not to think about how fucking good it felt to touch him again.

"Can I come in?" he asks, glancing toward my couch, that same brokenness from earlier returning ten-fold and reminding me that he really wasn't here to start a fight with me. Something's going on, and whatever it is is enough to bring him right to my door. "There's something . . . we need to talk."

Unease rocks through my veins as I nod and wave him toward my couch, silently welcoming him into my apartment. He visibly swallows before striding through my home and hastily dropping onto my couch, sitting too straight to possibly be comfortable.

A million things rush through my mind, each one worse than the last, and my hands start to shake, fearing what's about to come out of his mouth. Is he with someone else already? Did he knock some chick up and is going to give her the life I wanted? Fuck, I'm going to be sick thinking about this shit.

It feels weird having him here, and I stand by the kitchen, unsure of what to do. "Can I get you a coffee or something? Water?"

"No," he says with a subtle shake of his head, his eyes softening as he indicates with a slight chin lift for me to come and join him on the couch. "Can we skip over the pleasantries? The longer I wait, the harder it's going to be to get this out. Just . . . come and sit down."

Shit. He's not even going to ease me into it, just wants to rip it off like a Band-Aid.

Anxiety crashes through me as I shakily walk across my living room and take the furthest seat away from him, but perhaps I should have taken the seat closest to the door instead. There's no shame in making a quick escape.

The need to reach out and touch him runs through me, but I hold back. I can't go down that road. Touching him earlier was already too much for me to handle. After seeing him last week, I've barely gotten him out of my head, though what's new, right? I had only just gotten past the heaviness of seeing him at that bar, and now, here he is again, sending shockwaves through my body. Only this time it's worse. So much worse.

Taking a deep breath, I prepare for the worst, lifting my gaze to Carter's. "What's going on?" I finally ask, sick to my stomach.

His eyes close as if he's in an incredible amount of pain, and as his head hangs, I suddenly feel way too far away. I know I shouldn't, but I find myself getting up and crossing the living room before sitting down right beside him. "Carter," I prompt, really starting to get worried.

He takes a deep breath, and as he lifts that anguish-filled gaze to mine, he reaches across, scooping my hand into his and holding onto it as though it's his only lifeline. "Fuck, Bri. I don't know how to tell you this."

My brows furrow, but I stay silent, waiting for him to find the words. "Sara went into labor last night," he starts.

My heart sinks as I suck in a breath, the fear tightening its wicked hold on me. "The baby?" I breathe, my voice barely audible over the sound of my pulse thumping in my ears.

Carter gives me a sad smile, trying to be encouraging, but I can see that he's barely touched the surface of what's going on. "The baby is fine," he tells me. "They had a little girl."

Oh, thank God.

I let out a breath, the relief quickly thrumming through my body until it comes to a dead stop. If the baby is fine, then that could only mean . . .

No. No, he's not about to tell me what I think he's going to tell me. There has to be something else going on because the alternative simply isn't acceptable. I refuse to believe it.

Sensing my panic, Carter squeezes my hand and meets my stare once again. "The baby was stuck in the birth canal and Sara had to have an emergency C-section. The procedure went well, and the baby was delivered safely, but as they started to close Sara up, she began to hemorrhage," he tells me, pausing for just a moment as his voice breaks. "They couldn't save her, Bri. They couldn't stop the bleeding."

No, no, no. He isn't saying this. This isn't happening.

"Don't," I cry. "Don't say it."

"She's gone," he says softly.

Tears fill my eyes as words escape me, my heart shattering into a million pieces. How could this be so? I only saw Sara last week. She texted me a picture yesterday, showing off her pregnant belly. And now . . . No.

I gasp for air, struggling to catch my breath as grief claims me, darkening my soul and forcing painful sobs from deep in my chest. The realization that I'll never see her smiling face again tears me to shreds, but that precious baby. Did she even get to meet her mommy? Did Sara ever get the chance to hold her?

Fuck.

Sean. Poor Sean. The pain he must be feeling right now.

My head drops into my hands as Carter wraps his strong arms around me, and as agony filters through my body, I can't help but crawl up into his lap, straddling him as I bury my face into the curve of his neck with a desperate need for the safety and comfort only he can offer.

Carter leans back into my couch as we hold onto one another, and we sit for what could be minutes or hours, but when I finally come up for air, my eyes hurt and my body feels weak. "What's going to happen with the baby?" I ask, pulling back out of his hold and wiping my sore eyes on the back of my hands, knowing Sean wouldn't be in any state to look after a newborn so soon after his wife passed.

"Cassie is going to watch her for now, and I guess Sara's parents will help out too, but I'm sure they'll be busy with funeral arrangements. I can't picture Sean being up for that," he explains.

I nod, the tears still running down my cheeks. "Let them know that I'm here if it gets too hard, or if they just need a break. I can help."

"They know," he tells me, his hand dropping to my thigh and giving it a comforting squeeze.

Needing to put a little space between us, I clamber off his lap and sink into my couch, grabbing my throw blanket and pulling it right up to my chin. Carter and I sit in a numb silence, both of us lost in our thoughts, his hand not leaving my thigh for even a second.

He must sit with me for well over an hour before he sits forward on the couch, dragging a hand over his face. "I should probably get back to Sean," he says. "Are you going to be okay if I get going?"

"Yeah," I murmur, getting up, the heaviness in my heart making me feel as though I will never smile again. "I should probably check in on Cass. She'll need a friend right now."

"She's still at the hospital," he tells me. "Did you want me to give you a lift?"

"No," I say with a slight shake of my head, reality starting to creep back in. "That's probably not a good idea. This is . . . it's already too much."

Carter nods in agreement, and I feel an awkward goodbye coming along, and after just losing Sara, the thought of letting him walk out the door has new tears welling in my eyes. He rubs the back of his neck as he looks down. "I, umm . . . I didn't want you finding out through someone else," he says, slowly lifting his dark gaze back to mine. "And I just . . . I guess I just really needed to see you."

I nod but don't respond. I mean, what can I say? Thanks for showing up at my door at 6:30 in the morning and telling me that one of my best friends is dead—a woman I thought would be family one day.

Shit.

Not knowing what else to say, Carter gives me a forced smile before finally turning his back and walking around my couch, making his way to my door. He clutches the handle, and as he slowly pulls it open, he looks back at me, longing flashing in his eyes, and I realize just how much he needs me right now. His grief, on top of missing me, is eating him alive, and just as he is for me, I'm one of his only comforts. But he pushed me away, he let me go, and unfortunately, that means he doesn't get to come back and take what he needs from me when times get hard. That's not how a breakup is supposed to work.

His gaze falls away, and just as quickly as he barged in here, he disappears. As the soft thud of the door sounds through my small apartment, the tears return, and I break down all over again.

Chapter Thirteen

BRIANNA

I walk into the hospital and head straight for the maternity ward, following a family who's carrying a bundle of pink balloons that say *It's a girl* across the front. Shit, maybe I should have stopped to pick up something to say congratulations, but what do you get a newborn baby who just lost her mother?

I've never been in here and have no idea where I'm going, and I wander around for a few minutes before finally coming to the nursery, peering in to find the room filled with tiny little blue and pink bundles, each one of them so content in their bassinet.

Cass sits in a quiet corner with her hand on a crib, gently rocking it back and forth and looking as though she's about ready to pass out. My heart breaks for her. I can't imagine what fresh hell she's been through over the past twelve hours. She's gone from being excited about meeting her niece, to grieving a loved one, to now becoming a temporary, full-time caregiver for a newborn baby.

I gently knock on the window, hoping I don't wake up any of the babies, and I watch as Cassie's eyes ping open, her gaze lifting to meet mine through the glass. Her face lights up for the quickest moment, and as I smile back at her, the heaviness returns and the light completely disappears.

Her face breaks, and as her bottom lip starts to wobble, the tears spring from her eyes. And after looking down to check the baby, she rushes out of the nursery. I catch her in my arms, and the second her face smooshes into my neck, we each fall apart, weeping over the loss of our friend.

"Are you alright?" I ask a few minutes later as we both start wiping our eyes.

She sniffles and shakes her head. "No," she tells me. "I don't have a single clue what I'm doing here. I'm not maternal. Hell, I don't even know how to change a diaper. I'm so out of my depth, and it's only been a few hours. But there's nothing I can do. I've been trying to google everything, but it's just—I've never been a mom before or ever cared for someone other than myself. I don't know what I'm doing. I can't be responsible for a newborn, but none of the boys would be able to handle it."

"Hey," I say, trying to soothe her panic. "It's going to be alright.

The fact that you're standing here, willing to do this to help Sean, speaks volumes. We've just gotta figure out what she needs and take it one step at a time."

"I . . . I don't think I can," Cassie admits. "Every time she cries, I can't help but think that she needs her mommy." The second the word *mommy* comes out of her mouth, we both break down again, tears falling from our eyes. "Do you want to come and meet her?" Cass finally asks when we've both regained control of ourselves.

"Yeah, I'd love to," I tell her.

Cass takes my hand, and we walk into the nursery as quietly as possible. She leads me to her niece with a proud smile, and I peer over the edge of the bassinet, taking in the most precious angel I've ever seen. "Wow," I say as I look down at the gorgeous little soul. "She's beautiful."

A tear escapes my eye as I notice how most of her little features are an exact baby version of Sara's. The big eyes, the light hair, the cheeks. It goes on and on. "She looks just like her," I whisper.

"Yeah," Cass says. "She sure does."

Glancing up at her name card, I realize it's still empty. "Does she have a name yet?" I ask, noticing how all the other babies are perfectly filled out.

"No . . . actually, I don't know. She's just baby Waters for now. Sean came to see her for about thirty seconds. He took one look at her, and it's like his whole world just shattered all over again. I know she needs him right now, but he's not ready, and I don't want to force her on him until I know he's going to be able to care for her properly."

Damn. Every word she says is like taking a shot straight to the chest. I can't imagine how hard this must be for all of them, Sean in particular. "Do you know what you're going to do when she gets discharged?"

"No, I've been thinking about it. I'm not sure if I should move in with Sean until he can handle it or if I just set up a nursery at home and keep her with me. I guess it all comes down to Sean. She's either going to help him heal or make it harder."

"I can't imagine being in your position right now," I tell her. "Just remember, I'm here if you need me."

The baby cries and Cass looks up at the clock with an unsure cringe. "I think she's hungry again?" she says, but it comes out more like a question. "Or maybe she wants to sleep . . ."

"Okay, grab her a bottle and we'll give it a try," I tell her in a calming tone, trying to help her see that this doesn't need to be a panic. It's nothing but a little trial and error until you get it right. "If that's not what she wants, she'll tell you, and then we can try a sleep."

"Yeah, you're right," she says before disappearing and returning a minute later with a bottle in hand. "I don't know why I'm freaking out so much about this."

"Don't stress, it's normal," I tell her. "Most first-time moms freak out, and they have nine months to prepare. This has just been sprung on you at a moment's notice. No one expects you to be perfect. Just keep her safe until her daddy can take over."

She lets out a shaky breath before settling the bottle down and reaching in to pick up the baby before pausing and glancing at me. "Do you want to do it?" she asks.

A wide smile stretches across my face. "Oh God, I thought you'd never ask." Leaning over the side of the bassinet, I scoop the sweet little angel into my arms and take a seat on the nursery couch as Cass comes over with the bottle. She hands it to me and takes the seat beside me, watching as I help to push the bottle teat into the right position in her mouth. It takes the baby a few tries, but eventually she settles into it and takes her sweet-ass time drinking the bottle. But I can't blame her. She's barely a few hours old. She needs to work up the muscles before she'll be able to drink like her uncles.

"Wow, how did you get her to do that?" Cassie muses, watching with a keen eye. "She's been struggling with me."

"You just need to relax when you're with her. Babies feed off your emotions. They can sense when you're upset and anxious, and that makes them uneasy. If you're relaxed, the baby will be relaxed."

"Well I can't really help that right now," she scoffs.

"I know, but when you're with her, just be with her. Push everything else to the side and try to enjoy it," I tell her. "Everything with her parents is completely out of your control, so all you need to do is think about her. She needs to feel safe with you, and that will come with your confidence."

Cassie pushes out her bottom lip. "You know that's so much easier said than done," she says.

"I know, but I know you, Cass, and that's how I know you're going to rock this. Just give it a day or two and ease into it. I can stick around and help. We can tag-team it."

Cass leans into me, her head resting against my shoulder. "I love you," she murmurs just as an almighty yawn tears through her.

"I love you, too."

The baby is just about finished her bottle when the door to the nursery opens and Carter strides in. He glances up as he approaches us before coming to a startling stop, clearly having forgotten that I was going to be here with Cass. His jaw goes slack as he stands in silence, not knowing what to say as he takes it all in—more specifically, watching me with his newborn niece tucked securely in my arms.

He stands motionless, looking completely lost for words. "I, um . . . just wanted to check on the baby."

The thought of Carter looking out for this baby kills me, but then it makes me wonder if having this baby around might help change his view on the whole having kids thing. I mean, if he could negotiate on that, then I can negotiate on the marriage thing. As long as I can somehow have him in my life.

Shit. Wishful thinking has never got me far.

Passing the baby to Cassie, I stand and give her an encouraging smile, needing to be anywhere but here. "I'm gonna go and grab us something to eat," I tell her, watching as she awkwardly tries to hold the baby while balancing her bottle and keeping it from falling out of her mouth.

"What?" Cass panics, her eyes wide. "Don't leave. I need you."

I help make adjustments so they're both comfortable on the couch. "I'll be gone for fifteen minutes at most. You'll be fine," I tell her. "Once she's finished her bottle, sit her up on your lap and support her head, then gently pat her back until she burps. Then you should be good to change her diaper and put her to sleep."

"Okay," she says. "Wait. Why does she need to burp?"

A grin stretches across my face, and I lean in to give her the cold hard truth. "You know that pain you get in your guts when you really need to let one rip and you just can't?"

Cassie's eyes widen, understanding exactly where I'm going with this. "Right, okay. A burp is a must," she says. "And what do I do after all of that?"

"Breathe," I tell her with an encouraging smile, while desperately aware of the way Carter listens in on our conversation, his closeness making me need to reach out to him just as I did back in my apartment. "If she doesn't want to sleep after that, give her a cuddle and enjoy it. Let her know that she's got the best aunty in the world and that she's going to be just fine."

Cassie lets out a heavy breath, giving me a warm smile. "I swear, if you go any further than the hospital food court, I'm hunting you down."

"Fifteen minutes," I remind her before grabbing my phone and holding it up. "I'm keeping this on. Call me if you need me, okay?" And with that, I turn and make my way out of the nursery, keeping my head down and avoiding Carter's piercing stare with every last ounce of determination I have left.

Chapter Fourteen

BRIANNA

It's been four long days since Sara's death, and today we say goodbye.

I figured I'd head over to Cassie's place first to help her get ready because, let's face it, trying to do anything with a newborn isn't supposed to be easy. Plus, Jax tries, but the truth is that he's completely useless when it comes to this baby. At least he's trying though. They're both completely exhausted, and even though it's only been four days, I can see them starting to get into a routine that's working for them.

After getting myself dressed and ready, I grab my black purse off my kitchen counter and head out to my car—well, technically it's

Bobby's car. Though to be fair, he offered it up for me to use while I wait for my new car to come in, but that's on him. Bobby knows me well enough to know that I would claim it as my own. Besides, he's got more than enough cars over in New York, he doesn't need this one.

Putting the car into gear, I head over to Cassie's place, feeling the heaviness of Sara's loss on my heart today. Don't get me wrong, I've been feeling it every day. Every time I see her baby, I feel it. Every time someone mentions how Sean's doing, I feel it. But today, knowing we will gather to say our final goodbyes . . . shit. It stings in a way no one could ever prepare for.

As far as I'm aware, Sean hasn't found the courage to visit his daughter since he broke down in the hospital, and I can't blame him for that. Everybody deals with grief in different ways, and we all just have to come together to help him wherever he needs. But my heart breaks for his baby girl. She still doesn't have a name, and I know she's only a baby and has no idea what's going on, but I can't help but feel like she needs her daddy. I understand these are unusual circumstances, but he will come around. I'm sure of it.

Sara's parents have been helpful, but with their elderly age combined with the devastation over losing their only daughter, and making the funeral arrangements, there's only so much they've been able to do. So, unfortunately for Cass, all those responsibilities remain on her shoulders.

Parking my car in Cassie's big driveway, I make my way up the grand entrance and push through the front door, knocking on the wood as I go. "It's just me," I call out from the foyer.

The baby's cries are the first thing I hear, followed by Jax's voice politely asking her to go to sleep as though this were some kind of business meeting. I follow the sound into the living room and find Jax standing in nothing but a pair of sweatpants, looking as though he hasn't slept a wink as he bounces the little girl in his arms.

"Oh, thank fuck," Jax mutters the second he sees me. He strides across the room, and before I have a chance to put my purse down, he deposits the sweet little angel into my arms. "I love her and all, but I wasn't made for babies. Especially ones this small."

I laugh as I lay her down on the couch and fix up her blanket before cuddling the blonde beauty into my arms. "You'll pick it up eventually," I tell him, though to be honest, I'm hoping he won't have to. Sean is going to swoop in at some point and take this little girl, and the rest will be history. At least until Cass decides to pop out a baby of her own, but after this, I wouldn't be surprised if they wanted to wait a little.

"Yeah, I'm not too sure about that," Jax says, dragging his hands over his tired face. "Give me a toddler any day. I can drop one of those without breaking it."

I roll my eyes as I get comfortable on the couch, and as I glance down at the baby, I realize this little cherub is wide awake with no chance of sleep in her near future. "When was the last time she had a bottle?"

"I don't know," he says. "Cass is having a shower. She said all I had to do was watch her while she slept, but then she woke up and started crying."

"So . . . you're trying to put her back to sleep?" I grin.

"Well, yeah," he grunts as if it's a stupid question.

"She's hungry, dude," I tell him as I get up and head into the kitchen. Jax helps out, putting a bottle together and grabbing a towel in case she decides to hit me with one of her crowd-pleasing spit-ups. There's no faulting Jax here. While he's still uncomfortable with the baby, he's nailing everything else.

"God help you when you guys have kids," I tell him with a grin as I settle back on the couch, the bottle already in her mouth.

"Tell me about it," he replies, looking horrified for what his future will hold.

A moment later, we hear Cass on the stairs, and when she strides into the living room wrapped in a towel, a smile spreads across her face seeing me with her niece. "Hey," she says with a cringe. "Sorry that took so long. I kind of fell asleep while shaving my legs."

My gaze shifts down her body and I can't help the grin that pulls at the corner of my lips, seeing that after she fell asleep, she still couldn't be bothered finishing the job. "No problem," I tell her. "We're just chilling down here if you want to finish getting ready."

"Thank God," she mumbles, walking over to the back of the couch and peering over my shoulder at the little girl. "You all good? I thought we were meeting at the church."

"I couldn't sleep and was up and ready much earlier than I expected, so I thought I'd come over here to help you guys out. Today is gonna be hard for everyone, and if I can somehow make that a little easier, then here I am."

"Thank, fuck," Jax sighs in relief. "I was worried I'd have to do it."

Cass rolls her eyes at her husband. "Would you just go and get your ass ready?" she mutters. "You smell like baby shit and . . . is that vomit on your chest?"

Jax's eyes widen in horror, his head dropping to his chest where something white and crusty lingers to the right of his sculpted man-tit. His face goes pale, and he looks as though he's about to hurl as he turns on his heel and blasts out of here.

Cass laughs, more than happy with herself before looking back at me. "You wanna bring her upstairs? I could use some help figuring out what to wear."

With that, Cass helps pull me up from the couch without disturbing the baby drinking her bottle, and we hurry upstairs, more than aware of the time quickly running out. I make myself comfortable in Cassie's massive walk-in closet, which is practically the size of my whole apartment.

She riffles through her clothes, pulling out dress after dress and holding them up to her body before looking at me, her face scrunching with distaste after every single one. She's running out of options when she finally pulls one out that makes her take a second look. She moves in front of her mirror, and after holding it against her body, she finally loses her towel and gets her ass dressed. She matches it with a pair of heels before heading into the bathroom to start on her hair and makeup.

She's just about done when I look at the clock and realize that if we don't get going soon, we're going to be late. "Hey, Cass," I call out, realizing we haven't seen Jax since he left to get ready. "Maybe check Jax hasn't crashed somewhere. I'm gonna get the baby ready, and then I think it's time to go."

"Oh shit," she mutters, probably only halfway through her hair. "Okay."

Ducking out of her room with a near-sleeping baby attached to my chest, I stride down the hall and into the room they've made into a nursery. It's not exactly the best setup for a baby, and there are definitely a lot of things missing, but considering everything and what little time they've had to prepare for this, they're doing amazing. Besides, it's not like the baby actually sleeps in here. She has a little bassinet right beside Cass and Jax's bed, so this nursery is pretty much used as a changing station and storage for all her clothes, most of which are still in the shopping bags they came in.

Laying the baby down, I go through all the little outfits she has, but I can't really find anything appropriate for a funeral among the piles of white and pink clothes. I decide on a white dress thinking it could be symbolic of her innocence and unconditional love she's bound to have for her mommy.

Fuck, I know she didn't get a chance to really meet her properly, but I bet she's missing her.

With the baby ready, I head downstairs to find Cassie madly packing a diaper bag, filling it with hundreds of diapers, wipes, spare outfits, spare bottles, and practically a whole tin of formula. I grin to myself, able to see her future so perfectly in this moment.

Cass hears my heels clicking on the tiles and glances up, taking in the precious baby in my arms. A brilliant smile comes over her face, and her eyes fill with subtle tears. "Oh, look at you," she coos to the baby as she lifts her out of my arms. "You are the most beautiful creature in the world."

Jax appears from around the corner and grabs the diaper bag off the table, slinging it over his shoulder, doing what he can to be helpful. With everyone ready, we all head out to his truck. There's going to be a celebration of Sara's life here after the funeral, so I jump in Jax's truck, knowing I'm just going to end up here later anyway.

We arrive at the church, and I find it packed with Sara's friends and family, some who I know well, and some I'm only meeting for the first time today. We head on in and find Sean right up front, greeting everyone and putting on a show, pretending to be cheerful when we all know he's absolutely wrecked inside.

Knowing Carter is bound to be here somewhere, I scan the pews until I find him standing in the front of the church. He's wearing a suit that fits him just right, and something dies inside of me as I'm hit with the fleeting thought of him waiting for me at the very end of the church's center aisle on our wedding day.

Shit. I can't go there. Not today.

The last time I saw him in a suit was Cassie's wedding, the night he realized we couldn't continue, and it's a stark reminder of the white suit jacket that lives rent-free in the bottom of my closet. I try my hardest to push the thoughts away, needing today to be about Sara, not my broken heart.

Tearing my gaze from Carter, I make my way down the aisle with Cass and Jax, doing everything in my power not to look his way again. I push the stroller to give myself a distraction and head straight for Sean, stepping right into him and giving him a big hug. The second I pull back, he glances down at his little girl, his lips pressing into a hard line as if trying not to break. "How's she doing?" he asks quietly.

"Good," I say with an encouraging smile before taking a risk. "She could really use her daddy."

He doesn't respond, just watches her with longing, and I dip down into the stroller and pull the sleeping beauty out. "Here," I say, handing her over.

Sean starts to object, but I thrust her toward him and deposit her right into his arms. He awkwardly takes her from me, and I keep quiet as he adjusts her, getting comfortable. She instantly lets out a sigh and snuggles in closer, as if knowing perfectly well that her daddy's got her now.

Sean falls in love with her right before my eyes, and I realize this must be the first time he's actually held her. He shuffles over toward the front pew and takes a seat, ignoring all the people around him, each one of them solely here as a reminder of everything he's lost.

This was Sara's gift to him, and maybe all he needs is a moment to catch up.

I look around and see all eyes are on him. Cassie has soft tears falling from her eyes, while Logan and Carter look ridiculously identical, the heartbreak and sorrow written all over their faces.

Sean puts his finger into her little hand, and it crushes my heart to see his daughter latch onto it like she'll never let go. I take a seat beside him and look down at the sweet baby. "I think she misses her mommy," I tell him honestly.

"Why?" he questions.

"Because she spent the last nine months loving her unconditionally. Sara cradled her and talked to her every day. I know they didn't get a chance to bond face-to-face, but I like to think that she knew who her mommy was."

"Thanks, Bri," he says with sincerity.

"She's the closest link to Sara that you'll ever have," I tell him. "Embrace that. Don't push her away."

"Never," he whispers as he looks down at his baby girl who resembles her mother in the most incredible way.

The priest approaches Sean and lets him know it's time to get started, and with a nod, Sean hands the baby over to me and rounds up the boys. They head outside while the guests take their seats, and I lean over to Cass, letting her know that I'll watch the baby during the funeral. She's performing a few songs during the ceremony and I can give her one less thing to worry about.

A few minutes later, the priest welcomes everybody while Cassie gets up and adjusts the microphone. Music starts and the words of *Hallelujah* flow freely from her mouth, filling the church with its heartbreaking sound.

The triplets come in slowly, holding Sara's coffin along with Jax, her father, and her cousin. Watching them walk down the aisle breaks me, and tears start flowing from my eyes as I hold my dear friend's child while I tell her goodbye.

Nothing on this earth will ever make this moment okay.

Death is such a natural thing. It happens all the time, and eventually, it happens to us all. So why is it so hard to say goodbye?

The boys place Sara down gently at the front of the church and take their seats. Sean sits down on my right and reaches for the baby while Carter sits to my left. He pulls my hand into his and I allow him to, as quite frankly, I need him more than anything. I know letting go later is going to destroy me, but I can't find it within me to care. I need this just as much as he does.

We don't look at each other, and I think it's better that way. He rubs his thumb over my knuckles and gives me all the comfort he can offer. All I want in this moment is to curl into him and cry, but I hold myself together because, as much as I hate it, I'm no longer his, and I'm not entitled to that luxury anymore.

When Cassie's song ends, she comes to sit with Jax, tears in her eyes as the priest gets started.

The time comes for Sean's eulogy, and it's the most difficult thing to witness. He stands before the congregation with bloodshot eyes and takes a shaky breath. He waits a moment, finding it too hard to start, but then looks at his daughter to find the strength.

He starts talking about the type of wife and friend Sara was, telling us all how they met in high school and fell in love over movie dates and stupid parties. The further he gets through his speech, the harder the words are for him to deliver until grief completely takes over, and he can no longer go on.

Carter releases my hand and rises beside me before making his way to the altar. He embraces his brother before taking the speech out of his hands and making my tears fall that much stronger.

Sean takes his seat beside me, weeping with undeniable grief, and I hand him his baby girl, realizing he needs her now more than ever. He greedily takes her and pulls her right up to his face, holding her to him and taking comfort in her.

Carter watches Sean with tears in his eyes, but he remains strong just as I knew he would. He quickly searches through Sean's speech, and not a moment later, picks up where his brother left off.

It's hard to listen to the words spilling out of Carter's mouth, the agony and grief in his tone, every new sentence of Sean's eulogy tearing me to shreds. And as Carter finishes Sean's speech, pride surges through me for how he so effortlessly stood in front of all these people and poured his heart out through Sean's words, knowing these people needed to hear Sean and Sara's story. But I wouldn't have expected anything less, that's the kind of man he is.

Carter returns to my side and eagerly scoops my hand into his, and it doesn't go unnoticed how he holds onto me a little bit tighter. Completing Sean's speech definitely took a toll on his heart.

Cass gets up and sings *At Last*, and I realize this is the song she sang at Sean and Sara's wedding for their first dance. I wasn't there, but I've seen that moment caught on video, and it was just as beautiful as it is now. More tears spill from my eyes, and before I know it, Cassie's song is coming to an end and we're heading to the cemetery.

I thought it couldn't get much worse than listening to Sean's words in the church or hearing him as he wept beside me, but standing at Cassie's side, holding onto her as we watch the boys lower Sara into the ground is easily the hardest part of the day.

One by one, the guests leave the cemetery, leaving just us and Sara's closest friends and family behind. Everybody who stays behind receives an offer to come to Cassie's place for dinner and a celebration of Sara's life, and as expected, every single one of them shows up.

We sit around the massive living room, each with a drink in hand, toasting to our memories of the woman we never wanted to say goodbye to.

Sean sits with the baby in his arms, feeding her a bottle while everyone goes around the circle, telling their favorite stories of Sara. There's laughter, tears, smiles, and sobs coming from every direction of the room, and it's heartbreakingly beautiful, everything that Sara deserves.

I watch Sean as the stories are told, and I feel like today has given him just a little bit of closure. And while nothing is going to take away his pain, he was able to say goodbye on his own terms, and eventually, he will start to heal, but it's going to be one hell of a long journey. Having his daughter in his lap definitely helps, but hearing the sweet words of his loved ones talking about his wife and how much they adored her puts a smile on his face, and I couldn't have asked for anything more.

"She truly was a beautiful woman," I tell him as he catches me watching the smile on his face. "You know she will forever be looking down on you and that beautiful girl."

He raises his drink to me, and together we toast to Sara and the wonderful life she led.

Chapter Fifteen

CARTER

Today goes right up there as one of the hardest days of my life, right beside burying my parents and leaving Bri.

Most people have gone, leaving just my family and Bri behind, and I sit quietly, the heaviness still resting on my heart as I nurse a bottle of Jack. I'm glad today is coming to an end so I can try and put the pain behind me. I just want to live in a world of denial, one where I can pretend this never happened and Sara is right here with us—that this was all a sick fucking joke and soon enough, she's going to come waltzing through the door with a stupid grin and say *Gotcha*.

My gaze remains locked on Bri, just as it has for most of the day.

She doesn't know it, but she's the only reason I've been able to make it through the day. She's been a gift to my family during this time. She's been there for Cass, held her hand during the hardest part of the day, sat with Sean during the ceremony, and even got him to accept his daughter and find comfort within her—something I was truly starting to become concerned about.

And by some miracle, she even allowed me to hold her hand when I thought I couldn't go on any longer, but when I had to let go, it almost tore me to shreds.

The baby falls asleep in Sean's arms, and I find it impossible to tear my gaze away from her. I have completely fallen in love with this child, but by no means does that mean I've changed my mind about wanting to have one of my own. This baby is family and was created out of the love that Sean and Sara shared. She's a huge part of Sara that's been left behind, and because of that, I will protect and treasure this child for the rest of my life.

Sean looks up from his little bundle of joy and glances around the room. "Sara wanted to call her Georgia, but I think I'll add Sara's name in too. Georgia Sara Waters," he tells us.

"I love it," Cassie smiles as she holds up her drink. "To little baby Georgia."

We all greedily take another drink, which most of us follow up with another, and it's no surprise that within the space of thirty minutes, most of us are wasted. As the night becomes rowdy with laughter and stories, Logan hops up and offers to take little Georgia up to her bassinet, only he stumbles and nearly falls straight into the wall, making Sean hold onto his little angel just a little bit tighter.

"I'll take her," Bri offers, getting up and taking her out of Sean's arms. Sean gives her a gentle kiss on the forehead before reluctantly relaxing back onto the couch and watching Bri leave the room. Despite knowing I shouldn't, I find myself on my feet, quietly following her out of the room.

I walk up the stairs and follow the sound of the soft singing coming from the darkened nursery, and I lean against the doorframe, watching as she tucks Georgia into her bassinet. The baby stirs in her bed, but Bri gently rocks it while the words of *"Twinkle, Twinkle, Little Star"* flow beautifully from her mouth.

I'm struck with the memory of my mother singing this very song to us when we were kids. I always pretended that I was too tough to have my mom sing to me, especially a song I always considered to be for girls, but on the inside, I loved it. I just wish I would have told her that. Though I'm sure she knew. She always knew.

Watching how good Bri's been with this baby confirms that I was right. I did the right thing by ending it with her. I just wish it didn't hurt so much. She's going to make an amazing mother one day. Even with someone else's child, she's nurturing and loving.

Once Georgia is settled, she turns to leave but comes to a halt when she sees me in the doorway. Her back stiffens as her gorgeous green eyes flash with longing. "What are you doing?" she asks, pausing near the door and keeping her voice low to not wake the baby.

"I . . . I don't know," I admit. "I just had to see you."

Bri presses her lips together, and deciding she can't handle hearing it tonight, she heads for the door. She walks straight past me, but when I'm hit with that familiar smell of her perfume, I find myself reaching out and grabbing her arm.

She pauses and both of us stand in silence, and despite knowing how reckless this is, I can't stop myself from pulling her back and drawing her into my arms until her chest collides with mine. She gasps, her hand bracing against my chest as she looks up at me, and all I see is pain.

She's still hurting deeply, and I hate that I'm responsible for that. "Don't," she whispers, gently shaking her head. "Don't do this."

My gaze softens, my hand tightening around her waist and holding her to me. "You're going to make an amazing mother one day," I tell her.

Tears well in her eyes, but she refuses to let them fall. "Have you changed your mind?" she questions.

Pain rips through me as she watches me, waiting for my answer. I see the hope in her eyes, and knowing that I'm going to have to shut her down again kills me. I don't know if it's the alcohol in my system or the fact that I've been craving her for so long, but I reach out and run my finger down the side of her face, watching as she leans into my touch. "No, I haven't," I tell her regrettably.

Bri lets out a sigh, a single tear falling down her cheek. "Then I'll never be a mother."

Fuck. No.

"Don't say that, Brianna," I tell her, the idea of her never getting her happily ever after because of me makes me want to throw myself off the top of the tallest building. "You're going to be a mother someday, and it's going to be everything you've dreamed of."

"No," she says, determination in her tone as she looks away and rests her head against my chest. Out of habit, my hand curls into the back of her hair, holding her to me, terrified that she might decide to walk away. "I can't just turn off how I feel about you, and the thought of having anyone else's child but yours eats me up. It's always going to be you, Carter."

Fuck. That hurts.

"I'm sorry," I murmur. "You don't know how much I wish I could give you that. I've fucking destroyed myself over the last five months, willing myself to be able to take it all back and change my mind. I'm so fucking in love with you, Brianna. It kills me that I'm hurting you like this."

I feel her tears soaking through my shirt, and I do my best to wipe them away. She brings up her hands, and I crave for her to wrap them around me just like she used to, but instead, she presses against my chest and pushes me away.

Desperation gnaws at me. I'm not ready for this to end, and I grab her hand, not letting her go. "Don't go," I beg, feeling as though my whole fucking world will crumble if she walks away right now.

"Why?" she asks, those watery eyes piercing right through to my soul.

I pull her in close and tilt her face up to mine, her lips barely a breath away. "Because I can't handle watching you walk away again, not tonight."

Her eyes search mine, and I can't resist her any longer. I drop my face to hers, closing the gap as I take her warm lips in mine in a passionate, needy kiss, bringing me home for the first time in five long months. Brianna melts into me, her arms locking around my neck as she kisses me back, a soft moan rumbling through her chest.

I deepen our kiss and hate that her cheeks are still wet from her tears, wishing I could be the man she needs me to be.

Brianna is home to me, and being with her right now feels like being welcomed back after a million years away, but I know it's wrong. This is nothing more than a stolen moment that's only going to make it so much harder to let go. I ended it, I broke her heart and left her empty, but still, I'm standing here asking to take from her again when I know I don't deserve it.

I can handle hurting myself in order to touch her if only for a little while, but hurting her again is monstrous, and I should be ashamed of myself. Yet, I can't find it within me to stop. I take her in like a drug I've been starved of, a desperate craving that needs to be satisfied, because without it, I know I would certainly die. And after all this time, she's still my world.

"Fuck, I love you," I say against her lips. She doesn't say anything, and I realize that hearing those words probably isn't the greatest thing to help her move on, but it's not as though she hasn't always known it. My love for her is never going to change, even through the darkest storms. How could it?

Bri's hands find the top of my shirt, and she pops the first button as a wild desperation crashes through me, and yet I grab her hands, stopping her from going any further. She pulls back, looking up at me in confusion. There's only been once I've denied her. Apart from that, she knows I'm not the man to hold back when she needs me physically. "We shouldn't," I tell her, knowing that taking this any further could be detrimental to our health.

She takes a shaky breath before fisting her hand into the front of my shirt and pulling me back in. "Yeah, Carter. Yeah, we definitely should," she pants, a fire burning in her eyes, one that drives me crazy with hunger. "It's okay," she says, sensing my hesitation. "I know it means nothing."

"Bri, baby," I say, my fingers trailing down her body. "It will never mean nothing."

"I can handle it," she promises. "I need this. Please, Carter. I need it just as much as you do."

Fuck.

My lips slam back on hers as she grabs my shirt in both hands and tears it open, the buttons popping off and scattering through the hallway. Grasping her firm ass, I lift her and push her up against the wall, pinning her with my body as she winds her legs around my waist. I'm hard within seconds and grind against her, five long months of craving keeping me on edge.

My lips drop to her neck as she pushes the fabric of my torn shirt off my shoulders, and I rip the shirt off my body, letting it fall to the ground behind me. The second she can, she puts her hands on my bare skin, and the feel of her touch is like the sweetest sin. Fuck, I've missed her touch.

I close my eyes as the pure longing and satisfaction become too much to bear. I need so much more, but I'm terrified she's going to tell me to stop, push me away, and remind me that this is a terrible idea.

Feeling weird about doing this right near Georgia's room, I pull her away from the wall, holding onto her tightly as I walk back down the long hallway toward my old bedroom, the same room we were in when I first broke her heart.

With her lips on mine and her hands clawing into the muscles of my back, I reach for the door handle when Bri lifts her face from mine. "Not here," she murmurs against my lips.

Understanding tears at my chest. The last time we were in this room, we left with shattered hearts. Of course she's not going to want to go in there, I should have known. This room is tainted.

I keep walking down the hall and push through to the guest room, kicking the door shut behind me before lowering Bri to her feet and diving for her dress. If this were any other moment with her, I'd take my time. I'd start at the top and worship every inch of her body, not stopping until her throat is raw from screaming my name, but right now, we don't have time for that. The hunger and craving are too strong, and if I don't get to touch her soon, I'll surely crumble.

Bri's dress is unzipped as she works on my belt, yanking it out of my pants and dropping it to the ground with her dress. She steps out of the pool of fabric at her feet, leaving her in nothing but black lace underwear, a matching bra, and black high heels.

Fuck me. I could come just looking at her.

My gaze lingers on her body as my pants drop to the floor, and the second they're gone, we frantically collide. She jumps into my arms, all but clawing her way up my body as I walk us to the bed, crashing down onto the mattress with our lips fused together.

My hands roam over her silky smooth skin as the rush to rid ourselves of our underwear begins. She reaches down between us and works on freeing my straining cock as I slide one hand beneath her, quickly unclasping her bra.

I pull the straps off her arms and toss the black lace to the side, revealing her perfect tits that I've done nothing but dream of since the moment I walked away. Without a second thought, I lower my lips to her breast and close my mouth over her nipple, my tongue flicking over it as it hardens beneath my touch. Bri groans and arches her back off the mattress, pushing up against me, silently begging for more. And goddamn, I'm going to give it to her.

With my underwear now somewhere at the end of the bed, Bri closes her tight fist around the base of my cock, working her way up and down, her thumb roaming over my tip as I close my eyes in pure ecstasy.

Needing her to feel just as fucking alive, my hand trails down her body and slips inside her black, lace thong. I cup her pussy, and she grinds against the heel of my palm, groaning for more. "Fuck, Carter," she pants. "Please."

She's soaking wet, ready for me to give her everything she needs, and I don't hesitate, rubbing my fingers over her clit and loving the way her body jolts with undeniable pleasure beneath me. Keeping my thumb at her clit, I stretch my fingers down and slowly push inside her, feeling her walls squeezing around me. "Yes," she cries as I start to work her.

I add another finger, massaging her walls while moving in and out, not daring to let up on her sweet clit, and in return, she works my cock the way I like it. The closer she gets, her grip tightens, and I fucking crave her more. I need to fuck her and make sweet love, but at the same time, I'm desperate to take her mouth, desperate to feel her hands all over my body, and desperate to taste her as she comes.

I fucking need it all.

"Carter," Bri pants. "I need you inside me."

Fuck, yes.

Nothing holds me back as I pull my hand free from her sweet cunt and tear her thong right down the fucking seams. Then taking her thigh, I hitch it up and around my hip as I line myself up with her entrance, then finally bring us home as I push inside her, stretching her walls around me.

Bri arches her back off the mattress, tipping her head back as she bites down on her bottom lip. Her hand fists into the hair at the nape of my neck, and she pulls me down to her, closing the distance. I don't hesitate to drop my lips to hers and kiss her with the fierce need that blasts through my chest. She closes her eyes as the undiluted pleasure rocks through both of us, satisfying the wild hunger and craving we've each felt over the past five months.

Bri laces her fingers through mine, holding onto me with everything she's got as I really start working her body, feeling like the fucking stars are aligned for the first time in months. I move in and out while working her clit with my fingers, rubbing tight circles just as my other hand cups her tit, my thumb brushing right over her pebbled nipple and making her squirm beneath my touch.

I've always loved being physical with Bri, it's where we excelled, but this right here is so much more than we ever had before. A fucking nuclear bomb could detonate right now and we'd have no fucking clue. This woman right here is the only thing that exists in my world right now.

My lips come down on hers, and as I continue to thrust into her, taking her deeper with each new angle, she pushes up into me, needing so much more. Our bodies grow sweaty, and she squeezes my hands as she gets closer to the edge. I know I'm not going to be able to last, five months of jerking off doesn't compare to being inside this incredible woman.

I feel her walls start to contract, and I know she's right on the fucking edge, and I don't dare stop, desperate to feel the way her pussy comes undone around me. I hitch her thigh up higher, taking her even deeper, not daring to let up on her clit, and as I thrust into her one more time, her nails dig into my shoulders, and she cries out in undeniable ecstasy. Brianna explodes around me, her pussy clenching on my cock, and it's all I can fucking take before coming right along with her.

I keep moving as she rides out her high, her walls convulsing around me as I pour myself into her sweet pussy. "Holy fuck," she pants, throwing her head back with pleasure, looking more fucking radiant than ever before.

She reaches her climax, and as we both start coming down, I

collapse on top of her, bracing myself on my elbows to keep from squishing her beneath me. Neither of us move—Bri's thigh still hitched over my hip as I remain seated deep inside her sweet pussy, the idea of ever pulling out of her eating me alive.

Slipping my arms around her, I hold her tight as I roll us over on the bed, putting her on top so I don't crush her with my weight, a move I've made with her so many times before. She immediately lowers her head to my chest and lets out a heavy sigh as I run my fingers through her hair, my other hand resting against her ass.

Neither of us speak, knowing the second we do, it's all over, and the thought of having to let her go again kills me, especially now. If we just stay like this, keep pretending that everything is okay, we can make this moment last all night long.

My hand moves back and forth across Bri's back, and when her breathing becomes heavy and slow, I realize she's fallen asleep. Then instead of slipping away in the night, instead of doing the right thing and leaving her in peace, I wrap my arms tighter around her, pull the blanket higher over her, and spend the night holding her in my arms.

Light eventually starts to shine through the bedroom window, and with absolute regret, I slide out from under her and tuck her back into the sheets, making sure she's warm. "I'm sorry," I whisper into the silent room as I press a kiss to her forehead.

It's best if I'm gone when she wakes. That way I save her from the pain of having to say goodbye again. I watch her for a short moment, not wanting to leave, but I know I must. "I love you, Bri," I tell her unconscious mind before finally slipping out of the room.

I head downstairs in despair and grab my keys off the counter, passing Sean in the kitchen, who sits at the counter giving Georgia a bottle. He looks at me and gives me a sad smile, clearly realizing that something has happened between me and Bri after we disappeared from the party last night, and judging by the fact that I'm slipping out before the sun has finished rising, he understands that neither of us are on the same page.

I return his smile and head for the door. When I climb into my truck and look up at the house that holds my whole heart, I hesitate, hoping like fuck I'm truly doing the right thing.

I'm so fucking sorry, Bri.

And with that, I start it up and head down the tree-lined driveway, leaving her behind . . . again.

Chapter Sixteen

BRIANNA

The mid-morning sun shines through the window and I wake feeling incredible after sleeping so perfectly for the first time in five months. But that feeling slips away the second I realize that I've woken up in the Waters estate alone.

My heart shatters all over again. I don't know what I was thinking when I slept with Carter, again. I thought I was stronger. I thought I'd be able to handle it. Hell, I thought I would never fall into his arms again, but I should have known better. I allowed my alcohol-induced mind to make the decisions, and while I don't regret it one single bit, I can't stand the lingering pain it left on my heart.

God, I needed last night with him, needed that closeness, but all it did was bring me right back to being that broken girl he left behind five months ago.

I'm such a fucking idiot.

All I've done is broken my heart all over again. I thought I was finally starting to heal, but last night was just a reminder that I'm madly in love with a man who will never want the same things in life.

Last night replays like a movie in my mind, every single moment on repeat and making me miss him more. Carter touched me as though I was the most precious person in the world, but was also rough and demanding when he knew I needed it. He looked at me like I was the only woman he'd ever seen and never wanted to let go, and the way he smelled like the fondest memories of my past was the best feeling.

And then he went and pushed inside me. Fuck, he breathed life into me for the first time in five months. Every moment was filled with undiluted passion. It was nothing short of amazing. Hands down the best sex I've ever had.

And then it ended, and along with it came the realization that I would have to let go.

He said he hadn't changed his mind about having a future together, but I still so desperately want it. I was honest when I said I couldn't have a child with another man, the thought makes me sick to my stomach. But where the hell does that leave me?

I'm forever going to be the cat lady.

Tears begin to fall as I wrap myself up in the sheets. It's like losing him all over again. I feel like I'm right back at square one.

I lay in the used bed, not wanting to leave, when I realize that this is pathetic. The man doesn't want a future with me, yet I've spent the last five months pining over him. I didn't even give moving on a good try. Instead, I picked a guy I knew I'd never have a future with.

What the hell is wrong with me? I need to give myself space to heal. I need to not date losers and wait until I'm truly ready. And that shit is going to start today. I'm not a pathetic girl whose happiness is dependent on a man.

Fuck, that's a hard pill to swallow. The idea of moving on has me ready to fall to pieces, but I have to do it, otherwise, I'll be stuck in this endless cycle of heartbreak. But before I can do that, there's just one thing I need to do.

Using the sheet to dry my eyes, I clamber out of the bed before wrapping it around me like some kind of makeshift dress. Finding my scattered, torn clothes across the room, I shove them into a bag and strut out of the room with my head held high, promising myself that I will never fall victim to Carter Water's wicked charm again.

I mean, don't get me wrong, it was amazing, fucking incredible, mind-blowing even. And just the thought of never having him touch me like that again . . . Well, shit. It's a tragedy. I'll have to find some way to be satisfied with average sex with average men for the rest of my life.

I'm sure I'll eventually find someone to be happy with, someone I can train to get me off the way Carter does. It will be a long road, but after my poor heart heals, I need to give it a try. If that fails, then I can always turn to the monster dildo I keep stashed under my bed. It's gotta be good for something, right?

Walking down the hall, I knock on Cassie's bedroom door, not bothering to wait before pushing my way in. After living together for the last year of college, there isn't much we haven't seen of each other, and I guess that means Jax too. I mean, damn. The number of times I've accidentally seen that man's bare ass is astounding, but I'm not going to complain, he's got one of the best asses I've ever seen.

"Fuck," Jax groans as he takes one look at me, wrapped in the sheet with red, puffy eyes. He yawns and gets out of bed, dragging his feet, understanding that for the foreseeable future, his wife is mine.

Jax walks out of the room, leaving me and Cass alone, and I crawl in beside her as she rolls over and welcomes me into her arms. I cry on her shoulder as if I can magically expel the pain from my heart with my tears—the final tears I will allow myself to cry for Carter Waters.

Once they finally run their course, I get out of bed, steal one of Cassie's outfits, and get my ass home after stopping by the store, a new, fiercer determination pulsing through my veins.

Grabbing the bag from the store, I take the little box of chestnut hair dye and scan through the instructions before putting the color through my hair, finally reclaiming some lost, broken part of myself.

The second I get in the shower, I scrub my body and wash every inch of him off me before shampooing my hair. Half an hour later, I feel like a new me. Then just to prove some ridiculous point, I take the clothes from yesterday and dump them in the bathtub with the box of Carter memories in the back of my closet, and open the bathroom window. Then, hoping I don't accidentally burn the whole apartment complex to the ground, I light it up, more than ready to say goodbye.

It's been four weeks since that night with Carter, and I'm proud to say that I've actually been doing alright . . . mostly. Okay, that's complete bullshit. I'm still a mess, but I'm a mess who can wear a smile a little more often.

I still think about him all the time, but then I remember that I'm not a pathetic loser who's going to spend the rest of my life pining over someone I can't have. And honestly, that thought always manages to save me from falling down the rabbit hole.

I've embraced this whole *new me* bullshit. Though, after my fire singed the roof and left burn marks, I kinda have no choice but to follow through with it. After all, I'm not going to lose my rental bond for nothing.

I've spent these past few weeks being the healthiest version of myself. I've started taking yoga classes, and I'm pretty close to convincing Cassie to take pole dancing classes like we used to in college. I've started the whole clean eating crap and even invested in a few cooking classes, which means I'm saving a shitload of money by not purchasing takeout.

The only part I refuse to negotiate on is the wine. That stays. The wine is a necessity.

The whole cooking thing is taking a little longer to catch on than everything else, but I haven't given myself food poisoning or burned down my apartment yet, so that's a bonus. Though according to Cassie and Jax, the food could probably taste better.

It's been another great day where I've managed to stick to my new lifestyle. I sit in my classroom with a great big smile on my face as I watch my students draw up equations on the whiteboard for one another to solve. The kids have just started learning about addition, and I swear, it's the most amusing thing I've ever witnessed.

Hearing thunder booming through the sky, I glance out the window, watching the heavy rain slam against the window as the kids take a few minutes to work out the answers to their equations. As I wait, the rain turns to hail and the kids lose their tiny minds.

Just great. My brand-new car is parked out in that shit. Knowing my luck, it'll end up with hail damage and put me out a couple hundred dollars on the deductible for the insurance. That's what I get for trying to save money on takeout. It's like the world just knows when you've got some cash saved up and it's like *here, you don't need that. Let me hit you with a hail storm!*

"It looks like snow," little Isabelle squeals as the hail quickly blankets the school.

"Yeah, it looks pretty great," I tell her.

"Can we go outside?" Jack asks.

I think it over. I know Jack's idea of going outside probably consists of running through the hail, which I'd never allow, but I see no harm in going out and standing under the shelter. "Okay," I smile. "Put your pencils down. We can stand out under the shelter and watch the hail, but if anyone goes past the shelter, you'll be spending your lunchtime with me, understood? I don't feel like losing my job today."

"Yes, Miss Lucas," they reply in unison.

The sound of their chairs scraping against the floor echoes throughout the room along with their excited chatter. Being the best bunch of kids I know, they automatically line up at the door and wait for me to come open it. If only I had this kind of organization in my personal life.

We head out into the cold, and they rush toward the very edge of the shelter, knowing damn well they're pushing their luck. As if on cue, each one of them thrust their hands out to try and catch the hailstones.

"Why does it hail?" Jessica asks as she bends down to scoop a large hailstone off the ground before making a show of cleaning off the dirt and grass.

"Good question," I tell her. "Why don't we do a little research after lunch and see if we can figure it out?"

"Okay," she smiles.

I can already see my afternoon plans changing into a science lesson, so I decide I better make it fun. The hail comes to a stop, and soon after, the rain calms down to a sprinkle. "Alright guys. You have thirty seconds to go out there and find the biggest hailstone you can."

They lose their minds again, and I start counting down from thirty, putting on a big show, watching as they run for their lives. They scatter across the playground, picking up stones before tossing them back down and grabbing another. My countdown finishes, and they reluctantly make their way back to me, each with a single hailstone in their open palm.

Not wanting them to melt, I rush them back into the classroom and empty out one of the many crayon buckets. Reading my mind, they start rushing toward me and dumping their stones in. "Hurry up, guys," I tell them. "We don't want them to melt."

With the stones safely in the bucket, I look over my students. "Alright, who's the fastest runner?"

Every single hand flies up into the sky with a few of them going as far as jumping up and down to get noticed. I grin at the kids, absolutely loving my job. "Alright, Sam," I say, handing him the bucket, "run this down to the staff room and ask Miss Davies to put it in the freezer."

He nods eagerly, and like the damn Flash, he disappears out the door.

"Okay, the rest of you get your little tushies back in your seats and finish these equations." They all groan but reluctantly head back to their seats, a lot slower than when they vacated them. By some miracle, we get through the equations just in time for the lunch bell to ring.

Due to the wet weather, I ask the kids if any of them would like to stay inside during lunch, and with no takers, I head down to the staff room and eat my lunch among other adults. Taking advantage of the break, I look up more information about hail, just to make sure I'm telling the kids the right thing. Because honestly, who actually remembers this stuff?

My phone rings on the table, and I grin as Cassie's name flashes across my screen. "Hey, what's up?" I smile.

"Are you on your lunch break?" she questions, a cringe in her tone, never able to remember the right time to call.

"Sure am," I say. "I wouldn't be answering if I wasn't."

"Good point," she grunts. "Can you break your diet and have wine and ice cream with me tonight?"

I scrunch up my face. I really don't want to break my diet. I've been doing so well, but if she has a good reason, I might consider it. "Why? What's going on? Are you having a shit day?" I ask, wondering if something's going on with the baby. After the funeral, Cass and Jax temporarily moved in with Sean so she could help him transition into being a full-time daddy. So far, it seems to be going great. She'll hopefully be able to move back home soon.

"You could say that," she says. "I got my period."

"Oh," I pout, completely understanding. Cass and I usually get our periods at the same time, and most of the time, they're not so bad, but every now and then, Cassie's really sucks. It makes me wonder what's going on with me as I usually get mine a few days before Cassie does.

I've never been late before, so maybe Cassie's body is a little off and she's got it early, or maybe it's the healthy eating and exercise I've been doing that's throwing mine off. I highly doubt it, but either way, we're not synching up, and it causes a funny feeling in the pit of my stomach.

"Hold on a second," I tell her before pulling my phone away from my ear. I bring up my calendar and double check the date, then start counting back the weeks. Hmm, strange. It's definitely me. I'm late.

Oh, fuck. I'm late.

I've never been late in my life. I couldn't be . . . pregnant, could I? Noooooo. That's absurd.

Carter and I have always been safe during sex. It's not possible.

It must be the change of lifestyle screwing me up. I mean, I can't be pregnant. Carter and I aren't even together. He doesn't want kids.

"Hey, Cass," I say, bringing the phone back to my ear. "I've got to go."

"Oh, okay," she says. "Are we on for tonight?"

Shit. If I see her, I'm going to open my big mouth, and I don't want to do that. I'm not ready to accept it. Hell, I don't even know if there's anything to accept, but I'd like to live in denial a little longer. Besides, she'll force me to take a test and face it. And then there's the whole not wanting to put her in the middle situation. If I was pregnant, I'd ask her not to tell Carter until I figured everything out, and that's not fair to her. She's still his little sister and would want to do right by him.

"Um, no, sorry," I tell her before coming up with some excuse about a fellow teacher's farewell dinner and hating myself for lying to her.

"Okay, sure," she says, the disappointment strong in her tone.

Cassie ends the call and I'm left sitting at the table, staring into space as I try to work out any other reason for why my period could be late.

It doesn't matter anyway because I'm not pregnant. I couldn't be.

I try to think back to the night that I've been desperately trying to forget, but it's hard. I had a shitload to drink and the minor details are too fuzzy. Did he use a condom? Maybe he pulled out. I don't know, but the uncertainty rattles me to the bone. I mean, don't get me wrong, I'd love to be pregnant with Carter's child. It's everything I've always wanted, but only if he were on board. I wanted us to be a family, but this . . . no, this isn't even close to how I imagined it.

All I know is that if I am, I'm going to be doing this on my own.

I consider grabbing my shit and leaving for the day, faking a stomach bug so I can freak out at home by myself, but then I promised the kids a science lesson on frozen fucking water, and I'm not that teacher who's going to let them down.

I laugh at the irony of today's storm. When it rains, it fucking pours.

Can't I catch a fucking break?

Just when I thought I was moving on and could somehow find happiness without Carter, this happens. I swear, if I'm not pregnant, I'm going to dedicate my life to celibacy. This shit is freaking me out way too much.

The bell sounds through the school, and I reluctantly pack up my things and head out the door. I get halfway back to my classroom when I remember the damn hailstones in the freezer. Fuck. I need to get my head screwed on before I have to face a bunch of kids. Hell, at this rate, I'm going to get my lesson plan wrong.

Turning around, I hurry back to the staff room, collect the damn hailstones, and a few minutes later, I unlock my classroom door and watch as my rowdy kids hurry into the room, more than ready to finish off their day.

Chapter Seventeen

BRIANNA

Why the fuck are there so many different brands of pregnancy tests? This is ridiculous. I stand in the airport pharmacy, looking at the range of tests before me, and realize just how out of my depth I am.

It's been a week and three days since that phone call with Cassie, and I've been going insane. I don't know why it's taken me this long to even consider taking a test, but I guess the second I do it, it makes it all too real. And honestly, I'm terrified of what it might say.

Something inside me screams that it's real, and to tell the truth, I'm scared. I don't know what I'm going to do. Do I tell Carter and risk him hating me? Do I not tell him and risk him finding out through someone else? Do I raise this child on my own or force Carter into something he doesn't want?

Fuck. I hate this so much.

My tits have started hurting this week, which makes me realize that I'm living in denial, especially considering my period still hasn't shown up. I need to take this stupid test and confirm what I already know to be true so I can start taking the right precautions. I'll need to make a doctor's appointment and get an ultrasound, then I'll need a shitload of vitamins for my growing baby.

Crap. This isn't happening.

I've never felt so alone in my life.

This whole baby thing has consumed my every thought for the past ten days. I think I've slept maybe three or four hours each night, and that only comes from pure exhaustion. So here I am, taking the next few days off work to fly my ass to New York to see Bobby. Hopefully he can help me see things clearly, maybe even force me to get a few hours of sleep.

I haven't even confirmed it, and I feel as though I already love this little creature within me.

Hearing the announcement for my flight to board, I hastily grab one of every brand of pregnancy test off the shelf and rush through the self-service checkout, wanting to avoid the knowing looks I'm sure the old grandma behind the counter is bound to give me.

I race across the airport and join the line for my flight as I stuff the bag of tests into my handbag and search for my boarding pass.

A few hours later, the plane touches down, and I grab my luggage from the baggage claim before ordering an Uber and making my way outside. I eventually get my ass firmly seated in the back of a car before finally pulling up to the front of Bobby's building.

Getting in the elevator, I head all the way up to the top before entering his code to gain access to the penthouse.

Ever since Bobby signed on the dotted line and became the next best thing in the NHL, he's been living it up and enjoying life like the world's most eligible bachelor. I don't blame him. We don't come from a wealthy family, so it's a huge deal for him, and not to mention, he shares the love with his twin sister, and I'm always down with that. He loves spoiling me, and I can't find it within me to tell him no.

"Yo, Bobby?" I call out as the elevator opens straight into his fancy apartment.

Making my way inside his home, I start searching around when I get no response. Though it's not like I called first. There's a good chance he's not even home, and honestly, with these pregnancy tests burning a hole in my pocket, that's really going to piss me off.

Seeing his phone and wallet on the kitchen counter, I realize he must be here somewhere, so my searching kicks up to stalker mode.

Dumping my bag on the table, I head down the hallway and knock on the bathroom door, hoping like fuck I'm not catching him in the middle of taking a shit. Thankfully I get no response, leaving only his bedroom left to check.

Rolling my eyes, I keep striding down the hall. That big bastard has always loved a good afternoon nap. He's such a grandpa.

Carelessly pushing my way into his room, I throw my hand up and beam at the big asshole. "SURPRI—OH FUCK, NO!" My eyes burn as I come to a screeching halt, finding my twin brother with a girl wrapped around his body, bouncing up and down, the sound of her ass slapping against his thighs.

Bobby's eyes widen in horror, and he all but grabs the girl by the hips and launches her off the bed as I slap my hands over my eyes, hastily backing out of the room. "Fuck, fuck, FUCK. Yuck, Bobby."

I hear the dickhead laughing as his date bitches at him, and I can't help but wonder why I'm the one who feels humiliated. Making my way to the living room, I get comfortable with a glass of water as I look out through Bobby's massive floor-to-ceiling windows that capture the magnificent views of New York. God, I wanna smack him right now, but I can't help but feel so incredibly proud of him. Hell, I feel this way every time I visit him out here. He's doing so well for himself and is the perfect example of what happens when you truly believe in yourself and keep working until you reach your dreams.

Bobby emerges a few minutes later and shuffles his hooker into the elevator before dropping down on the couch beside me, his arms spread out on the backrest, making himself comfortable. "What the fuck are you doing here?" he asks with a cheesy grin.

I look at him, and while I so desperately want to bitch at him for what I just walked in on, all that manages to come out is a terrified whimper before I burst into uncontrollable tears.

"Woah," Bobby says, springing into overprotective brother mode and yanking me into his chest, wrapping me up in a warm hug. "What the fuck is going on?"

I let out a breath as I prepare to make this way too real. "I'm pregnant."

His eyes bulge out of his head. "You're what?" he demands, flying up off the couch and gaping at me in horror.

"Well . . . I'm pretty sure anyway."

"What?" he repeats.

"Yeah . . ."

"Shit, Brianna," he breathes, quickly pacing up and down the length of the couch before finally dropping back down beside me, his head in his hands as though I just told him that the second I give birth to this crotch monster, I'll be dropping it on his doorstep. "How did this happen?"

"Really?" I ask, giving him a blank stare. "Do you need me to explain?"

Bobby rolls his eyes as he watches me. "You know what I meant," he says. "But how the hell can you only be pretty sure? You either are or you're not. There's no in-between."

I let out a heavy sigh and prepare myself for the onslaught of bullshit that's going to follow after this. "I haven't taken the test yet," I admit.

"Fuck, Brianna. Are you shitting me?" he scoffs. "You came all the way here without taking the fucking test first?"

"Umm . . . yeah," I say.

He lets out a frustrated groan before standing up and grabbing his keys off the counter. "Come on."

I get to my feet, my brows furrowed. "Huh? Where are we going?"

"To go get the fucking test, dumbass. Where do you think we're going?" he says as if it's the most obvious thing in the world.

Crossing the living room, I grab my bag before scrambling through it until my hand closes around the bag of tests I'd bought at the airport drug store. "Ahh, here's one I prepared earlier," I tell him in a stupid voice, knowing damn well now isn't the time for jokes, but fuck, I couldn't pass up the opportunity.

Bobby looks at me as though I've gone insane. "Then what the fuck are you waiting for? Get on with it."

I stand motionless, not wanting to make the move, my hands shaking at my sides. "I'm scared. What if it's positive?"

A softness creeps into his eyes, and he steps into me before wrapping me in those big, warm arms. "Then you'll make one hell of a great mother." I don't respond, just stand in his arms, taking comfort in my brother's kindness. "I'm assuming it's Carter's," he grunts as an afterthought. "What does he say about all of this? I thought he didn't want kids."

"I haven't told him yet," I admit, peering up at him with a cringe. "I haven't seen him since Sara's funeral, and I was trying to keep it like that. It hurts too much when I see him. Besides, I wanna be certain before I go dumping news like this on him."

"You can't avoid him forever," he says. "Especially now."

"I can try," I grunt.

"Don't be stupid," Bobby scolds as he pushes me out of his arms and leads me toward the bathroom. He comes right on in and steals the bag of tests out of my hands before dumping them out on the bathroom vanity. He picks up one of the boxes and makes himself comfortable on the edge of the bathtub, scanning over the instructions. "How the hell do these things work?" he questions as he studies the test.

"I don't know," I say, picking one up and having a look. "I've never had to do one before. I guess you just pee on it and wait."

"No, I don't think so," he says in confusion. "This one has a little tub you have to pee into and then you put the test in it."

"Not this one," I say, holding it up in my hand.

"Fuck, Bri. How many of these little bastards did you get?" he questions. "There's too many of them. I think I'm breaking out in hives."

"There's never too many," I tell him. "If I'm going to freak out then I want to know I'm freaking out for the right reason. I'm peeing on all of them."

He rolls his eyes and puts the test down on the vanity before pulling out his phone. "Where do you think I can order *world's best uncle* mugs from?" At my lack of response, he looks up at me with a blank expression, his brows starting to furrow with confusion. "What the hell are you waiting for? An invitation? Get on with it."

Uhhh . . . is this guy for real? I mean, I know we're twins and shared a womb, but this is definitely pushing the friendship. Crossing my arms over my chest, I fix him with a hard glare. "Were you going to leave?" I question, my brows raised.

Bobby scoffs and gives me a blank stare. "No. I want to be the first to know."

"There's no one else here, Bobby," I remind him, pointing a finger toward the door. "Get the hell out."

"Uggghhhhh," he groans as he gets up, rolling his eyes. "Fine. But if I hear you on the phone or even get the feeling you're gonna text someone before me, I'm barging right back in here." With that, my moronic twin strides out the door and pulls it closed behind him, leaving me to grow the fuck up and do the one thing I've been avoiding for the past ten days.

Tearing open the packet, I pull out the test and give the instructions a good read, though I'm pretty sure I know what I'm doing. It couldn't be that complicated, right? Sitting on the toilet, I shove the test between my legs and do my best to pee, but hearing Bobby hovering by the door makes me feel a little shy.

A minute passes when I hear him start to pace. "What's taking so long?" he groans through the door.

"I can hear you breathing against the door, asshole. You're giving me stage fright."

"For fuck's sake," he grunts before finally getting the hint and taking off down the hallway. "Call me when you're done."

With Bobby out of the way, I get down to business, and like magic, the river starts flowing free, and I do everything in my power to make sure I don't accidentally pee all over myself. Certain I've done it right, I clean myself up and pop the test on the vanity before starting the longest waiting game of my life.

Pulling out my phone, I set a timer for two minutes, and as I watch it countdown, my nerves start getting the best of me. My hands shake, and I have to force myself to turn around. I drop onto the edge of the bathtub, right where Bobby had been only a few short minutes ago, my heart racing, having no idea how I want this to go.

I can't help but feel as though this moment is going to define the rest of my life. It's either going to go one way or the other, and to be honest, I already feel attached to the idea of having a child, but I don't know if it's the actual child I'm attached to or the idea of it being Carter's.

Surely I couldn't be attached to a baby so soon. I haven't even confirmed I'm pregnant yet.

Unable to help myself, I glance back at the timer. One minute to go.

Shit.

My palms grow sweaty, and I feel as though I could be sick, anxiety gripping hold of me and threatening to send me right over the edge.

The timer goes off, and I shoot up off the edge of the marble bathtub before turning to the test, only I can't look. Damn it, why does it have to be so hard? I start pacing the length of the bathroom, desperately trying to pump myself up as though I'm some kind of athlete getting ready for the biggest game of my life.

I shake my hands, my shoulders bouncing, and just when I think I'm ready, I go to position myself back in front of the sink, but like the little bitch I am, I crumble, unable to even glance down at the stupid piss stick.

Letting out a breath, I give in to the big buffoon out in the living room. Grabbing the door handle, I yank it open before shoving my head out into the hallway. "Bobby," I call, my voice bouncing off the walls.

"What?" he yells back, that same hint of frustration still lingering in his deep tone.

"I can't do it."

"You can't pee?" he questions with a scoff. "I moved away. You've been in there for ages."

"No, dickhead," I grumble, rolling my eyes. "I can't look at it."

"Oh." A soft chuckle comes from the living room, and in the blink of an eye, Bobby appears at the end of the hallway, all but rushing toward me. He barges past me as he moves into the bathroom, his gaze sweeping high and low before zeroing in on the test on the vanity. He scoops it up eagerly, and I cringe, all too aware that I just peed on that.

He looks at it for a minute, and with every passing second, my nerves get worse. "Fucking hell, Bobby," I groan. "What does it say?"

"I, uhh . . . don't know," he grunts, his face scrunching as he tries to figure it out. "Where are the instructions for this shit?"

I find the piece of paper that came with the box and open it up, groaning at how long it takes. I mean, damn. Why are these instructions bigger than the world map I have pinned to my classroom wall? "Um . . ." I say, scanning the page. "One line; not pregnant. Two lines; pregnant."

Bobby lets out a breath. "What do you want it to be?" he asks as he turns to face me, his eyes giving nothing away.

I think it over for a moment, wanting to be honest, but I already know my answer, despite how much I've denied it. "Positive," I tell him, even though the idea of carrying Carter's child makes me want to crumble.

Relief flashes in Bobby's eyes just as a wide grin splits his face in two. "Congratulations, Momma. We're having a baby."

"Are you sure?" I question, my eyes wide as I yank the piss stick out of his hand, ignoring the way he said *we're*. Glancing down, I feast my gaze upon the pregnancy test, and sure enough, right there in front of my very eyes are two solid lines, telling me exactly what I've been needing to hear.

Hoooooooly shit. Two lines.

I look up at Bobby as a smile slowly starts to cross my face. "I'm pregnant," I breathe, trying to wrap my head around it before the excitement comes blasting through my veins. "Holy fucking shit. I'M PREGNANT!"

"Hell, yeah. You are," Bobby booms, yanking me into his wide chest and lifting me off my feet before spinning us around. "I'm going to be the best fucking uncle ever."

Laughter overwhelms me and I shove against him. "Yeah, well you can start by putting me down," I tell him. "This probably isn't too good for the baby."

The baby.

"Oh, shit," Bobby says, dropping me back to my feet with wide eyes. "You're right. When was the last time you ate? Have you been drinking? I hope you haven't been eating anything you shouldn't be."

"I'm fine," I tell him. "I've been eating clean for the past few weeks and keeping the alcohol to a limit. I haven't done anything that isn't safe during pregnancy."

"Good," he says, "I'm gonna feed you anyway."

Bobby all but drags me out of the bathroom and deposits me into the stool at the island counter and I watch as he starts pulling random shit out of his fridge and starts putting lunch together. "Fuck," he grunts a moment later. "That chick really wore me out."

I grab an empty drink bottle off the counter and launch it at the big bastard. "Ugh, I don't want to know," I tell him.

"Shut up," he demands. "Over the last six months, I've had to listen to all your *I love Carter, no I hate Carter. Oh wait, I love him* bullshit. I've let you ugly cry all over me, and I've just checked your fucking pregnancy test for you. Which was covered in piss by the way. So if I want to tell you about the chick I just fucked, you're going to listen, and you're going to listen good."

"Fineee," I groan, rolling my eyes, hating that he has a point.

"Good. And while you're at it, put a fucking smile on your face and pretend you're rooting for me."

Twisting a fake smile from ear to ear, I beam at the moron. "Oh my God, Bobby! Tell me all about it. I bet she was soaking wet for you. Did you take her raw? Bend her over your fucking bed and take her hard? Did she scream for you? I bet she did. She looked like the kind of bitch that could take it hard."

Bobby's face twists with disgust. "You're right. We can't do this. I'll call Jax and tell him about it instead."

"Thank God," I say in relief.

Finishing up with the mess of ingredients on the counter, Bobby hands me a plate of . . . I don't even know what, but the second it's settled in front of me, my stomach grumbles, and I gobble it down, not realizing just how hungry I was. "So, how do you feel?" he asks.

"I umm . . . I actually have no idea," I tell him. "I'm excited and freaked out at the same time, plus there's the whole telling Carter thing."

"What's freaking you out so much?" he questions as he finishes his lunch and starts packing up his kitchen. "You've got this. We already know that you're going to be an amazing mom. You're like the baby whisperer."

A soft smile settles across my lips at his comments. "I'm scared I'm going to be doing it all alone," I tell him honestly. "I've come to terms with the fact that Carter doesn't want kids and isn't going to be in the picture. But now that I'm going to have a child, I don't want him to go without a daddy."

Bobby fixes me with a pointed stare, his brow arching in question. "Him?"

I shrug my shoulders, the idea of having a boy making my smile widen. "It's just a feeling," I tell him. "Ever since Carter and I first got together, I would picture our future. Our kids, our home, everything. And when I saw our kids, it was always boys—miniature Carters."

A sad smile settles across his lips, and he moves around the island counter and pulls me into his arms. "Don't be upset, Bri. I know you're still hurting, but this is what you've always wanted, whether it's Carter's baby or anyone else's. And don't act like this baby is ever going to go without. He's got you and he's got me. I'll be there so much you'll never feel alone, and if you don't think you're coping, I can move you to New York to be here, or I can somehow see if the Colorado Thunder wants me. Though, I'm not gonna lie, playing with Jax again would be good."

"Thanks," I smile, "but there's no way in hell I'm about to let you do all of that. I'm going to be okay. Besides, I can't leave my students or Cassie. They're the only things that keep me sane. Not to mention, Mom and Dad would kill me if I even considered moving their first grandbaby away."

"Shit. Mom and Dad! What are you going to tell them?" Bobby rushes out in a panic. "They're going to send you to bible camp again."

"Ugh, don't remind me," I say as the worst memories of my childhood come crashing back. "Just promise me you won't say anything. I want to be the one to tell them."

"And when is that going to be?" he challenges, knowing me too damn well.

I shrug my shoulders, averting my gaze. "When the baby is starting college."

"Bri," he groans. "They're bound to notice when your baby bump is knocking all the plates off the table at Christmas dinner."

"Shut up," I groan, realizing just how many things I haven't considered yet.

By the time night comes, I find myself curling up in Bobby's spare bed. I have so many thoughts rushing through my mind, but the only thing I'm certain of is that I'm going to have a baby, with or without

Carter.

I start making a mental list of all the things I'm going to have to do, like searching for the best baby doctor in Denver. But more importantly, I need to keep taking care of myself, keep my body healthy, strong, and happy, which includes actually getting some sleep

And with that, I pull the blanket right up to my chin as my hand rests against my belly, more than ready for the incredible adventure to come.

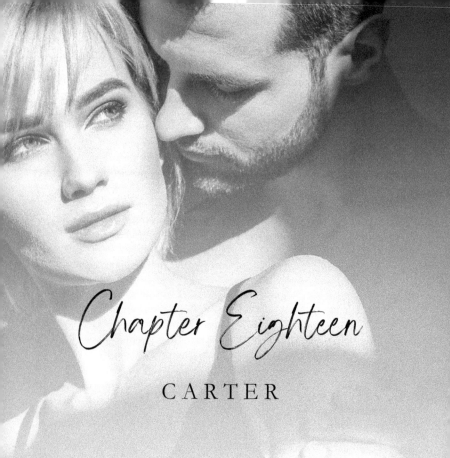

Chapter Eighteen

CARTER

It's been six weeks since I last saw her, and I can't fucking take it. Cassie has been giving me updates, but I can tell she's only giving me the bare minimum, but from what I can tell, Bri is doing really well. And honestly, this might make me the most selfish bastard out there, but I fucking hate it.

For the past six months, all I've wanted was for Bri to stop hurting and move on, despite how desperately I wanted to hold onto her. But now that she is . . . fuck. It's killing me.

Does that mean she doesn't love me anymore? Is she forgetting about me? The idea of not owning her whole fucking heart is the most devastating thought to ever enter my head. Not being her man, the one she trusts, the one she comes home to and holds through the night. I fucking hate it, but it's on my shoulders. I pushed her away, I forced her to go. Hell, all this time I've been saying she should try to move on to get her happily ever after, but it's not as though I've taken my own advice. I've been holding on so tight that I don't think it's even possible to let go now.

Cassie says Bri has been doing yoga and taking cooking classes, which sounds great, but I need something more, some kind of sign that she's still mine. I knew it would hurt when she finally moved on, but I'm not ready for it to happen just yet.

"Carter?" Mr. Wilder's voice calls out, breaking me out of my endless thoughts of Brianna. "Are you listening to me?"

Shit.

"Yes, I certainly am," I say, my gaze flicking toward him across the boardroom table as I try not to grit my teeth. Mr. Wilder is, hands down, the biggest pain-in-the-ass client I've ever met. Waters Construction has been working with him for over three years creating a new build for his multi-million-dollar home, and what we've built is incredible, probably the biggest residential property we've ever put our name on—the only problem is his wife.

Every time we get close to completion, she makes changes, and I swear, I'm so damn close to telling them to shove their house up their asses. It's fucking ridiculous. This is the seventh time I have sat across from him with the finished plans in my hands, crossing shit out and starting over.

The meeting always goes fine, then he goes home to his wife, who decides she needs a fucking ten-foot water feature to be built into the design of her over-the-top foyer. Every time I tell my men that they need to knock down something that's already been finalized, it breaks each one of their hearts. They value their work, just as I do, but clients like this make me want to throw in the towel.

Don't get me wrong, I love my job. I studied architecture and design in college, wanting to be taken on as a consultant in my father's company, and when he passed, the whole thing came my way. It's the most bittersweet moment I've ever experienced.

Dad had amazing grand designs, which we still offer. My clients love the originals, but since I've taken the reins, we've been doing more extreme builds that have put me on the map. To say it's fucking awesome is an understatement.

Waters Construction is now known as the go-to company for high-end clients and celebrities who are looking for luxury and extreme designs. They're after the *wow* factor and something to add to their portfolios to show off to their rich friends. Not once have I let a client down. We always come through. Seeing the look on the clients' faces when they see their designer home for the first time is fucking priceless. It's a high I will never stop chasing.

Just like Brianna Lucas.

But right now, dealing with these particular clients is a fucking nightmare. I mean, sure, this happens all the time. When people are paying a shitload of money, their expectations are nothing short of perfection. It's understandable, and on builds like this, the clients will often request two or three changes to the plan after thinking on it for a hot minute. Not these assholes. They take nitpicking to a whole new level.

"So, where are we at with these new changes?" Mr. Wilder asks.

"All good," I tell him. "All that's left to do is to get your written consent on the new updates, then we can inform our builders."

"Excellent," he says, leaning across the table to shake my hand. He stands and rolls up the final plans before shoving them under his arm and making me cringe as he crinkles the paper I just spent the last hour working on. "I'll get my wife to review this tonight, and I'll be in touch tomorrow."

"Wonderful," I say with a fake smile, the one I reserve for the hardest of clients. I show him out the door and let out a groan the second it closes behind him. "Thank fuck, that's over," I say to my secretary with a sigh before handing her a pile of papers and a copy of the latest updates from the meeting.

"Sooooo, after these final changes that should be a wrap on the Wilder property, right?" she questions as she starts going through the paperwork.

"I fucking hope so," I tell her. "He needs the okay from the wife first, and we all know how that usually goes."

"Ugh," she groans. "The guy should just grow a pair of balls and tell her how it's going to be."

"That, he should," I agree, "But I can't deny that with her eye for detail and over-the-top taste, they're going to have a picture-perfect home."

"They will," she agrees before putting her head down and diving straight into her work.

Making my way back to my office, I close the door behind me and drop down into my chair, swiveling to look out the window of my penthouse office suite. I let out a heavy sigh, bracing my hand behind my neck. I need a fucking drink after dealing with that.

My office takes up the two top floors of one of the biggest skyscrapers in Denver. It's located in the heart of the city, with hundreds of employees that keep it running, and I get to be the lucky bastard at the top.

My phone beeps on my desk behind me, and I let out a groan as I spin back around, certain it's work calling all too soon. Only finding a missed call from Logan, I let out a relieved breath and quickly call him back. "What's up?" I say as he answers the call.

"Just checking in," he says, a strange, jittery nervousness in his tone. Though that's expected, especially considering today is one of the biggest days of his whole career. "Are you coming to my game tonight?"

"It's the fucking championship game," I remind him as if he didn't know. "Like fuck I'll be missing that."

"Cool," he says, drawing it out as though hesitating. "Um . . ."

Fuck. What's this asshole done now?

"Spit it out," I demand.

I can practically hear the cringe in his tone. "Cass is bringing Bri to the game," he tells me. "Figured I should let you know. I didn't want you to feel blindsided by her being there."

Shit. I didn't even think about that, but of course she's going to be there. The Colorado Thunder are battling it out against the LA Storm, with a bunch of guys Jax used to play college hockey with—Miller Cain and Tank Meyers, some of the best players in the league. Nobody is going to miss this game. Hell, I'm sure Bobby is even going to be there.

"Okay, sure," I say, pretending as though the mere thought of seeing my girl doesn't make my heart start racing. But one thing is for sure, I'm going to need a few drinks before I see her. I don't think I'll be able to watch her so effortlessly pretend I don't exist.

Fuck. Why am I being such a pussy about this?

Seeing her is going to be a good thing. Hell, it's exactly what I've craved every day for nearly seven months. I don't necessarily have to talk to her, but just seeing her and making sure she's safe and happy would do wonders for my soul. I just hope seeing me isn't going to fuck up any progress she's made.

Knowing there's no way I'm going to be able to concentrate on my work now, I pack up my shit and bail before jumping in my truck and getting the fuck out of there.

The rest of my day drags by, and I spend most of it pacing through my living room until it's finally time to get going. Making sure to wear my Thunder jersey to play the role of the most supportive brother in history, I get myself ready, and before I know it, I'm pulling up at the arena.

Making my way up the grandstand to the VIP section, I'm surprised to see Sean here and even more surprised to see that he's brought Georgia with him, to a fucking hockey game, but ever since Sara's funeral, Sean hasn't let her out of his sight for even a second. "Hey man," I say, taking the seat beside him and lifting the baby right out of his arms. "How are you doing?"

"Not bad," he replies. His usual charm is still missing, but I can't blame the guy. It hasn't been that long since he lost his wife, and it's a huge adjustment, especially with a newborn to care for.

Looking down at the baby, I watch as she settles into a peaceful sleep and a chuckle rumbles through my chest. The noise in this area is loud enough to wake the dead, and yet here's Georgia, settling in for a nap. "God, she's precious," I murmur.

"She is," he tells me. "I don't know how I'd be coping without her."

I nod in agreement. It's damn clear that Georgia has become the reason he breathes. Since the second he held her, he fell in love. If anything were to happen to this little girl . . . fuck, I know without a doubt that we'd lose Sean too, and honestly, that scares the shit out of me.

"Hey," a familiar voice says, coming up the grandstand. Nervousness blasts through my veins at my sister's voice knowing damn well Bri would be right there with her. And sure enough, as I glance up at Cassie's smiling face, I find Bri right behind her shoulder, her gaze cast down, probably trying to avoid any form of eye contact.

I can't stop staring.

Fuck, she looks radiant, but what's new? She's always looked like a fucking angel to me. Only this time, she's different. She's dyed her hair, a rich brunette, and goddammit, it has me desperate to run my fingers through it. There's almost a glow about her, an undeniable happiness that shines through her gorgeous green eyes, and it pains me not to know what has her feeling this way, especially in the face of having to see me.

Cassie walks along the row in front of us and grabs Georgia out of my hands before shooting me a warning look, silently asking me not to do anything stupid, and as I roll my eyes, she takes the seat directly in front of me. Bri, on the other hand, gives Sean a bright smile before leaning over the row of chairs and giving him a kiss on the cheek, that rich brunette hair falling forward and brushing along my arm. Her gaze briefly flashes to me, but that's all she gives me before taking her seat right beside Cass.

She leans over into Cassie's space and gives Georgia a beaming smile, and just like that, the two of them start fighting over who gets to hold the sleeping baby. And fuck, it shouldn't have me smiling like this.

The arena eventually fills and Bobby joins the girls, but not before giving me a look that tells me to watch myself. But what else should I have expected? I'm sure Bobby has played a vital part in keeping Bri together, and for that I have nothing but respect and gratitude for him, even if it means he desperately wants to kick my ass.

As the game begins, the atmosphere in the arena picks up. Cassie, Bri, and Bobby are all on their feet cheering while Sean and I sit back, neither of us particularly in the mood. But the second Logan looks up here, we'll both be sure to slap on a smile, maybe even wave our hands around a little.

As Bri sits down in her chair, her long hair flows over the backrest, and I try my hardest not to reach out and run my fingers through it. I can't stop thinking about how good she's doing. There's no pouting or secret tears, and I realize Cassie was right, Bri really is starting to heal.

Her cheeks are no longer hollowed out, she's laughing and looks strong. It's fucking beautiful. She's drinking a bottle of water rather than a soda, she ignores the guy walking around selling hot dogs, and the way her ass sits in those jeans also doesn't go unnoticed.

As she watches the game, she reaches down into her handbag and pulls out a bottle of pills, and I lean forward in my seat, trying to peer at the label as she drops one into her hand and swallows it dry. My brows furrow. What the hell are they for? Is she sick or is she doing the whole *healthy me daily vitamin* thing? Bri's hand is covering the label, and the curiosity is eating me up inside, but as Cass has pointed out a million times before, I haven't got a right to know what's going on in her life.

Bri drops the pills back into her handbag, and I start to convince myself that they're just vitamins. She would have absolutely no need to be taking medication, and even if she did, I'm sure Cassie would have told me if she was sick.

Satisfied with my conclusion, I sit back in my chair and try to relax, but it doesn't stop the overwhelming need to dive over the seats and run away with her handbag until I can uncover all her secrets. Fuck, I'm so pathetic.

Bri finally gets to steal Georgia, and in the move, accidentally wakes her up. Her little blue eyes look up at Bri, and a smile instantly lights up her beautiful face. "Hi, princess. Did you have a good sleep?" she coos, her voice flowing to me even over the noise of the rowdy crowd. "You're so beautiful. I can't wait to have one of you."

I watch in adoration as two of the world's most beautiful creatures find comfort in one another, and as I do, Sean leans into my side, motioning down to Bri and Georgia. "You can't tell me you don't want that."

"If I did, don't you think I would have knocked her up already?"

"Quit lying to yourself," he scoffs, almost sounding frustrated with the situation. "Since Georgia was born, you've been different. You do everything for that baby, and it fucking terrifies you that you love her so much."

I let out a breath. "I don't know, man," I say. "She's my niece. Of course I'm going to love her, but that doesn't automatically mean I want one of my own."

Sean lets out a heavy breath and shakes his head, averting his gaze back to the game as he prepares to give me some kind of deep wisdom. "Look, I've kept my mouth shut hoping you'd figure it out on your own, but you're being a fucking idiot," he growls under his breath, making sure the girls can't overhear us. "Surely Sara's death has shown you just how fucking precious life is. It's unpredictable, and in the blink of an eye, it could all be gone. And what you have with Bri, that's fucking rare, man, and you're throwing it all away. Stop being such a scared prick and take a chance. I was terrified when I found out Sara was pregnant, but that's no excuse not to give it a fucking try. Now that Georgia is here, I've realized how much of a gift a child is. My wife is dead, Carter, and I'd do anything to get her back, while you're sitting here, selfishly pushing Bri aside because you're too fucking scared to admit what you really want in life." He takes a quick moment to compose himself before continuing. "You're missing out on a chance to find the greatest happiness, and fulfillment known to man because you're too busy being a fucking pussy, and it's really starting to piss me off. Fucking grab her and don't let go. Have all the children in the world. Marry her and wake up every fucking morning seeing the smile on her face, because when it's gone, *like really fucking gone*, you would have wished that you gave her the world."

His words hit me hard, every last one of them searing me right through the chest and leaving a stain on my soul. I sit in silence, the heaviness weighing me down. Could he be right that I'm throwing away a chance to have a happy, complete life with the woman I love because I'm scared? I've never thought of it that way, but maybe he's right.

The thought of committing to a marriage scares the shit out of me. Before Bri, I'd never even had a long-term relationship. My life was about fucking around and getting laid. How do I know I won't revert back to my old ways and destroy it? The thought of doing that to Bri, especially if we had kids, is just too much. Shit, I wouldn't even know the first thing about being a father. It's best to just avoid that ship altogether. I'm not like Sean or Logan. I don't have that natural instinct with kids.

"If I go down that road, I'm just going to end up hurting her," I tell Sean.

"Yeah, well it's a little too late for that," he scoffs, managing to make me feel like an absolute dick again.

I let out a breath. "I need some air," I say, getting up and making my way down the grandstand. As I walk around the arena, I glance back up at my family and see Bri looking down at me with that gorgeous baby in her arms. And just like that, I see the future I so willingly gave away.

It's like taking a bullet straight to the fucking chest.

Agony tears through me as I realize just how right Sean is. I've pushed Bri away. I've caused her all this pain because I'm scared. I've put tears on her face, shattered her heart, and left her questioning her whole future, all because of my own insecurities and fear. And now, it's too fucking late.

The knowledge of what I've done and the unnecessary hurt I've caused us both is too much to bear. She's moved on and is finally in a good place. She's happy in her new life without me, trying to figure out her next steps and learn what her new version of happiness includes.

I've destroyed the best thing that ever happened to me because I'm a fucking pussy, terrified of commitment.

Not being able to even face her, I walk straight out of the arena and get in my truck, feeling like an absolute prick for doing this to Logan and Jax, but I can't be here right now. I can't even begin to face what I've done. So with the images of Bri holding Georgia seared into my mind, I get the fuck out of here.

Chapter Nineteen

BRIANNA

I did it. I saw him and didn't freak out. I was strong. I mean, I was definitely dying on the inside. All I wanted was to turn around and throw myself into his warm arms just to feel his skin on mine, but the important thing is that I didn't.

I kept it together and honestly, I think it's this tiny little baby inside me that gave me the strength to do it. Everything I do from now on is for my child, and I need to make sure I do what's best for his future . . . or hers.

Something was going on with him though. He was too quiet, barely even cheering for Logan and Jax, and that's very unlike him.

Hockey isn't exactly his favorite sport, but he always makes sure to support his family. I don't think Carter even said a single word the whole time he was there, and then he got up and left, leaving me desperate for answers. I managed to push the feeling away, it's none of my business what's going on in his life anymore. Besides, if it was something ridiculously crazy, he knows he can come to me . . . well, at least, I think he knows that.

I'll always be there for him. After all, this baby is going to keep us connected for the rest of our lives.

Walking up the stairs of the grandstand and having to pretend like everything was okay was the hardest part. I nearly lost it. I could feel the tears stinging my eyes, but somehow, I managed to reel them in. I was so nervous. Carter has always been so in tune with me, and I was certain with just one look, he would know my secret, but perhaps our time apart has dulled his senses because I don't think he suspected a thing.

What's the point in hiding it though? He's going to find out sooner or later, and I have all intentions of telling him, I just don't know how. I can't keep this from Cassie for much longer, and the second she figures it out, it's game over. Hell, she's going to be so angry with me when she realizes I've known this for two weeks now.

Shit. I'm such an awful person.

Opening the door to the doctor's office, I make my way up to the reception desk as I nervously fidget with the hem of my shirt. I'm so freaking anxious. It's been eight weeks since that night with Carter, and this is my first OBGYN appointment. Well, technically it's my second. I went for an appointment a few days ago and the doctor gave me weird vibes before asking me to drop my pants in a less than professional way. I've never run away faster in my life. So here I am, meeting with a nice lady doctor, and hopefully, I'm going to love her.

After giving the receptionist my name, I'm lumped with a stack of paperwork and invited to take a seat in the waiting room. There are a few people in line ahead of me, and I carefully select my spot, not wanting to intrude on anyone's personal space. After taking my seat, I get busy filling out the paperwork, only faltering when it starts asking about the father.

I keep it vague, and before I know it, I hear my name called across the waiting room. Grabbing my bag, I scurry after the doctor, not wanting to keep her waiting. The doctor ushers me into her office, and I quickly take a look around, taking in the clinical, clean space and the subtle hues of pastel purple and yellow decorating the walls. I instantly feel at ease.

The doctor offers me a seat, and I get comfortable before giving her a nervous smile, having no idea what to expect from this appointment. "Welcome, Brianna. I'm Doctor Thompson. I understand you're newly pregnant?"

"Yes," I tell her.

She glances down at the paperwork on her desk, her red-rimmed glasses low on her nose. "And is this your first pregnancy?"

I nod my head, despite her averted gaze. "Yes, it is."

"Alright, I'm assuming that must mean you have plenty of questions and are possibly feeling a little anxious about everything that's going to happen during your pregnancy. However, you are in good hands, and I'll do my best to make this journey as carefree and enjoyable as possible. But let's be real, pregnancy isn't designed to be easy."

Dr. Thompson gives me a comforting smile, and I think she can see the nervousness wafting off of me. "First up, I am assuming you completed all the necessary blood work prior to your appointment?"

"Yes," I say with a nod. "I was assured you would have the results ready to go."

"Wonderful," she murmurs, her gaze shifting to her computer. She starts clicking buttons and soon enough, she finds what she's looking for. "Uh-huh," she declares. "Here they are."

She takes her time scanning through my test results, and as she does, she asks me questions about my last menstrual cycle and when I believe this baby was conceived. We chat for a minute, and after confirming my HCG levels are a little more elevated than expected, she stands and waves me into her procedure room. "Come on through, Brianna," she says. "We're going to do an internal ultrasound to determine how far along you are and see if we can get a reading on a heartbeat yet."

Excitement drums through my veins at getting to see my baby for the first time, plus also the possibility of hearing his little heartbeat, and as I get to my feet to follow her, I pause, my brows furrowed. Did she say *internal* ultrasound? As in something getting shoved up my coochie?

Ahh shit. What do I have to lose? After all, shoving something up my coochie is how I got in this mess to start with.

Following Dr. Thompson into her procedure room, I take a quick glance around. There's a small patient bed with stirrups attached and a table set up with a big machine connected to a little remote TV, not to mention an industrial-sized bottle of what looks like lube.

The doctor pulls a curtain for privacy and asks me to undress from the waist down and lay on the bed with a blanket covering my bottom half. I quickly do as I'm asked, more than ready to get this over and done with. I mean, women do this every day. Surely it couldn't be that bad, right?

Dr. Thompson gets comfortable on a rolling stool and flicks some switches on what I'm assuming is the ultrasound machine. She pulls out a long wand and explains exactly where it's going as I look at it in fear, my eyes wide as my heart starts to race.

"Don't they usually do ultrasounds from the outside?" I question.

"Usually, yes," she says as she starts putting a lubricant on the end of the wand. "But as you are still so early in your pregnancy, we'll get a clearer view of the fetus with an internal wand. Plus, we have a much higher chance of hearing the heartbeat this way, assuming we can hear one at all, that is. It's still a little early."

"Oh, okay," I say, starting to get a little more comfortable with the idea. "Is it safe for the baby?"

"Yes," she smiles before moving the wand between my legs and giving me a comforting stare. "Alright, Brianna. We're going to get started. I need you to take a deep breath and relax. The gel will be cold, so be prepared for that."

With that, Dr. Thompson gently pushes the wand inside me, and

I'm distracted by the alien feeling, but it quickly fades away the second an image appears on the screen. I have absolutely no idea what I'm looking at. It all looks like weird mush to me, but I know my baby is somewhere inside that image.

Dr. Thompson moves the wand around, and I try not to think about it as she busily takes measurements. "Okay," she says a few minutes later once she's finally finished, pushing the screen aside to better face me. "You're measuring seven weeks and four days. Unfortunately, I couldn't quite get the heartbeat today, but we'll be able to hear it at your next appointment."

I let out a heavy sigh, a little disappointed but still so excited to be hearing any kind of news at all. "Does everything look okay? Is he developing as he should?"

She gives me a knowing smile, her eyes sparkling with some kind of secret. "I think you mean *they*."

My brows furrow and I hold her stare, certain I heard her wrong. "I'm sorry?" I ask, my heart kicking into gear as my hands instantly grow clammy. She didn't just say *they*, did she? I mean, is she trying to use pronouns in a bid to be politically correct since no gender has been allocated to the baby yet, or does she mean *they*, as in multiple? Because that's simply insane. I can barely handle having to tell Carter that I'm pregnant with one baby, let alone two.

Dr. Thompson turns the screen right around and points at the black-and-white image. "Congratulations, Brianna. You've got twins in there," she tells me, indicating separate areas of the screen. "This is baby A," she says, pointing to a black blob before moving to the right, "and this here is baby B. You can see they share a sack which means they're identical."

Holy fucking shit.

This can't be real, but there they are, right in front of my face, and I find myself shaking my head, unease blasting through my veins. One baby I could handle. One baby would be manageable on my own. But two? Fuck. "Are you sure?" I ask her, more than ready to bail and find a second or third opinion—a million of them if that's what it'll take to make sure this ultrasound has been read correctly.

"Yes," she laughs. "I'm positive. Do twins run in your family?"

Dread settles over my shoulders, weighing me down and keeping me pinned to the patient bed. "Uh-huh. I have a twin brother, and the father is an identical triplet," I explain as my breath starts to come in hard, sharp pants. Hell, the more I think about it, the worse my gasps get. "Shit, I can't breathe."

"Okay," the doctor says, helping me to sit up. She leans me forward so my head is practically between my legs, and I close my eyes, desperately trying to calm myself. "Take slow deep breaths. You're okay. You're just having a slight panic attack. It will pass in a moment."

I do as she says and concentrate on the oxygen being sucked into my lungs before I slowly blow it back out again, and soon enough, I start feeling like my normal self again.

I slowly sit back up as she fills a glass of water and presses it into my hand. "Feeling better?" she questions, real concern in her eyes

"Better isn't the right word for it," I admit. "But you don't need to worry about me passing out."

"I'm glad," she says with a soft chuckle before excusing herself to give me a little privacy to get my pants back on, and as she goes, my gaze lingers on the screen.

Twins.

Crap.

I get dressed and meet the doctor back in her office before taking a seat. She hands me a shitload of paperwork for more scans and blood work, then she talks to me about the importance of choosing the correct hospital and discussing all the millions of things I need to know about not only having one baby, but having twins.

At the end of the appointment, Dr. Thompson hands me a copy of the ultrasound that she has slid into a little cardboard frame, and the longer I sit with the idea of having two babies, the quicker my heart swells with overwhelming joy.

I grab my bag and go to leave her office before finding myself hovering in her doorway. "Definitely twins?" I question, one last time. After all, one could never be too sure.

"Definitely."

Jesus. A bottle of wine would go down really well right now.

I let out a breath and give her a warm smile before making my way out of the office, telling myself that I can handle this. I have Bobby by my side, and eventually, I'll find the balls to tell Cass.

I'm going to be okay because, at the end of the day, I'm going to have two beautiful babies to love unconditionally, and I can't fucking wait. A part of me hopes they're little boys who'll grow up looking just like their daddy with that same dark hair and gorgeous eyes. But the other part of me wishes they'll look nothing like him because the constant reminder of Carter might just kill me.

Dropping into my car, I kick over the engine, but I just sit in my parking space, needing a moment to come to terms with everything. After twenty minutes pass, I decide it's time to pull myself together. I have homework to do. I need to figure out which hospital I'd like to be admitted to, my birthing plan, who I want in the room, and if I'm going to be using the drugs, and well . . . obviously. I'm pushing out two babies. I'm gonna need all the drugs!

On top of all of this, I'm going to have to calculate twice the amount of supplies. Bottles, bassinets, maybe a double stroller. There is just so much to do.

Backing out of my parking space and getting back on the road, my gaze shifts across the screen of my car. Bobby's number stares back at me from the home screen, and I can't resist hitting call. It rings through Bluetooth a few times before his deep tone fills my car. "What's up, assface?"

"You know that tiny one-bedroom apartment I have?" I ask, knowing just how fond he is of my new home.

"Yeah?" he questions, clearly having no idea where I'm going with this.

"I'm going to need a bigger one. I'm having twins."

There's only a second of silence before his booming laughter tears through my car and his amusement instantly has me wanting to claw his eyes out with a rusty fork. Then just to be a petty bitch and teach him a lesson, I end the call and drive my ass home.

Chapter Twenty

BRIANNA

B arely three months pregnant, and I already feel like a beached whale.

What the hell was I thinking?

I can't do this.

My bump is already protruding from my stomach, and I'm simply flabbergasted. Obviously I knew there would be a bump at some point, and considering there are two little crotch goblins in there, it would be bigger than any usual pregnancy, but this? Shit.

I'm already showing through my baggiest clothes. Not even a big winter coat can hide this pregnancy, and sooner rather than later, I'm going to have to admit defeat and start looking at maternity clothing.

Shit. Just thinking about how big I'm going to get makes me sick. I can't even imagine it. When someone is full term, they're huge, but with two . . . ugh. I'm terrified. Like how do I roll over in bed? How do I put my shoes on? Fuck, how will I pee a million times a day and reach between my legs simply to wipe? Holy cow. Though despite all of this, I know it'll be worth it because in the end, after all the discomfort and agony of trying to propel them from my womb, I'll have two gorgeous little munchkins that I will love and adore with everything I am. Hell, I already do.

I've been an awful friend to Cassie. I still haven't told her, and I'm now at the stage where I can't even say that I was waiting until the fear of an early miscarriage was over. The *I just had a big lunch* excuse is no longer going to work either, and when she realizes I've kept this from her, she's going to be devastated. What kind of friend keeps something so huge from their best friend? These babies are going to be her nieces or nephews. She's going to hate me.

Carter, on the other hand, deserves to know more than anyone. It's disgusting that I haven't told him yet, but I can't bring myself to march over there and tear his world to shreds. He's been a ghost since the hockey game, and I don't know how I feel about it. I've been using the excuse that I want to wait until I see him to spill the news, but then I purposefully go about not seeing him to avoid the conversation.

In fact, I've avoided everyone I know, apart from Bobby, but he's been holed up in New York, even though the hockey season is over, which makes me wonder if there's someone special keeping him there.

I go to work, specifically driving the long way to avoid *his* current builds just so I don't have to see him on a job site, then I go straight back home and to bed.

I haven't even told my parents yet.

For the first time in my life, I feel truly alone, and I only have myself to blame. To fill the void, I've started following a blog, and to be honest, I'm quite surprised by how much I'm enjoying it. I've never been one to indulge in blogs, but this one has me feeling as though I'm actually ready for how my life is going to change when these two crotch goblins arrive.

I found this blogger right after I got back from visiting Bobby in New York, and I've spent a lot of spare time reading her posts, not that I really have that much spare time between work and preparing for life with two babies. In one of the posts, she raved about how she'd written a week-by-week journal of her pregnancy that her baby would be able to enjoy when she grew up.

The idea sat with me, and I soon found myself browsing my selection of empty notepads and selecting the prettiest one before diving straight in to document this crazy journey.

Week 1 – 4

I'm sorry, baby. I don't really know what to write here. I guess . . . welcome to my guts! At this stage, I didn't know you existed, sorry 'bout that! I wasn't sick and didn't have any of the signs that come along with the early stage of pregnancy, but if it makes it any better, I was on a health kick, so I was eating well and taking care of you, even though I had no idea you were there. I've even been exercising.

One day, when you're older, you'll appreciate what a big deal that is!
So . . . I suppose, buckle in and get ready for what I'm sure is about to be a wild ride! I'll be checking in with you soon.

<u>Week 5</u>

So . . . uhhhhh. I'm pretty sure I know you're in there now after your Aunty Cassie made me realize I'm late for that time of the month—not that you want to hear about that. I'm sure that if you're a boy, you're thoroughly disgusted right now.

To be honest with you, I was kinda living in denial. Too scared to go to the drug store and grab a pregnancy test, because woah! Having a baby is a big deal, but I flew to New York to visit your Uncle Bobby and he knocked some sense into me. (By the way, the big buffoon is going to tell you all about his big hockey career and how he rocked it in New York. A word from the wise—it's best just to smile and nod. Do not, under any circumstances, joke around and insist that your Uncle Jax is better. Trust me, it doesn't end well!)

Anyway, I think I love you already. Who am I kidding? I know I do!
Mommy.

<u>Week 7</u>

Woah!!!!! There are two of you. What the hell, you guys? Way to throw a curve-ball at me. You've been cooking in there for seven weeks and only just decided to tell me? Poor form, guys!

I nearly collapsed in the doctor's office. The poor woman had to sit me up and remind me how to breathe! Though I learned that you're identical, just like your daddy and his brothers, but there are three of him. Kinda trippy if you ask me. Good thing I've got a good job since I'll have twice the baby shopping to do. I'll probably have to start doing all that kinda stuff soon. Though I don't know if I'm supposed to be buying pink or blue stuff. I'm thinking you're blue babies, but just to play it safe, I think I'll stick with neutral colors.

One thing is for sure, we're not all going to fit in my small, one-bedroom apartment. I'm going to have to start looking for something bigger for us, but I suppose we'll be alright until you guys start moving. Though, the thought of having to move after you're born seems like a challenge I don't want to face.

Do you think the city or the suburbs? I'm thinking a house in the suburbs with a yard for you two to run around in. How does that sound?

You sure are keeping me busy.

I saw your daddy this week, and to be honest, it was a little weird, but that's a different story—one I'm sure I'll spend hours telling you about when you're bigger. Anyway, I was a bad mommy. It was the perfect opportunity to tell him about you guys, and I chickened out. I'm so sorry. I promise, I'll tell him soon . . . I hope. I might be lying. There's no telling just yet! I'll keep you posted!

I know you need a daddy in your life, so even if Mommy and Daddy keep being silly, I promise, I'll make sure he's around for you. He truly is amazing, you're going to love him just like I do.

It's been a strange week. A new development has gone up in that massive space on the way to work with a big sign saying Waters Construction. That's your daddy's company, by the way. It's huge and he builds amazing houses for very rich, hoity-toity people. It's kinda cool actually. He's worked with a bunch of celebrities and important people. Don't ask for introductions though. It'll never happen. But then, you're his babies, and one day, I'm sure he'll move heaven and earth to give you the world.

Just like I will.

It's weird driving past the construction site every day, but so far, I haven't seen his truck there, so we're safe to keep living in our delusional bubble.

Anyway, I'm signing off for tonight. I'll check in again soon.

Mommy.

Week 9

Great news, munchkins. I can feel you guys doing backflips in the middle of the night. My tummy has gotten firmer and not because of all the yoga I've been doing!!!! It sticks out a tiny bit, but not enough that I have to get new clothes. Give it a few more weeks and people will start to notice.

It's one thing feeling you moving around inside of me, but actually seeing the bump makes this so much more real. I'm kinda scared, but I know we're going to be okay. Your uncle Bobby has a hero complex, so even if I'm freaking out, he's going to make sure we're all happy and healthy because that's what he does best.

Oooop . . . hold up. I need a quick power vomit.

. . . . . .

Okay, I'm back. But also, now that you're moving around a lot more, these little power vomits are becoming all too regular. Do you think you could move around with caution maybe? I spent over an hour cooking that dinner, and now it's chilling out with the fish.

Also, ignore those smudges. I swear, it's not vomit. Really, it's not . . . I promise. Ahhh, who am I kidding? It's definitely vomit, but I cleaned it up the best I could. Besides, it's your fault it's there anyway!

Anywhooooo . . . We're flying through this pregnancy. We're just past the two-

month mark. It's going so fast, and I'm enjoying 99.9% of it. Okay, maybe more like 90%. Pregnancy is hard and exhausting, and I fear it's only going to get harder from here.

How crazy is it to think I'm growing you guys inside my tummy? When you think about it, it's such a wild concept. I can't wait for my next scan so I can see you again. I downloaded an app that tells me you're the size of a green olive right now.

I haven't told your aunty Cass yet, and I'm nervous she's going to hate me, but it's . . . it's complicated.

I love you both so much. I hope you're happy and healthy in there.

I miss your daddy.

Mommy.

Week 10

Mommy has been busy! I found us a beautiful home in the suburbs, one with a huge yard that has space to build a pool (something I'm sure I could eventually convince your daddy to build for us) . . . buuuuut then we missed out on it.

I'll keep searching. I promise I'll find us an awesome home that we're all going to love.

The good news is that your Uncle Bobby came to visit this week. He stayed for a few days and then hurried back to New York. I think he has a girlfriend, but he won't admit it yet. Don't worry, I'll get it out of him. (I just hope it's not the girl I caught him with in New York . . . again, something I'll tell you about when you're thirty)

Mommy.

Week 11

Apparently you're the size of figs this week. You're still so small, so help me make sense of how I'm getting so big? This is ridiculous (Is now the time to admit that I don't actually know what a fig is?)

You're making my jeans very tight. Stop growing! I don't want to buy maternity clothes yet. I'm not ready for that step. Right now, I'm able to hide you under baggy hoodies and winter coats, but it's getting hard. I've seen people looking at me, their gazes lingering just a little too long, but I'm not big enough for anyone to risk asking just in case they're wrong. We're in that weird stage!

Aunty Cassie took me on a shopping trip, and I was such a bad mommy and didn't tell her about you yet. I want to keep you all to myself—that's a lame excuse, isn't it? Aunty Cass is so close with all of your uncles, and I just don't want to put her in the position of having to keep it from your daddy. It's only right for him to hear it from me. Though to be honest, I'm surprised Cass didn't notice our little bump, but she was very busy and concerned about finding some new "special" clothes for Uncle Jax.

Shit. You probably didn't need to know about that.

Also, I think it's time you learned that Mommy has a foul mouth. I'll do my best to try and keep it clean, but sometimes those naughty words just slip right out.

Mommy.

Week 12

I'm tired.

I've been sleeping a lot while you guys keep growing.

I saw your daddy at his construction site today. He looked pretty handsome just like you guys will be (that's assuming you're boys, otherwise, I just know you're going to be absolutely gorgeous little girls). The place Daddy is building looks like it's going to be huge. I'll show you guys when you arrive. You'll be so proud of the amazing things he can do.

Mommy loves him very much, and I miss him too, but that's our little secret. Can you believe we've made it to 3 months already?

This time with you is going so fast. In a blink of an eye, I'll have you both in my arms, struggling to figure out how to feed you at the same time. I swear, we've got some fun times ahead of us, but promise you'll take it easy on me. Also, I did some research on babies who bite their mommy's nipples while breastfeeding, and I've been having nightmares. Please don't do that to me. I don't think I could handle that kind of stress.

Though, speaking of stress. I watched a movie tonight that showed exactly how you guys are supposed to come out of me, and to be honest, I should not have watched it. It's . . . gross. I think society is wanting me to boast about how beautiful and natural childbirth is, but they couldn't be more wrong. There's nothing natural about that! You're going to come out all squishy and covered in slimy stuff, not to mention, if your head gets stuck down there, you're gonna look like an alien. So let's get this out of the way now . . . I'm not going to be a regular mommy, but I promise, I'm going to try my best. But if mommy looks a little frazzled, just smile and remind me how much you love me.

Anyway, I have another scan tomorrow, I'm so excited to see you. It's a big one where they're going to measure you both to make sure you're growing just right. I'll let you know how it goes.

Love you to the moon and back.

Mommy.

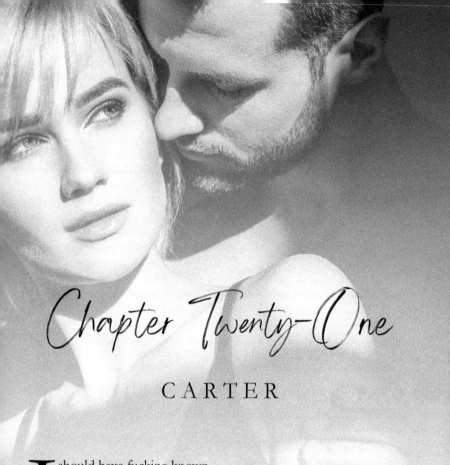

Chapter Twenty-One

CARTER

I should have fucking known.

Anger drums through my veins as I drive across town to the Wilder's new build, first thing on a Friday morning because, surprise, surprise, the idiot's wife decided she wants to make a few more fucking changes that can't possibly wait until Monday.

For fuck's sake. When Waters Construction received the formal approval to complete the Wilder build and hand over their keys, I should have known that wasn't the last I'd be seeing of them.

I've never regretted a build, nor have I ever regretted taking on particular clients, but the Wilders are close to being my first. I'm lost in my thoughts as I take a shortcut through the city, trying to figure out what other changes Mrs. Wilder could possibly make, and the more I think about it, the more frustrated I become.

I'm busy fighting with the woman in my head, really giving her a piece of my mind, when a brunette steps off the curb, completely engrossed with the papers in her hand, and walks straight out into traffic.

My eyes widen as I slam on my brakes, the tires screeching across the road. I lay on the horn, the sound booming through the city as my grip tightens on the steering wheel, my stomach falling out of my ass.

Fuck. Fuck. Fuck. *Please don't hit her.*

The woman frets, her head whipping in my direction, her eyes wide and filled with fear, and the second her gaze locks on mine through the windshield, my whole fucking world crumbles with horror.

Brianna.

My truck continues screeching toward her, and I press on the brakes even harder, my foot all but slamming right through the bottom of the truck. Fear grips her, and she stands motionless in the middle of the road, not having enough time to react and lunge away. Instead, she wraps her arms around herself and hopes like hell that I can stop in time.

Fuck. If this truck touches even a single hair on her body, I'd never forgive myself.

The moment seems to go on forever, but in reality, it happens in the blink of an eye. My truck hurtles toward her, the horn still blaring through the street, when finally I come to a halt just inches away from her.

My chest rises and falls with wild gasps as I try to catch my breath, the relief pounding through my veins. My head falls forward, dropping onto the top of my steering wheel, feeling as though I could be sick.

That was way too fucking close for my liking. I almost killed the woman I love in the middle of the fucking city.

After catching my breath and taking a minute for my heart to stop racing, I move to get out and check on her, desperate to grab her and pull her into my arms, when two angry fists slam down on the hood of my truck, her ferocious glare meeting mine through the windshield. "What the fuck is your problem?" she yells for the whole fucking street to hear. "You could have killed me."

Oh, hell no.

Rage bursts through me, and I throw my door open, not even sparing a second to cut the engine. I slam the door behind me and fly around the front of my truck until I'm standing right in front of the woman of my dreams—the one thing I have needed since the night of Logan's championship game. But I'm far too angry to appreciate that fact.

"Are you fucking kidding me?" I roar. "Do you always make a habit of crossing the road without looking, or are you so fucking self-centered that you just assume everyone will magically stop for you?"

"No. No fucking way are you blaming me for this," she grunts, that familiar angry crease appearing right between her eyebrows, the one I've been dying to see for the past eight months.

"What the fuck is wrong with you, Brianna? You literally stepped off the fucking sidewalk without even bothering to look up. You were too fucking distracted by reading," I say pointing to the paper in her hand. "I could have fucking killed you."

She narrows that blazing green gaze on me as her hand discretely moves out of sight, and I watch as she starts to reach her boiling point, only moments from blowing up at me just like she used to. And fuck, despite my rage, I need it. I fucking need her to throw herself at me, need her to slam those feisty little fists into my chest, need her to make me feel something for the first time in eight months.

She steps in closer, her jaw clenches, and just as she goes to let me have it, a nosey bystander steps up beside us. "Are you alright, Miss?" the old guy asks, discreetly trying to get between us and stop us from ripping each other's heads off.

"She's fine," I grunt, not needing a third party trying to insert themselves into our bullshit.

"I can speak for myself," Bri seethes, her glare not leaving mine for even a second.

I clench my jaw, the anger blasting through me like never before, but fuck, I love it. How is it this woman still manages to get such a reaction out of me? I've been missing her so much, I don't even care that she's furious with me. Though, if anything, she should be fucking thankful that I was watching the road and able to stop before turning her into minced meat.

"Sir," the old man says in disapproval, fixing me with a hard stare. "I was talking to the lady."

Bri rolls her eyes, clearly not appreciating his help either, but not having it in her to be impolite to someone who's simply trying to care. Me though, I don't hold the same reservations, especially where my girl is involved.

"I'm fine," Bri grits through her teeth, trying to force a reassuring smile for the old man.

"Good, I'm glad we got that sorted," I tell her, stepping back to my truck, more than ready to haul her over my shoulder and get her ass out of here. Preferably back to my place where I can pin her against my bedroom wall and work out our issues in sexual favors, though somehow, I don't think that's gonna happen. "Get in my fucking truck. I'm taking you home."

Brianna gapes at me as though I've lost my mind, her brows arching, and I swear, she looks as though she's two seconds from exploding. "Like fuck I'm going anywhere with you, asshole," she spits, "You nearly killed me."

"Again. Not my fucking fault."

She glares at me again, standing still as if trying to set some kind of challenge, but if she thinks she's going to win this, she's got another thing coming. Though there's no denying just how fucking beautiful she looks, even when she's about to tear my ballsack right off my body.

"That is hardly a way to speak to a woman, young man," the intruder reprimands.

Get fucked.

My anger turns into red-hot rage, and I turn on the old man. "Look, I get it, you're trying to protect the little damsel in distress, trying to be her hero, but she doesn't need a fucking hero. She never has."

"That's no excuse to speak to her in that way," he fires back.

"Can't you see this is a private conversation?" I question. "She's my fucking girlfr—"

Fuck. This day just keeps getting worse.

Letting out a sigh, I prepare for the onslaught from Brianna, watching as she sucks in a furious gasp, her eyes going wide.

In three.

Two.

One.

"I dare you to finish that sentence, Carter Waters," she seethes as I notice a shitload of people standing around, some horrified by what's going on while others look as though they're settling in for a show.

"Calm down. It was a slip of the tongue."

Her eyes grow watery, and this time, I know it's out of pure rage rather than confused feelings. She must hate me. I've never seen her get quite this angry before, though I guess it's fair, I nearly killed her.

"Oh, a slip of the tongue," she scoffs. "That's bullshit and you know it. You just want to keep fucking me around and messing with my emotions. Well, guess what, Carter? You've well and truly fucked me up." Brianna takes a shaky breath before gathering herself, realizing she's already said too much before lowering her tone and trying to find just a sliver of self-control. "You can't just keep showing up in my life and making things harder for me."

"What?" I sputter, taken back. "You think I planned this? You think I woke up bright and early on my Friday morning and thought, hmm, today's the day I'm gonna run over the fucking love of my life?"

"Sir," the old man cuts in, making me realize he's still here, still butting in on something that's clearly none of his business. "Where's your morality? You can't talk to a pregnant woman this way. This kind of stress is not good for the baby."

Brianna's eyes go wide, but I'm too busy turning to the old man to figure out why. "What the fuck are you talking about?" I demand, looking at him like he's fucking crazy before turning back to Bri. "She's not . . ."

The horrified look on her face has my gaze trailing down her body, over her much fuller tits, to her stomach, then I stumble back, my ribs slamming into the grille of my truck, finding her swollen stomach—a perfect fucking baby bump staring right at me like a brutal reminder of everything I gave up.

I can't fucking breathe, feeling my heart falling right out of my goddamn chest and shattering on the dirty pavement. She's not just pregnant. *She's pregnant.* A bump like this could only be for someone who's at least six months along.

How could I have missed that?

My stomach drops. No wonder she's been so distant lately. She got herself knocked up, and fuck, if she's at least six months then she would have already been pregnant when we hooked up after the funeral. I know that day was hard for everyone, but that night with her was special, and now . . . fuck. Now it's tainted.

A mix of emotions fires through me. Anger. Emptiness. Betrayal. Did she do this on purpose to make sure there would never be a future between us, or is it just out of spite? There are other ways she could have gone about hurting me that would have been better than this. "You got yourself knocked up?" I question, feeling as though I'm moments from falling to my knees, the agony soaring through my chest and eating me alive. I knew one day she'd have a baby, but I wasn't expecting it so soon. I feel fucking blindsided. "Who's the lucky guy?"

I thought she would have waited to find someone special. Dated for a few years before finally tying the knot. Then sure, the kids would have come along soon after that. But she didn't have to go and jump in bed with the first asshole who said she was hot.

Tears fall from her eyes, and for the first time, I'm far too broken for them to have an effect on me. How could she do this? Doesn't she realize that I'm still in love with her? I would have tried to make it work if I thought there was even a slight chance. But not now . . . I can barely even meet her eyes.

Brianna steps forward, pushing the guy out of her way, and slams the piece of paper against my chest. "You're the lucky guy, asshole," she says, her voice breaking as the tears stream down her face. "Congratulations, it's twins."

Without another word, Brianna walks away, and I barely have time to catch the piece of paper as it starts floating to the ground. My world crumbles, unease blasting through my veins and bringing me to my knees as the cars stopped behind my truck start honking for me to move out of the way. But I can't fucking move. I can't fucking breathe.

Watching her as she goes, she drops down into her car across the street, and in an instant, she crumbles over the steering wheel, utterly broken, and I want nothing more than to go to her, to pull her into my arms and tell her everything is going to be alright, but I don't. I don't move a fucking inch.

Brianna Lucas is pregnant with my child. Children. *Twins*. It's not possible.

I told her I didn't want kids. We broke up so this exact thing couldn't happen, yet here we are. I handed her the dynamite, and she lit the fuse right under me.

Betrayal grabs hold of my chest and refuses to release me, like a vice tightening further by the second.

Brianna got pregnant and didn't tell me, then decided to keep it without telling me, and waited three long months before letting me in on the secret. And fuck, I know damn well she wasn't knocking down my door to do it. I'm sure when she first found out, she probably had every intention of letting me know, but three months? No, she was going to keep this dirty little secret buried down as long as she could. Fuck, I know Brianna doesn't owe me anything, but as the father of those children, I had the right to know.

What really guts me, what really tears me at the seams, is how Cassandra could possibly keep this from me. She's my baby sister and didn't even have the decency to tell me. Where's her fucking loyalty? I've given everything to Cass, made sure she has the world in the palm of her hands, and this is how she repays me.

Is this some kind of twisted revenge for hurting her best friend? Because if it is, that's fucked up. That's taking it too far. I understood the months of silent treatment, but you don't bring children into this shit. If she wanted to hurt me, she could have easily trashed my truck or cut me out, but this? There's no coming back from this.

My hands ball into fists when I recall the piece of paper she slammed into my chest. I open my hand and find it crumpled into a tight ball under the pressure of my fist. After smoothing it out and seeing a blank page, I flip it over to find an ultrasound image with two perfect little babies growing inside their mother's womb.

My babies. *My children.* The very children I always swore I never wanted, but looking at them now . . . fuck. How could any man stand in my position and say they don't want this? How could I ever deny such angelic creatures?

I've made the biggest mistake of my fucking life.

My head spins with the betrayal and hurt, not able to even string a sentence together, but the one thing I do know is that I would go to the ends of the earth, fight my way through the darkest pits of hell just to protect those two tiny humans.

My children.

Twins.

Fuck. I'm going to have twins.

My life is never going to be the same, and yet, as I remain here on my knees in the middle of the fucking road, I realize that I don't want it to be. I'm fucking terrified. I never thought I would want this, but I was wrong, so fucking wrong. I knew I'd make a mistake the night of Logan's championship game, but I didn't understand the extent of it until this very moment.

I want it all, and I'm going to do everything in my power to make that happen.

Looking across the road, I go to find Bri, more than ready to make this right, when I realize she's gone. Shit, of course, she's gone. I shouldn't have expected anything different. After all, I've been a mess on the road for twenty fucking minutes.

I consider going after her, but knowing Bri, I need to give her space to breathe, time to calm down and collect her wild emotions. She's not in the right mind frame to have to deal with confrontation, but at the very least, I could text. I could let her know that she has no reason to fear this, that I'm fully on board and want this just as much as she does. That these children are never going to go without.

Pulling out my phone, I see seven missed calls from Mr. Wilder, and going against my every instinct, I swipe the notifications away and pull up Bri's name in my phone.

My thumb is just moments from pressing down on her number when I pause, realizing this is not a conversation that can be had over the phone. I need to do this in person, and she needs to be able to see the honesty in my eyes when I tell her that I will never let her go.

But before I can do that, she needs today to chill, then come tomorrow, it's on!

As for right now, Cassandra and I need to have a little chat.

Chapter Twenty-Two

BRIANNA

Week 12

I know I've already written this week but there's been a little development.

Uhhhhh . . . your daddy knows, and considering he almost passed out in the street

after almost running me over, I don't think it's going to go down well.

Brace yourselves, babies. Shit is about to get real!

.

Chapter Twenty-Three

BRIANNA

"**B**rianna Fucking Lucas."

Ahhh, shit.

My apartment door is flung open by my best friend, and I suck in a breath, preparing for the worst as she storms through my apartment. Her usual happy face is long gone, replaced with absolute rage, and it's clear she just spoke with her brother.

I give her a tight smile from the kitchen, but her eyes don't meet mine, they go straight to my stomach as if not really believing anything Carter had to say. But there's no denying it now, I've been strutting around in nothing but my underwear all day. She can see my baby bump just as clearly as I can see the hurt in her eyes.

After sitting in my car and crying over the top of my steering wheel, I had to get out of there. Seeing him crumble to the ground like that, completely broken and lost, reminded me of the day he first broke up with me. I couldn't handle the pain that came along with it. But the way he looked at me, the betrayal in his eyes . . . There's no doubt about it, Carter Waters despises me. I went and did the one thing he always said he didn't want.

I didn't want him to find out like this. I've been wracking my brain for ways to tell him since the moment I peed on the pregnancy test, and out of all the different scenarios I came up with, that was definitely not one of them. If there was a way to go back and do it all over, to tell him in another way, I would do it in a heartbeat.

I've never felt rage like that before. I could see the wheels turning in his mind, judging the size of my bump, and I know he was thinking the worst—assuming I'd been sleeping around. Despite wanting to run at the first second, I couldn't leave him without telling him the truth. I only wish I didn't do it like a fucking psycho.

I'm almost positive he's sitting in some filthy dive bar, drinking bottle after bottle of whiskey. Logan will probably have to go and scrape him off the sidewalk tonight or go searching through the hospitals just to make sure he's still alive.

He'll never forgive me for this, and even though it takes two to tango, I could have been honest with him and given him the chance to have a say. I stole that from him knowing what he would have wanted. I betrayed him in the worst way, and he has every right to hate me for it.

Carter never would have asked me to have an abortion, especially considering how I feel about having children, but he would have absolved himself of any parental rights and I would have truly been doing this alone. The second I realized I was pregnant, the babies became the best thing I ever did. They were already a done deal, already a permanent fixture in my life. I was going to be their mommy and nothing Carter said could have changed that.

The door slams behind Cass, and it's so loud, I can hear it echoing right down the hallway. "So, it's true?" Cass grunts, looking at me through tears as if I'm the worst person in the world.

My brows furrow as a large lump forms in my throat, making me feel as though I'm going to break. "I'm sorry," I whisper, not needing to confirm what she already knows.

Cassie braces her hands against my kitchen counter, gripping the marble and trying to keep herself from shaking, her gaze locked on my protruding stomach. "How long have you known?" she asks, her voice breaking.

Letting out a breath, I walk around my kitchen counter and into the small living room, nodding my head for her to follow. Taking a seat on the couch, I pat the space beside me, welcoming her to sit, but I'm not sure if she will, and it kills me how that's even a thought that enters my head. "I found out at four weeks."

"But," she says, her gaze flicking back to my stomach as she reluctantly drops down at the other end of the couch, keeping as far as the couch will allow. "How far along are you?"

"Three months."

A tear escapes her eye, and I hate that I put it there. A moment passes before she finally finds the strength to lift her gaze to mine, and the betrayal in her eyes is like a knife right through the chest. "I get that you're in a bad situation with Carter, but how could you not tell me?"

"God, Cass. You have no idea how much I wanted to," I say as my own tears start to fall down my cheeks and drop to my chest. "I couldn't. You love your brothers so much, and I love that about you, but I could never put you in the position where you would have to lie to them—to Carter. He needed to hear it from me, and if you knew . . . it would have torn you to pieces."

"I just . . . I really want to hate you," she cries. "You have no idea how much it hurts. I thought I was your best friend. We were supposed to tell each other everything, and this . . . it's huge."

"You should hate me, Cass," I tell her. "I've been agonizing over not telling you, but I just couldn't. At the start, I was in denial. I couldn't even bring myself to take the test. I didn't want to believe it was true, and I was so scared of how Carter would react, and now it's worse than ever. I couldn't even bring myself to tell my parents. Bobby is the only one who knows."

Cassie nods as she looks down at her lap and plays with her rings. She's silent for a while, and I want to scream at her to hurry up and say something, even if it's just to yell at me, anything would be better than the silence. "So, there's two of them?" she finally asks.

"There are," I tell her, slowly inching across the couch until I'm close enough to grab her hand.

Cass doesn't pull back from my touch, and as she latches onto my hand and holds it tight, relief starts pulsing through my veins. "Keeping this from me . . . I don't know. I'm really hurt. I feel like I've missed out on so much of this. I could have been there for you, helped you through everything, and while I don't necessarily agree with your reasons for hiding it, I understand it," she says. "But at the end of the day, these babies are my nieces or nephews, and you will always be my best friend."

I give her a small smile, bringing our joined hands into my lap. "Believe me, if I could change that, I would, but what's important is that these two crotch goblins are going to need an aunty who loves them just as much as their mommy does."

She gives me a sad smile before launching across the couch, closing the small gap between us, and throwing her arms around me. "I'm going to love them so much, they'll hate me."

"Not possible," I smile as I wipe away a tear, pulling back to meet her eyes. "Cass?" I question, a seriousness creeping into my tone. "I'm terrified, after what happened to Sara, I—"

"Don't," she says, cutting me off. "What happened to Sara was a tragedy, but that's not going to happen to you. You don't need to be scared."

My hands shake, needing to get the words out. "You don't know that. Women die from childbirth and post-delivery complications all the time. And I can deal with that. It would really suck, but I need to know that if I'm doing this alone, if Carter doesn't want to be a part of this, you'll give these babies a loving home. I don't want to leave them without a mommy or daddy."

"Me?" she breathes, wide-eyed. "Are you sure? I'm honored, but what about Bobby?"

I shake my head. "Bobby would honestly love to have them, but he's not ready for something like this. He has his career ahead of him and needs to figure himself out. He's going to be an amazing uncle to these rugrats, but he's in New York. You're here where their daddy and their family is. This is where I want them to call home."

"Okay," Cass breathes. "You've got my word."

Tears fall from my eyes as I reach in and pull Cass back into me. "Make sure they know their father," I tell her. "I want them to love him like I do."

"Always."

A minute passes as we each wipe our tears, and as Cass leans back, she forces a smile across her face, desperately trying to lighten the mood. "I feel like a fool for not noticing earlier," she tells me, her fingers brushing over my bump. "You're kinda huge."

"Don't. I went out of my way to make sure nobody would find out. The number of winter coats I've worn during fall is just ridiculous."

Cass scoffs. "Well, looks like that plan crashed and burned."

I smile to myself before muttering under my breath. "Tell me about it."

Cass gives me a tight smile, glancing up at me and cringing. "I heard he nearly ran you over," she questions.

"Yeah," I grunt, my hands still shaking with the thought, that moment easily being the most terrifying moment of my life, thinking

I was about to lose my sweet babies. "You were pretty damn close to visiting me in the morgue."

Cassie's eyes widen in shock. "Really?" she questions. "It was that close?"

"Uh-huh. There's skid marks on the road to prove it. There wasn't even enough time to jump out of the way."

"Shit. He never would have forgiven himself if he had hurt you."

"I know," I agree with a heavy sigh. "I'll deny I ever said it, but it wasn't his fault. I'd just been at the doctor's office and was distracted by the ultrasound picture. I wasn't looking and just stepped out onto the road. It was stupid. My head is so consumed with these babies that I'm not thinking about the little things, and it's getting me into trouble."

Cass gives me a tight smile that's followed up with a shitload of sympathy. "I bet," she says. "I think I'm actually a little jealous. After Georgia was born, I've been thinking about having one of my own."

"No, don't do that," I tell her with a laugh, the stress of those first few nights with little Georgia still so fresh in my mind. "I'm having two. We can share."

"I don't think it works like that," she laughs.

The room falls quiet, and as I take a deep breath, I look up at her and press my lips into a hard line, willing myself not to be so obvious, but the curiosity gets the better of me. "How's he doing?"

"Honestly, I don't know," she says. "I think he's in shock and doesn't know how to handle it. He only talked to me because he assumed I already knew and didn't tell him. But the second he found out I had no idea, he completely shut off and didn't say another word.

Which is why I had to come here for myself. I needed answers."

Shit. This isn't good.

"I'm really sorry, Cass," I tell her again.

She squeezes my hand again, giving me a small, encouraging smile. "It's okay."

I appreciate her trying, but we both know nothing about this is okay. "No, it's really not."

"You're right. It's not. But there's nothing we can do about it now apart from moving forward and figuring out the best way for you to have a healthy, happy pregnancy."

I give her a smile, which is when she finally relaxes into the couch and hits me with all the pregnancy questions. We settle into our usual friendship, and while it's still a little strained, I know we'll be fine. After all, I'm growing her newest family members inside of me.

I'm in the middle of telling her about the nipple biting dream I had when a banging sounds at the door. We look at each other, both our brows furrowed, but it doesn't take long to figure out who could be trying to bust down my door.

"Brianna Lucas, open this damn door," Carter calls from the other side.

"Shit," Cassie mutters with a cringe. "I think I better go."

"What? No. Don't you dare leave me with him," I beg. "He's probably made his way through a whole bar by now and is on the rampage looking for more."

"Sorry, girl," she grins, the amusement in her eyes making me wonder if this is some kind of payback for lying to her for three months. "You got yourself into this mess."

"Cass," I whine, sounding like a child whose mom just told her she couldn't have any candy.

The banging continues at the door. "Brianna," Carter grunts in warning. "I know you're in there. I can smell the deception wafting through the door."

Fucking hell.

Cassie gives me a wide smile, enjoying this way too much. "You two need to sort this shit out, and soon. It's in both of your best interests to find middle ground. Otherwise, this pregnancy is going to be a pain in everyones' asses."

I couldn't agree more.

She starts to leave, and I grab hold of her, giving her my award-winning puppy dog eyes. "Please."

"Nope," she says, getting up and reminding me that those puppy dog eyes only ever worked on the asshole at the door, and something tells me they're not going to work this time.

Carter bangs against the wooden door again, and I roll my eyes at his determination, but honestly, Cassie didn't lock it behind her when she came storming in here. All he'd have to do is try the handle.

Cass strides across my apartment before grabbing hold of the handle and yanking the door open, and before she even gets a chance to move, Carter is storming in, stepping right into her and invading her personal space, his finger against her chest, more than ready to say what's on his mind.

His eyes widen briefly, quickly realizing it's Cass before backing up and pointing out the door and down the hallway. "Out," he rumbles, that single word and the authority in his tone making chills race through my body.

"Already on it, brother," Cass says, reaching up onto her tippy toes and pressing a kiss to his cheek. "Try not to be too hard on her. I know she hurt you, but she's still my best friend. Besides, she's in no state for stress."

Cassie ducks under his arm and quickly disappears down the hallway as his piercing stare lifts to mine. My heart races, nervousness blooming through me, while distantly aware that I'm wearing nothing but my underwear.

I swallow hard, watching as Carter slams the door behind him and makes his way toward me. Neither of us says a word, and the silence is agonizing. His gaze travels down my body, taking in the entirety of my bump, and a part of me is grateful that he's able to see me like this, taking it all in. No more hiding.

He's only three steps away now, and I bunch my hands into fists at my sides, keeping myself from reaching out and falling into his arms, begging him not to hate me, to tell me that everything is going to be okay.

Two steps to go and my knees become weak.

One.

Shit.

Chapter Twenty-Four

BRIANNA

Carter steps in front of me, and before I even get a chance to breathe him in or figure out what I'm going to say, he reaches out and grabs my waist, his strong hands so firm on my body. Then in a moment of complete perfection, Carter pulls me into his wide chest before slamming his warm lips down on mine, bringing me home for the first time in months.

I melt into him as need blasts through my veins and fills me with the sweetest ecstasy.

My arms lock around his neck as my lips start moving with his, the hunger for him like nothing I've ever felt. His familiar scent wraps around me, drowning me in him, and if the choice was up to me, I would never let him go.

Wait. What am I doing?

My day from hell comes crashing back to me, the way he almost ran me over, the tension out on the road, and the way he gaped at me, realizing the extent of my disgusting betrayal.

Despite the way every cell in my body yearns for him, I shove my hand against his chest and push him back, tears threatening to well in my eyes. I look up at him, taking in the hunger in his expression and watching the way he tries to reach for me again, barely able to hold himself back. "What the hell do you think you're doing?"

"Wow. This whole pregnancy thing really gets you fired up, huh?"

Fuck. I could kill him for that, but he's right. My emotions are all over the place, and I have nothing to blame but my stupid pregnancy hormones, but that doesn't give him the right to point it out. It's like telling a woman on her period that she's a moody bitch. No matter how true it might be, you just can't say it.

Crossing my arms over my chest, I fix the greatest love of my life with the most ferocious glare I can possibly muster. "Get out," I demand.

Carter scoffs, a smile pulling at his lips as though he were playing with a feisty kitty with an attitude. "No," he says.

Frustration burns through me, and I throw my hands up before balling them into fists at my side, hating how hard it is to control myself. Though while I could certainly blame the pregnancy hormones, there's no denying that Carter Waters has a gift for driving me insane. "Then what the hell are you doing here, Carter?" I repeat. "This doesn't make sense. I thought you were coming in here to rage at me. Call me names, fall apart, or demand an explanation, not try to get me in bed."

Carter's gaze softens and he hesitantly steps back into me, taking his time as if not to spook me, but the moment his hands land on my bump, my chest swells with undeniable joy, having dreamed about this moment since the second the test came back positive.

Tears well in my eyes, but I keep my gaze locked on his, waiting to hear what he has to say. "I needed to see you, Bri. I need to know why you thought it was okay not to tell me about this," he says, his thumb moving back and forth over my bump.

"What does it matter?" I question, reaching up and curling my hand around the back of his neck, desperately needing to touch him despite the heavy conversation. "You don't want this. You said it yourself and were so adamant about it that you left me. The idea of telling you and having you despise me for deciding to keep them . . . fuck, Carter. I could never live with myself knowing you hated me."

"I could never hate you, Bri. You drive me insane and make me want to strangle you sometimes, but no matter how far you push me, I will never hate you." He pauses, watching as the tears spill down my cheeks. "I'm sorry, baby. I hate that I made you feel that you couldn't come to me with this."

My gaze drops away, not knowing how to respond, and he simply pulls me into his chest, holding me close as I listen to the rapid beat of his heart. "You're fucking radiant, Brianna. Pregnancy suits you."

"You wouldn't be saying that if you saw the way these little monsters have me throwing up my lunch every afternoon. There's nothing radiant about that."

A breathy chuckle escapes him before the seriousness becomes so heavy in the room, it has me ready to run for the fucking hills. "Brianna," he murmurs, his tone having me pull back an inch to see his eyes. "I fucked up. The night of Logan's championship game, I realized I'd made the biggest mistake of my life, seeing you sitting up in the grandstand with my family, holding little Georgia. I knew I'd given up my whole fucking future, but seeing you today, seeing the way you were glowing with my babies in your womb . . . fuck, Bri. I don't ever want to let you go."

I shake my head, needing to step out of his arms, confusion gripping me and pulling me down into the dark abyss below. "Don't," I tell him, the tears so heavy in my eyes. "Don't bullshit me like that. You can't come in here and promise me the world when I know you can't give it to me. You're drunk, Carter. You've been drinking, and suddenly you think you want all these things you've sworn to me you'd never want, but come morning when that wicked hangover sets in, you're gonna pull the rug out from under me and destroy me all over again. You've already broken me, and I somehow clawed my way back, but I won't let you do it again. I'm having these babies on my own. I've already come to terms with it. I don't need anything from you, so don't feel like you need to come in here like some kind of hero that's going to save the day. You can be as involved in their lives as you want. I wouldn't dream of trying to hinder that, but when you broke me, you ensured we could never be a family."

"You can't do this on your own," he says.

"I can. Women all over the world do it every day."

"You're not hearing me, Bri," he says, starting to creep in again. "I want to do this with you. I want to wake up every fucking morning with you in my arms. I want to raise these babies with you. I want the memories and good times. I want it all."

"I don't believe you," I whisper, hating how the words feel on my tongue, "and I don't want your help. You left me. You ruined a perfectly good thing because of this very reason, and I'm supposed to just believe that you want to be a part of it now?"

"Yes," he says. "I fucked up. Big time. But you know me, Bri. You know me better than anyone in this world, and you know that I wouldn't just come to you like this without thinking it through."

I shake my head, the tears rolling down my cheeks. "You need to leave, Carter. I . . . I can't do this," I tell him, needing a moment to take it all in and wrap my head around everything he's trying to say. The words are so perfect, it's what I dream about every night, but how the hell am I supposed to believe them? He's just overwhelmed by the emotions of learning he's going to be a father, and his strong sense of morality has kicked in, telling him he needs to do the right thing by the mother of his children.

He doesn't truly want this. I know he doesn't.

Carter fixes me with a hard stare, letting me see the determination in his dark eyes. "I'm not walking away from this. I want to make this work. I want to be here and be their father."

I let out a sigh. "Look, Carter. Like I said, I'm more than happy for you to be in these babies' lives. I want you to be in their lives. They need to grow up knowing who their daddy is, but they're not born yet, and I can't handle this," I say, indicating the space between us. "You and I are not a thing anymore, and you made damn sure of that. So, until they're born, you don't need to be here. I'll let you know when I have doctor's appointments and you're more than welcome to attend them with me, but you need to respect my space. These babies are yours, but I'm not."

"Please, Brianna. You know we belong together, you, me, and these babies. We're a family. The second I saw that ultrasound it all became clear to me, and I'll do whatever it takes for you to see how badly I want this."

"What?" I scoff. "You had an epiphany, did you? Eight months ago, you said you didn't see marriage and babies in your future, and I'm supposed to suddenly believe that you want that now? You're riding high on the emotions, Carter, and I appreciate you coming and saying what you needed to say, but all you're doing is hurting me more."

Carter shakes his head, his eyes glistening with overwhelming happiness as his hands come back to my waist. He leans in and presses a gentle kiss to my forehead, lingering there as though he's been craving it just as much as I have. "Let me take you to dinner."

My brows furrow and I look back up at him, trying to figure out his angle. "No."

"Brianna," he says more firmly. "Let me take you to dinner."

"Absolutely not. I know I'm not exactly your favorite person after keeping this pregnancy from you, but that doesn't mean I owe you my time."

"Let me try this again," he says, taking his time as he crowds me, walking into me and forcing me to back up until my spine is pressed against the wall and he hovers over me, making my breath catch in my throat as my hands fall to his chest. "Go get your stubborn ass dressed, Brianna. I'm taking you to dinner whether you fucking like it or not."

I swallow hard, so unbelievably affected by this man. I start melting into him, needing him to hold me, needing him to love me so damn fiercely he could never let go. "Fine," I finally whisper, needing him to back up before I cross a line I won't be able to save myself from. "But only because I'm hungry and too tired to cook."

"Noted," he says with a triumphant grin, stepping back and allowing me space to breathe.

I hastily slip around him and hurry down my hallway, peeking back over my shoulder only to see his hungry gaze still locked on me. "Jackass," I grumble before disappearing into my bedroom.

I throw on some clothes, not even caring if I look good, too irritated by this whole situation, but what am I supposed to do? He's right, these children are his, and I would never keep them from him. Since the second I fell pregnant, our lives became intertwined. Getting along with Carter Waters is just something I'm going to have to learn how to do . . . preferably without throwing myself at him in the process.

Running my fingers through my hair and trying to control the mess, I hear my phone buzz on the bedside table and make my way across my room, scooping it up to find a text from Cass.

Cassie – Is everything okay?

I scoff as I start typing out a quick reply.

Bri – Your brother is an ass.
Cassie – Yeah . . . he is. Love you xx.

Grabbing my purse, I make my way back up the hall and stop by the kitchen to scoop my keys off the counter, then without sparing him a single glance, I storm to the door while sensing him following behind.

After locking up behind me, we make our way out of my apartment complex, and I feel his stare on me the whole way out to his truck. Being the gentleman he is, he opens my door for me, and I bypass his hand as I try to get up into his truck on my own. "Come on, babe," he says, watching me struggle. "Let me help you."

I ignore him like the child I am and struggle to hoist myself up, a firm believer that pregnancy isn't a handicap. "This is so fucking wrong," Carter mutters, watching the show.

He thankfully keeps his hands to himself, and the second I'm settled in his truck, he closes the door and makes his way around to the driver's side. The truck smells just like him, and I want nothing more than to burst into tears, too overwhelmed by everything that's going on. Why am I doing this? I should have kicked him out.

Carter gets in, and just as he goes to start the engine, my eyes widen, and a gasp sails between my lips. "What now?" he mutters.

"You're drunk. You shouldn't be driving."

"I'm not drunk," he argues. "I haven't had a single drink. I've been pacing my fucking living room all afternoon trying to give you space."

I scoff. "Wow, let's hope our children don't have your lack of self-control."

Carter rolls his eyes, and after taking a calming breath, he starts up the truck and pulls out onto the road. "What do you feel like?" he asks, referring to dinner.

I shrug my shoulders and he groans, knowing this routine a little too well. We drive in silence, and as he flies through the beautiful Denver city, my gaze falls to his hand on the gear shift. I want to reach out and hold it like I used to. In fact, I want to throw myself across the console and ride him like a fucking cowgirl, but that seems a little inappropriate. What can I say? This pregnancy has me horny as fuck.

He finally pulls into one of the many restaurants he knows I like, and I can't keep the snide comment from flying out. "Are you sure this is where you want to eat?" I question. "We wouldn't want to get right to the door only for you to change your mind. I know how you struggle with such big commitments."

He narrows his eyes at me. "Yes, I'm sure," he says, clearly not very impressed with my snide comments, though there's no denying I'm funny as fuck. But now that the words have flown out of my mind, I'm all too aware of just how immature I'm being about it, yet I can't seem to help myself.

Carter jumps down from the truck and walks around the front, knowing better than to come help me, despite his chivalrous needs.

Opening my door, I swivel in my chair to get out, but I find myself unable to move, and after taking too long, Carter walks around and comes to stand in the open door, peering up at me in concern. "What's wrong?"

"This isn't a good idea," I tell him, the heaviness weighing on my heart, fear gripping me in a choke hold.

"I think you're wrong," he murmurs, stepping closer into the open door and pushing himself between my knees, his hand falling to my thigh as those dark eyes remain on mine. "I want to make this work, Bri. I swear to you, I'm not going to change my mind, and I'm sure as fuck never going to hurt you again. We're going to be a family."

I shake my head, desperately wishing I could believe him. "I can't, Carter. You broke me. I don't trust you anymore."

Devastation clouds his stare after taking that hit, but he doesn't back down as he reaches up and trails his fingers down the side of my face in the same way he used to.

My face falls into his hand and he presses his lips to my forehead. "Please, Brianna. I've lived the last eight months without you, and it's been the hardest time of my life. I love you, and I can see it in your eyes that you still love me, too. Just give me a chance to prove to you that I truly do want this. We can take it slow, baby. I'm not expecting you to just fall in where we left off, but it'd kill me if we couldn't at least try. I know we can make this work."

His words are like music to my ears. It's everything I've been needing to hear from him, but it comes far too late. The trust is gone and the damage he's left behind is irreparable. "You're going to hurt me again, and this time, there's so much more at stake."

"I swear to you, Brianna, I won't," he says, looking deep into my eyes. A tear falls, but he catches it with his thumb and wipes it away, leaning in and kissing me right there.

"I don't know," I murmur, my hands shaking with fear, the idea of Carter hurting me again making me want to crumble right here in the parking lot.

"I know I've fucked up, Bri. I've made the biggest mistake of my life by letting you go, and I will do anything it takes to get you back. You're it for me. You and these babies," he says as he moves his hands to my stomach and cradles our children. "What if we make a deal?" he asks, a sparkle in his dark eyes.

"I don't know, Carter."

"We take it slow. I'll work on earning back your trust, and if I can, then you can decide if this is something worth fighting for, but you and I both know it is. Nobody loves like we do."

Fuck, he's such a smooth talker. It makes it so hard to deny him.

I watch him as I think it over, those dark, piercing eyes boring straight back into mine, and I can see he truly means what he says, and it confuses the shit out of me. "You won't change your mind?" I ask, feeling way too nervous about this.

Emotion shines through his eyes, and I have to resist reaching out and pulling him back into me. "I'm certain, Bri. I'm not changing my mind. I fell in love with those babies the second I saw the ultrasound, and I've been madly in love with you since the day I met you. I'm going to be their daddy, and not a damn thing is going to keep us from being a family, not even you. I pushed you away because I was scared of making those commitments, but I'm not anymore. I was a fool, and I don't want you to do it alone. I want to earn your trust back. I want to raise these babies together. Hell, I'm even looking forward to the sleepless nights and dirty diapers. And then, once the dust has settled and we have our babies in our arms, I'm going to make you my wife, and there's not a damn thing you can do about it."

Fuck, those words hold the weight of the world. They're everything I've ever wanted.

I search his eyes again as I think it over. How could I ever say no to him? He's the father of my children and the love of my life. It would be criminal not to try. "You really were a fool," I tell him. "I'll give you a chance to earn my trust, but if you fuck up, I'm done. There's no going back for us after that."

"I won't fuck it up," he promises as his eyes light with pure elation. "I know what it's like to live without you, and I won't do that again, especially when my kids are involved."

A soft smile creeps across my face as my heart starts to beat right out of my chest, a little piece of me coming back to life. There might still be a chance for my happy ending. "You earn my trust back first, then maybe I'll give us a shot," I tell him, only giving an inch.

Carter leans into me, pressing a kiss to my cheek, and it's all I can do not to pull him into me and have my way with him right here in the open doorway. "Thank you," he murmurs before stepping back and looking like a whole new man. He offers me his hand, and I graciously accept it. "Can I take you to dinner now?"

A wide smile settles across my lips, and with that, Carter helps me out of the truck before leading me inside. He wraps his arm around my waist, and I melt into his side, just like it was always meant to be.

Chapter Twenty-Five

CARTER

Making my way around the store, I stare at the shelves, never having felt so overwhelmed and out of my depth in my life. I mean, fuck. There are rows upon rows of baby shit. Bassinets, bottles, breast pumps, bedding, and strollers. I was supposed to be heading out to the Wilder mansion to check off a few of the most recent changes, but when I drove past this store, I found myself parking my truck and heading in.

Brianna is close to seven months pregnant now, and so far, it's been going well. She's slotted straight back into my life minus anything intimate. It's driving me crazy, but that's the deal I made. She needs to trust me, but not knowing how long that's going to take is honestly sending me up the fucking wall. But this is too important, and I get that she needs to take her time. I'm not about to fuck this up by rushing into it or pushing her too fast.

Seeing her every day, having her come over to my place, cooking in my kitchen, spending time with my family, and smiling that beautiful smile. Fuck. I'd do just about anything to be able to touch her and let her know just how much I love her, but I respect that she needs her space, and if that's what she needs to help us move on, then that's what I'm going to do.

And I have to admit, I've been using this time to trust her again too. The road goes both ways. After knowing she was pregnant with my children for three months and not telling me, it left a scar. I know she was scared, and I hadn't left her with many options, but I can't help but feel that betrayal right down to the core. The more time we're spending together, the quicker that scar has begun to heal.

Watching her stomach swell with our growing babies isn't something I ever thought I'd enjoy, but seeing her like this? Nothing has ever made me feel so good. I've become a different man—fiercely protective of her and our children, and I want this more than I could have ever known.

Brianna is nothing short of stunning. Every time she feels those little babies move inside her, her whole face lights up like Christmas morning, and it's honestly the greatest thing I've ever seen. Though truth be told, I kind of find it creepy. I don't know how I'd feel if there were little alien-looking things inside my guts, swimming around, kicking me in the ribs, and growing. I mean . . . Do they shit in there? How does it even work?

Over the past four months, I've realized the extent of just how badly I fucked up. Don't get me wrong, the second I learned she was pregnant, I knew I'd made the greatest mistake of my life. However, these past few months have taught me exactly what I was throwing away.

There's no doubt about it—Brianna Lucas is my life. She's my world, and I'd do anything to prove to her that I'm in it for the long haul. Just the thought of us growing old together and raising our babies is enough to get me off. My heart aches for her every time I see her, and as she sets her gaze on mine, those green eyes filled with hesitation, it tears me up inside. When she walks past, I have to resist reaching out to her. When she laughs, I have to force myself not to stare. When she sings to our children . . . fuck, I can't help but fall in love with her more.

If only she could see that.

I never knew just how hard it was to earn someone's trust once it had been broken. As it's not a physical thing that I can see, it makes it a nearly impossible task. I never know where I stand. I mean, shit. It would be helpful if she could get a container or something like that and fill it up a little each time I earn a bit of her trust, and when it's full . . . BAM, I'm back in the game.

On my imaginary trust scale, I think I'm doing alright. Each day, she allows me to touch her for just a little longer. Yesterday, she let me hold her hand while I was driving her back to her apartment after having a family dinner at Sean's place. It was only for a moment, and she refused to make eye contact with me the whole time, but it was a step in the right direction. It felt good having her soft hand in mine again. Apart from that, she allows me to live with my hands on her stomach, feeling our babies as they grow and move inside her.

It's so fucking incredible to feel, and while I love being able to touch her like that, I'd give my left nut just to be able to kiss her and take her to bed, to really show her how much she means to me.

How could I have been such a fool to not want this? I just wish I hadn't wasted all that time and hurt her. Our future could have been a reality a long time ago if it wasn't for me.

"Excuse me, Sir," a chirpy voice asks from beside me. I'm ripped out of my longing thoughts for Bri as I turn to the tiny saleswoman beside me. "Do you need help with anything?"

Glancing back to the massive range of bassinets before me and knowing damn well I don't know how to navigate this shit, I turn back to the woman with a tight smile. "Yeah, actually, that would be great. My . . . ahh," shit. What do I call her? My girlfriend, my friend, my partner, my baby momma? Fucked if I know, but I should at least enjoy the moment. "My wife is seven months pregnant, and we haven't got a thing, so I thought I'd surprise her and get it all."

The woman's face lights up as she gives me a beaming smile, looking at me like some kind of sucker she can milk every last dollar out of, and it's clear. "Well, you've come to the right place," she tells me. "Do you know the sex of the baby?

"No, but my wife believes they're boys," I explain.

"Plural?" she questions. "Twins?"

"Indeed."

Her grin widens, and I can practically see the dollar signs in her eyes

"Oh, beautiful," the woman coos. "Where would you like to start?"

"Umm . . . I don't know. I've never done this before," I tell her as my eyes scan the store again.

"Okay, sure," she says as though preparing to take on the challenge. "When you said you haven't got anything, how literal were you being?"

"Extremely," I grunt.

"Right," she says. "Well, how about we start with furniture and then we can move to the smaller things?"

"Sounds like a plan."

Before I know it, we both get carried away. We pick out a bedroom suite with cribs, a changing table, a set of drawers, and shelves for all their toys; which is when she convinces me that a nice soft mat for the babies to play on would look great on the floor, so I pick one of them too.

We move to the next section and add two mattresses to the list and a shitload of neutral-colored bedding. I would have liked to pick out a blue or pink bedding set, but that's just something I'll have to learn to get over. Besides, knowing Bri, she would have gone for the neutral colors too.

Oh, what the hell? I grab two sets of the blue bedding off the shelf and throw them into the very full cart anyway. If the babies turn out to be little girls, we could always keep the blue bedding on hand just in case. At least, that's what the saleswoman tells me right before convincing me to pick up a handful of pink sets too.

Next up, a bath and bassinets.

The further we get through the store, the more excited I become, like a child in a candy store who was just given an unlimited credit card. I think I'm finally understanding why chicks enjoy shopping so much. I honestly thought this shit was going to be daunting and boring, but knowing I'm setting my kids up with a good start at life makes me feel like I'm going to be the best goddamn daddy on the planet. Hell, I might even give Sean a run for his money.

We pick out a shitload of toys, towels, and blankets when she asks me a question that completely stumps me. "Is your wife going to be breastfeeding or bottle feeding?"

Fuck. I should definitely know this, and if I weren't so caught up on the way the word *wife* sounded, I might just have the brain cells to figure it out. "Ahh . . . I'm going to assume breastfeeding," I tell her.

The woman goes about getting everything Bri could possibly need and then throws in some bottles, a sterilizer, and some newborn formula just in case.

"Thank you so much for this," I tell the woman as I stand at the cash register, feeling a massive weight lifting off my shoulders. "My wife is going to be thrilled."

"Good, I'm glad I could help. Now, when would you like all of this delivered?"

Hmm. Good question. A plan starts forming, and I arch a brow as I look at the woman. "Is it all in stock?"

She quickly flicks through her computer before nodding. "It sure is."

"Is it too much to ask to get it all sorted and sent out this morning?"

"No problem at all," she says, probably not wanting to let down the guy who just bought nearly everything in her store.

I give her the address and she tells me it will be there in an hour, and I hand over my credit card, settling the bill before ducking out of the store. I look down at my watch and realize I should have just enough time to approve the changes on the Wilder mansion before getting back for the delivery to arrive.

An hour later, I pull up at Brianna's apartment just in time for the delivery truck to pull in behind me.

I hop out of my truck and thank the delivery guys for showing up right when they said they would, especially considering the late notice. They follow me into the building and right up to Brianna's door which is when I run into my first problem—getting through the fucking door.

Searching around, I find her spare key hidden in the light fixture above her door and smile to myself, wondering how the hell she was able to reach it in the first place. I open up her door and head inside with the delivery guys following behind. I head down the hallway to the bedroom which is when I realize, she only has a one-bedroom apartment.

"What the fuck?" I mutter to myself. How the hell did she expect to have twins living in this place and how the fuck did I not realize this earlier? Apart from the first time I was in here, she's only ever allowed me to drop her at her door, never welcomed me in, terrified because neither of us has even a shred of self-control.

An idea shoots through my mind and the second it's there, it won't be leaving.

Pulling my wallet out of my back pocket, I turn to the delivery guys before taking five hundred dollars out of my wallet. "What's it going to take to convince you guys to take the rest of the day off work and help me move all of my girl's shit into my place?"

Grins spread wide over each of their faces as the guy closest to me reaches out and gingerly plucks the money out of my hand. "No problem at all," he says. "What do you need?"

Two hours later, Brianna's apartment is packed up.

She's going to kill me, and it's definitely going to make the whole earning her trust thing just that little bit harder, but it's for the best. She can't raise twins in this tiny apartment. They need space to run, to grow, and I have just what they need at my place. It just makes perfect sense. I want them with me anyway, so as much as I say it's for their own good, a part of it is also for my own selfish needs.

Then because I have absolutely no intention of texting her to let her know what's going on, I leave a note on her counter so she doesn't think she's been robbed, then get on my way.

Fifteen minutes later, I turn down my long-ass driveway and indicate to the delivery driver to pull up right out front. I check my watch and realize we have just over three hours to get all this shit inside and set up before Brianna comes knocking down my door and cursing me out.

She's going to be pissed, but it will be worth it to have her living under my roof once again, where we can truly be a family.

Most of her stuff gets put downstairs so she can decide where she'd like it to go, but all her clothes and precious things are taken right up to my room because I wouldn't want her anywhere else, and honestly, that's not going to go down well.

Either way, I'm a fucking genius. I might be a dead genius, but I deserve a medal for this shit. I can't believe it's taken me this long to move her back in with me.

A few hours later, and after an extra hundred dollars each, the delivery guys finished helping me set up the nursery and were finally able to get on their way.

I stand in the room that's going to hold my children's sweetest, innocent dreams and look around at our handy work. The room is perfect. It looks like a baby bedroom designer has come and turned this place into a baby wonderland. I can't wait for Bri to see this. She's going to be blown away.

Two little cribs line the back wall, and a fully stocked toy shelf lines another. There's two little rocking horses, a closet filled with matching sets of clothes, and the woman even threw in a few boxes of diapers and wet wipes to get us started.

I owe that woman a bouquet of flowers or something to thank her for all the help she gave me today. Not to mention, I should also apologize for stealing her delivery drivers for the whole day. Without her, I would have been lost. I would have purchased just a handful of things and walked out. Clearly I had no idea what I was doing.

With a smile, I gently close the door to the nursery and head into my room and start hanging up all Bri's clothes in my closet, truly moving her in. I don't know what I'm going to do with all her other stuff, like the couch and bedroom suite, but I don't really care. Though, the monster cock I found hiding under her bed goes straight into my bedside drawer. I couldn't believe it when I saw it, but if that's how she wants to get down, then I'm all here for it.

Finishing up, I glance around my masterpiece, knowing damn well that she's going to hate this, but it's too late to go back now. She'll eventually get over it and see it's the best thing for us, but it'll be a journey getting there. She's too fucking stubborn to admit it right away, just as she still tries to tell me that the whole almost running her over incident was my fault.

Either way, I can't wait to see that angry little line appear between her brows as she screams at me for being the biggest jerk she knows. It's going to be amazing, and the whole time, I'm going to be doing everything in my power not to get hard and keep a straight face. God, she's so fucking hot when she's mad.

With an exhausted sigh, I head into my bathroom. After all the heavy lifting I've been doing today, I could really use a shower. After quickly stripping off, I get straight in and let the hot water wash over my sore muscles. Don't get me wrong, I fucking love my home and it's going to be an incredible place to raise my family, but when it comes to things like moving, it fucking sucks. Carrying endless boxes of furniture up and down those stairs has scarred me for life.

Unable to keep from picturing the feisty woman who's going to break down my door later tonight, my dick starts growing hard, and before I know it, I'm closing my fist around my cock and getting straight to work. After not having sex for seven months, and another five before that, jerking off has become a daily occurrence in this bathroom . . . and my bed, and the living room. Really, anywhere within the walls of this house.

But it's worth it because when the time comes for me and Bri to truly be together again, when I've finally earned back her trust, it'll just make it that much better. When I finally get her back into my arms, I'm going to show her things she could only imagine in her wildest dreams, and what's more, it's going to be fucking magical.

Chapter Twenty-Six

BRIANNA

"How was your day?" Cassie asks as I climb out of my car and struggle to lock the door with my purse in one hand and phone in the other.

"Hold on a sec," I mutter, jamming the phone between my ear and shoulder before locking the door properly. Double checking I have everything I need, I head up to the door of my apartment complex. "Sorry," I tell her. "Today's been huge. We had the science fair at school and my kids were so excited."

"Oh, really?" she coos, always loving to hear about my students. "I always loved the science fair. Did they enter any projects?"

"Not really," I say, walking into my building. "They're a bit young to be creating such elaborate things and actually understand what they're doing, so we built a volcano as a group. They loved it, especially when we made it explode." Reaching my door, I stop to riffle through my bag and search for my keys. Finding them in the very bottom of my bag, I curl my fingers around the cool metal and jam the key into the lock. "You should have seen their tiny faces. They loved it."

"I bet," she laughs.

I struggle with my stupid door and give the key a wiggle as a frustrated groan tears from the back of my throat. This damn door has been a nightmare since the day I moved in. Needing two hands, I drop my bag to the ground and squish my phone between my shoulder and ear again. "Fuck you, you stupid fucking door," I grunt at the bastard.

"What's going on?" Cassie laughs.

"My stupid door is jammed again."

"Give it a kick," she offers.

I do just that and get an odd satisfaction out of it, and after wiggling the key again, the door opens right up. Grabbing my bag off the floor, I step over the threshold and come to a startled halt. "Shit," I screech through the phone, fear pounding through my veins. "I've been robbed."

"What?" Cassie gasps.

"Shit. Shit. Shit. What do I do? What do I do?" I rush out, motionless in the doorway.

"Fuck. Fuck . . . um. I don't know," she panics. "Is anything gone?"

"I . . ." I can hardly talk as I look around. Everything is gone.

My whole life is completely gone. It looks as though someone has literally come through here and decided they liked my setup and stolen everything, right down to the dirty dishes I'd left on the coffee table.

My hand cradles my stomach as the tears take over. Fuck these stupid pregnancy hormones. I don't have the energy for this shit.

"Jax," Cassie yells. "We need to go."

"Huh? What's wrong?" I hear him ask in the background.

"Bri's place was broken into."

"Fuck," he curses before a shitload of rustling. "Bri?" Jax asks, and I realize Cass has put me on speaker. "Are you okay?"

Tears spill down my cheeks, feeling completely deflated. "Yeah," I whisper, slowly creeping deeper into my empty apartment.

"Was anything taken?" he questions.

"Yeah," I scoff as I look around the bare apartment. "Everything's gone. My couch, my TV, even my fucking coffee table and wall art. It looks like the day I moved in."

"Shit," he grunts. "You need to call the police," he says as I continue looking around.

"Don't hang up on me," I rush out, terrified of being alone right now. I mean, I know I'm technically alone, but once they hang up, I'll really feel alone.

"We won't," Cassie says, softly, trying to soothe my nerves before speaking a little quieter to Jax, commenting how strange it is for someone to have taken all of that stuff when usually break-ins are more focused on finding valuables and getting in and out as fast as possible, but something like this would have taken someone hours.

Not to mention, they'd need a truck to haul all my shit away.

I make my way down the hallway, making sure to give them a step-by-step rundown of every little thing that's happening before thinking better of it and switching to Facetime. "The bathroom's been used," I whisper.

"Ewww," Cassie says as Jax cuts her off. "Why are you whispering?"

"What if they're still here?"

"If you think they're still there, then you need to leave."

Fuck. Duh.

I stand motionless and hold my breath while I listen out for any noise, and after a good minute of listening, I decide I'm definitely alone in my apartment.

Heading down to the bedroom, I look into my closet cautiously, just in case anyone feels like jumping out at me today. "Shit, Cass. All my fucking clothes are gone."

"Are you serious? Who the fuck steals clothes?" she grunts. "It looks like someone has literally come and moved you out. Are you sure you've been paying your rent properly? Perhaps you need to put in a call with your landlord."

"Yeah, maybe," I mutter, not having any better ideas as I hear Jax cursing and offering to call the police for me.

Devastation swirls within me and the need to sit on my bed and cry comes over me, but I can't because I have no fucking bed, not even a fucking bedsheet or towel to wipe my face on. Hell, even my monster cock that was hiding under my bed is gone.

I hear Jax on the phone with the police, and I make my way back out to the living room, knowing they'll probably be here in a few minutes. I start checking through the kitchen drawers when I distantly notice the carpets have been vacuumed. What the fuck? Am I in the wrong apartment?

I'm about to tell Cassie all about it when my gaze narrows on a note that's been left on the counter. I scurry across the kitchen and hastily pick it up, hoping it offers some kind of explanation as to why my fucking apartment has been opened for the public to take whatever the hell they want.

Scanning over it, I see red.

Babe,

Don't be mad but . . . I sort of moved you into my place.

Dinner at 7?

Carter.

My stomach drops. That fucking bastard.

"What the fuck?" I grunt as anger crashes through me like a fucking tsunami, making me want to punch a hole in the wall or better yet, go over there and strangle the dickhead. How dare he do this?

"What is it?" Cass asks, taking in my tone. "What's wrong?"

"Tell Jax to tell the police it was a mistake," I tell her, though perhaps he should warn them about a murder that's about to go down. I just hope they don't beat me there because if I don't get my chance to curl my fingers around his throat, I'm gonna be pissed.

"What?" Cass grunts. "What's going on?"

"Just do it," I instruct as I try to calm my nerves by taking slow deep breaths.

After hearing Jax tell the police that it was a mistake, I get straight into my explanation, turning the camera on the note, knowing they're both crowding around Cassie's phone to see what's going on. "The asshole left me a note."

A booming laugh rips out of Jax as they read the note, and I hear the *oomph* from Cass nailing him—hopefully where it hurts. "Are you shitting me?" Cass questions. "I'm going to kill him."

"Not before I do!" I seethe, my whole body shaking with rage. I mean, fuck. On what planet would he think this was a good idea? "Fuck. I need to throw something, but there's nothing here to fucking throw."

"I know," she says in a soothing tone. "Try and calm down. Stress isn't good for my babies." I try to focus on taking deep breaths, but the more I think about it the worse it gets. "Do you want to come and stay at my place?"

"Can I let you know?" I ask. "I'm going to head over to Carter's place and rip him a new asshole."

"Okay," she says. "Rip him an extra one for me, too."

"You got it," I say before ending the call and heading for the door. I slam it behind me, not bothering to lock the door as it's not like there's anything to steal.

After getting in my car, I kick over the engine before taking off like a bat out of hell, going way too fast for a pregnant mother of twins. Within ten minutes, I screech into his driveway, not caring that

I took out half of his hedge—the very hedge I planted two years ago. The fucker can deal with it himself, and while he's at it, he can also fix the scratches his stupid hedge left on my car.

Coming to a stop right at the top of the circular driveway, I bail out of my car and slam the door behind me, realizing that a good door slamming is the only thing making me feel better right now. I storm up his front steps while clenching my hands into tight fists, trying to figure out how to articulate my rage without actually kicking him in the balls.

Reaching the front door, I push my way in, not bothering to ring the doorbell or knock because casually welcoming yourself straight into someone else's home seems to be the going trend. "Where the hell are you, you big bastard?" I call out over the massive foyer of the rich prick's home.

No answer. Fucking great.

I get searching, and it takes all of three seconds to find a shitload of my stuff sitting in the dining hall which never gets used, and seeing it here only manages to infuriate me further. "Carter?" I yell.

No answer.

Jerk.

Heading into the kitchen I used to call my own, I find nothing before checking the living room. Nothing. I dart up the stairs, having to wrap my hands around my stomach because my pace is too fast for comfort. I get only halfway before having to walk because, let's face it, being seven months pregnant with twins isn't easy.

Reaching the top, I push through every door and take a quick look inside, but come to a screeching stop when I push open the door right next to Carter's bedroom and find it completely dressed with the sweetest nursery I've ever seen.

Two beautiful cribs look back at me with a soft mat in the center, and a fully stocked changing table stands in the corner of the room. My emotions start swirling up inside of me, and I suck in a subtle gasp, my hand over my mouth as I step deeper into the beautiful nursery.

My eyes sting with unshed tears.

Fuck, I can't handle these hormones.

Making my way around the room, I notice how there are two of everything, even in the closet, matching little suits and booties. Fuck me. The tears start to fall, and I can barely hold myself together. My bottom lip wobbles, and I find myself breaking into a box of tissues to dry my face.

This is fucking perfect, but it'd be so much better if I wasn't so mad at Carter.

As I take in the room, I can picture it all. I'd come in with my little boys. Have one playing on the mat with his daddy while I get the other dressed and ready for the day. I can't fucking wait. This is everything I wanted and more.

But I'm not going to let him know that. At least, not yet.

The past couple of months have been incredible as we've been reconnecting. I can tell he's trying so hard, and I truly believe he wants this, I'm just not entirely convinced that he's ready. He's going to make the perfect daddy. My boys are so lucky to have him, especially now that I realize he's the kind to spoil them rotten. But this . . . this has me questioning just how ready he is, but what man ever is?

Knowing if I linger too long, I'll get too emotional, I quickly dry my eyes. Before I can thank him for this wonderful nursery he's created for our children, I need to deal with the fact that he had the audacity to move me out of my own home without even the hint of a conversation for my consent.

Grabbing another tissue just to be on the safe side, I go to close the door when I think better of it. The room is too beautiful to have the door closed, it needs to be seen. Then just because I can't help myself, I take a quick photo and send it as a text to Cassie, because who wouldn't want to see such beauty?

Backing away from the nursery, I take the few steps to Carter's bedroom and push my way in. A lifetime ago, this used to be the bedroom we shared and the memories that come crashing back almost have me gasping for air.

Pushing it all aside, I walk into the room, and the first thing I hear is the sound of the shower running in the private bathroom. No wonder he didn't answer when I called out.

I head straight for the bathroom door when I think better of it and detour to his closet, my stomach sinking. Pushing open the double doors, I peer inside and grit my teeth, finding all my clothes right where they used to live this time last year. My dresses, pants, shirts, and even my fucking underwear is in here.

That rat bastard.

Unable to stand another minute without confronting him, I storm right into the bathroom, practically kicking down the door as I go.

"You big fucking bastard. Where the hell do you get off moving all my shit into your place?" I demand, my gaze feasting upon the very naked man with water running down his perfectly sculpted body, who just happens to have his very large and very hard cock right in the palm of his hand.

Carter looks at me with hooded eyes, and I do my best to ignore it and pretend like the sight of his glistening body doesn't affect me. But fuck, he's amazing. I'd do anything to strip off and get in that shower with him. To have him bend me over as I desperately try to clutch onto the slippery tiles, all while he vigorously fucks me within an inch of my life.

In, out, in, out.

Oh God, I need him so bad. I want to be his needy whore again. The way I'd scream his name until the neighbors called the police.

Carter doesn't dare stop, only inches toward the shower door, more than welcoming me in, watching the way my thighs clench and seeing the overwhelming desire in my eyes. I'm fucking starving for him and he knows it.

Dragging my bottom lip between my teeth, I watch his hand slowly move up and down his impressively thick cock, and my knees begin to weaken. "Come on, baby," he murmurs with those sexy, hooded eyes focused so heavily on me. "Let me give you what you need."

My feet involuntarily begin to creep toward him when I realize what the fuck I'm doing. This man just moved me into his home without my consent. I need to be bitching at him, not about ready to drop onto my knees and take that delicious cock into my mouth.

Fuck.

"No," I demand, forcing myself to stop in the middle of the bathroom, the idea of not running right into that shower with him causing me physical pain. I shake my head, blinking as I try to find just a semblance of control. I hold my finger up and point out the door. "Get the fuck out."

Carter chuckles at me, and I swear, I nearly come in my pants. "Can I finish first?" he asks as he continues teasing me, his hand grazing up and down, squeezing at his tip. Shit, I need to get out of here and finish myself off in private.

"No," I snap before making a hasty exit out of the bathroom, panting like a fucking bitch.

Fuck. I need him.

My back falls against the closed bathroom door, and I'm left so fucking worked up, that just the thought of Carter on the other side getting off has my hand slipping into the waistband of my pants, which at seven months pregnant isn't as easy as it sounds.

My greedy fingers roll over my clit, and I suck in a breath, visualizing the way Carter stroked his cock, and his subtle grunts and groans from within the bathroom go a long fucking way in getting me off.

I'm so fucking needy that it takes no time at all, and as I hear Carter coming on the other side of the door, I come right along with him. My orgasm explodes through my body with a fierce desperation, and I'm barely able to keep on my feet.

I groan low, gasping for breath, but as I hear the shower cut off, I tear my hand out of my pants and race across the room, dropping onto the edge of our . . . his bed and prepare myself for the onslaught of bullshit that's about to come flying out of my mouth.

The bathroom door opens, and a cloud of steam rushes out before him, and I roll my eyes. The fucker never could remember to use the bathroom fan. Carter comes strutting out with a towel wrapped around his hips, looking like a god with the little beads of water covering his chest.

Shit, am I drooling?

He takes one look at me, and I know exactly what he's seeing—my flushed cheeks, the satisfaction in my eyes, and the way my chest rises and falls with rapid movement, looking like a woman who's just been thoroughly fucked.

A smirk pulls across his lips, knowing exactly what just went down in here, but thankfully he doesn't say a word. "Is something wrong, babe?" he questions, walking past me and into the open closet like he doesn't have a care in the world.

"Are you shitting me?" I demand, flying to my feet in outrage. "You had no right to do that."

"Babe," he says, turning around, dropping the towel and pulling on a pair of jeans, bypassing the underwear and making me hungry for him all over again.

"Don't *babe* me," I seethe as the stupid hormones bring tears to my furious eyes. "What the hell were you thinking?"

Carter pulls on a shirt and strides toward me. "You wanna know what I was thinking?" he murmurs, reaching up and wiping my tears away with his thumbs before placing a gentle hand on our kicking babies. "I was thinking that I love you and these babies, and I want you guys here with me. I know it was stupid, and I should have talked to you first, but the opportunity kind of presented itself, so I took it."

"You're an idiot," I tell him. "Did you consider that I might not want to live here with you?"

"I did," he says, that same stupid smirk pulling at his lips again, his eyes sparkling with amusement. "But then I remembered that I'm a fucking legend and you'd be crazy not to want that."

I hold back a smile, wanting so desperately to hate him, but fuck, he makes it so hard. "Call me crazy then because I don't want to live with you."

He leans into me, watching the way I respond to his touch, reading me so fucking well. "You're a liar, Brianna," he accuses, his eyes dancing with excitement.

"So, what if I am?" I breathe, desperate for him to close the gap and give me what I need, but damn it, what I need and what I want are two very different things right now.

Carter grins before reaching up and smoothing his fingers over the little crease between my brows—the one that only shows up when I'm angry, and usually, Carter Waters is the only one who could possibly make me angry enough for it to come out. "You're so fucking gorgeous," he murmurs. "I love you so goddamn much."

"Don't," I demand, pushing his hand away. "You don't get to do that, especially now. I'm so mad at you."

"I know you are, but if you give it a chance, you'll see how fucking perfect this is."

I shake my head, not wanting to believe him, but damn it, what could possibly be better than having our family living together in Carter's home? The very home I always imagined we'd be in. Needing a moment to calm down, I turn away and storm into the closet before grabbing a handful of clothes and heading for the door.

"Are you going to stay?" he questions, a hint of fear in his deep tone.

I turn around and fix him with a heavy glare. "Only because moving everything out is going to be too exhausting."

Carter's whole face lights up, and I want nothing more than to throw myself into his warm arms and go back to how things used to be. Then before I confuse my feelings, I finish storming out and make a show of slamming another door before I find one of his many spare bedrooms and slam that door as well.

Throwing my clothes on the end of the bed, I drop down and start rifling through my bag until my hand curls around my journal. Pulling it out, I find a pen and turn to the next page.

Week 26

Your father is an asshole.

An hour later, the door opens and I find Carter standing before me with Chinese food in hand. My stomach grumbles, and he doesn't wait for me to invite him in, just strolls right on over, makes himself comfortable on my newly-claimed bed, and starts digging into his dinner.

The smell is too much for me to handle, and I find myself digging in as well, the babies needing to be fed. Once we're done, Carter puts the empty containers on the floor and pulls me into his arms. I want nothing more than to push him away and put my walls back up, but I simply can't. My body yearns for his touch, and that need for him is just too strong.

I melt into him, and he lays us back on the bed, his arm locked securely around my waist as though he will never let me go. "I love you, Brianna. You know that right?" he murmurs as his fingers trail back and forth across my skin. "If I could take back all that hurt, you know I would."

"I know," I murmur, my hand falling to his chest and feeling the heavy thumping of his heartbeat. "I love you too."

His fingers pause, and I sense him begin to hesitate before letting the words fill the room. "Will you consider sleeping in my room?"

I smile up at him, a laugh catching in my throat. "Over my dead body," I tell him.

"It was worth a try," he chuckles, resting his other hand on my protruding stomach. He presses a kiss to my forehead, and I find myself beginning to grow sleepy, so content in his arms. "Are you going to stay?" he questions. "I want you here."

"And I want a castle in the South of France," I scoff.

"Babe," he groans.

"Yeah," I tell him, finally giving in to the inevitable. "I'm going to stay. I wouldn't want to be anywhere else." And with that, I fall into a deep, peaceful sleep as I lay in the arms of the man who owns my whole heart.

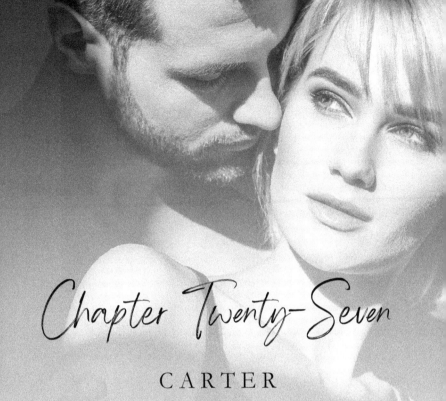

Chapter Twenty-Seven

CARTER

The fucking Wilder mansion is finally complete. I handed over the keys and I'll never have to deal with the mind-changing idiots again. I've never experienced such a frustrating build in my life, but there's no denying that the home I built was incredible. I even took Bri for a walk-through just to show off how fucking flawless my architecture and design skills are, simply because I knew how she'd stroke my ego and tell me how fucking amazing I am.

Naturally, the Wilders were thrilled, and even though they've been a thorn in my side for nearly two years, I couldn't wait to hand it over and see the look on their faces when they stepped through the threshold of their new home. I love doing custom designs, but man, they take a lot out of me. Though I suppose it comes with the territory when you're slapping a multi-million-dollar price tag on it.

Getting home after a rewarding day at work, I find my girl in nothing but her underwear, dancing through our kitchen as she works on dinner. Music blasts through the speakers as Bri sways her hips, singing along to the lyrics and getting every single one of the words wrong.

I grin as I take her in. She's been living with me for a few weeks now, and she still refuses to move out of the spare room. While I understand that she's trying to prove a point, all it means is that instead of being comfortable in my bed, I've been sleeping in there with her.

Brianna is slowly coming back to me and slowly beginning to trust me again. I've been with her as much as possible since the day I found out she was pregnant, but having her here under the same roof as me and being able to watch her tummy grow is everything.

Standing against the doorframe, I watch as she moves her body. She clearly hasn't figured out that she has an audience, and I sure as fuck don't let her in on the secret. Watching Bri just being herself is incredible and goes to show just how comfortable she is living here with me again.

I'd do just about anything to let her know I'm in it for the long haul. I swear, she's had enough foot rubs to last a lifetime. Call me pussy-whipped if you must, but I don't care. Being able to do this shit for her is more rewarding than any build I've ever done. I fucking love her, and if she needs me to scratch her ass because she can't reach it anymore, then you better fucking believe that I'm going to scratch that fine ass.

Bri's just over eight months pregnant now, which apparently, with twins means they could come any moment. She's been nervous and doing everything in her power to try and hide that, but I know her like the back of my hand, she can't hide shit from me . . . apart from a pregnancy, of course.

She finished work two weeks ago because her body physically can't handle it anymore, and I can tell how much she misses her students. I don't doubt that the second these babies pop out of her, she'll be taking them for a trip to the school to meet the other loves of her life.

The music changes to something with more of a beat, and she really gets into it, moving her fine body and shaking that sexy ass. Watching her move as she stirs a pot of pasta has me growing hard, and I simply can't wait any longer. She's my girl and it's about time I prove it to her.

Striding through the kitchen, I place my phone, wallet, and keys on the counter, keeping my gaze locked on her perfect body. The keys rattle as they land, and I expect her to hear me approaching, but she's too caught up in the song.

Moving in behind her, my hand slides onto her hip, and I press my body up against her. Bri stiffens at the touch, but quickly relaxes, realizing it's me and not some axe-wielding murderer. "What are you doing?" she murmurs, continuing to stir the pasta, only now her movements are a lot slower, distracted.

Reaching around her, I take the utensil out of her hand before turning off the stove. Bri turns in my arms and has to take a step back as her belly pushes up against me, and as she looks up at me, I let her see the intention in my eyes.

My hand comes up and wraps around her neck and jaw, tilting her chin up toward me, and she allows it. Like putty in my fucking hands, she leans into my touch, and I move in closer, leaving barely a breath between us.

"I love you, Brianna," I murmur. Her hand travels up my body and stops at my chest, her fingers splaying over my heart and I realize this is it; she's finished pushing me away. A tear falls from her eye, and I push my thumb out to catch it, quickly wiping it away. "Don't cry, baby."

Bri's hand fists into my shirt and she gives it a tug, pulling me closer and closing the gap. I rest my forehead against hers and she closes her eyes, soaking up every second of this precious moment. "I love you, too," she whispers with an open heart.

I can't hold back anymore. She's been here for weeks, and I've respected the space she needs, but it's time for her to see that this is where she belongs, wholeheartedly. Without another second of hesitation, I press my lips against hers and kiss her, feeling all my fears slipping away as she melts into me. Bri moves her lips against mine as she brings her hand up and around the back of my neck, holding onto me as though she'll never let go.

She deepens the kiss, and need rumbles through my chest, but I feel myself pulling back until there's only the slightest gap between us. Bri's brows furrow, her green gaze searching mine. "What's wrong?" she whispers, reluctantly starting to pull away, but I don't dare let her.

"Nothing," I smile, giving her all my love and trying to put her at ease. "Do you trust me?"

Understanding dawns in her eyes as a breathtaking smile spreads across her beautiful face. "I do," she tells me.

Relief surges through me. I could feel her trust beginning to return in the way she was so effortlessly falling back into our old relationship, the way she would beam at me as though she couldn't stand for me to go to work, the way she was right there when I got home, ready to hear all about my day. But nothing feels better than hearing her confirm that after everything we've been through, she's finally able to trust me again. I feel like I've been given a second chance at life—something I don't deserve but I'd give anything to have. And fuck, I'm going to savor every second of it.

There's no doubt about it, Brianna Lucas is my whole fucking world.

I smile down at her, letting her see the undeniable happiness in my eyes before pressing my lips back to hers. I kiss her deeply, and as she melts in my arms, her smile becomes too wide, making it impossible to not claim those lips for a second longer. I reach up and grip her chin, holding that gorgeous green gaze hostage. "And you're ready to give this another try?"

"I am."

Fuck me. It's like music to my ears.

Forcing myself to keep my composure, I release my hold on her before slipping my hand into my pocket and finding the white gold engagement ring that's been living there for the past five months.

The diamond catches Bri's eyes, and she sucks in a gasp, not having time to question it before I take her hands and drop down on one knee. "Marry me, Brianna," I tell her. "I know I've hurt you, and I've done everything in my power to be able to call you mine again, but now that I have you, I don't ever want to let you go. I want to marry you, Bri. I want to call you my wife and raise our babies as a family together, under one roof, and I hope like fuck you want this too."

Bri just gapes at me, her jaw slack and those gorgeous eyes focused heavily on mine. "Whaaa . . ."

I smile at her blank expression before getting back to my feet and cupping her face. I hold her stare, letting her know I'm not trying to fuck with her. I mean every fucking word. "You heard me, Brianna. Marry me."

"Are . . . are you sure?" she questions, shaking her head in disbelief. "I thought . . . I thought you didn't want this. I thought just wrapping your head around the whole baby thing was already pushing the limits."

"Five months ago, I might have agreed with you," I tell her, taking her hand and sliding the white gold engagement ring into place, right where it was always meant to be. "I was scared. I couldn't picture marriage or children because I had no idea what it meant not to have that in my life. I didn't know what the fuck I was missing, but baby, now I do, and I don't ever wanna give that up. I want it all with you. I once told you I couldn't give you the world, but if that's what you still want, then please, Bri. Please allow me to give you everything. I don't want to go back to a world where we don't exist."

She looks down at the ring on her finger again before looking up at me, tears brimming in her eyes. "When did you get this?" she whispers, barely able to find her voice as her hands shake.

"The night of Logan's championship game."

"You left the game early," she says. "I thought you left because I was there."

"No, I left because I realized I'd lost the best thing that ever happened to me."

Her eyes begin to sparkle as she starts putting the small pieces of our puzzle together. "That was before you found out I was pregnant," she says, realizing that this proposal has nothing to do with the fact she's pregnant with my children, but all to do with the way I love her.

"Yeah," I tell her, a smile pulling at the corner of my lips. "You're kinda leaving me hanging here."

"Oh shit," she laughs, her tears falling a little faster. "So, this really has nothing to do with the babies?"

"No, but I won't lie—they definitely sweeten the deal."

She wipes her tear-stained face and meets my stare. "All this time, I was worried that you wanted to get back together because it was the right thing to do for the babies, like you were just trying to man up. I was worried you might have thought I was trying to trap you in this."

"No, babe," I say, running my hands down her body and picking her up. I slide her back onto the kitchen counter to take the pressure off her swollen feet and step forward to place myself right between her legs.

Bri places her hand around my neck and pulls me in tighter. "If you knew so long ago, why'd you wait so long to ask?"

I lean in and press a kiss to her neck before answering. "Because I needed to give your heart a moment to heal first, then you threw me a curveball and said you didn't trust me anymore. That day I came to your apartment after finding out about the babies, I was going to ask you then. I had this whole thing planned, but I realized we couldn't start a marriage like that. It was important to me to earn your trust before taking our next step together."

I see the wheels turning in her mind and know she's on the verge of asking another question, but the wait is killing me. "Babe, you can ask me a million questions later. Right now, I need you to put me out of my misery. Tell me that you'll marry me and become my wife."

Bri pulls back ever so slightly so she can look me in the eye. She's quiet for a moment, and it's the worst kind of torture I've ever experienced. A slow smile begins lighting up her beautiful face as her eyes sparkle with the utmost love, blowing me the fuck away. "Nothing would make me happier than becoming your wife."

Elation crashes through me, filling my veins with the sweetest ecstasy as I let out a heavy, relief-filled sigh, barely getting a chance to take another breath before her warm lips are crushing down on mine.

Brianna kisses me deeply, and I wrap her into my arms, no moment in time could possibly get better than this. You know, apart from the obvious. The moment Brianna gives birth to my children will be magical, as will the day she walks down the aisle and becomes my wife, but there's something special about this. It's the start of a new journey with Brianna at my side. All the pain and agony of the past thirteen months is now firmly behind us.

"Does this mean you'll move out of the spare room?" I question.

Bri laughs, pulling back just enough to capture my stare. "Depends," she murmurs in a seductive tone as a mischievous sparkle hits her eyes. "Are you going to make it worth my while?"

"Fuck, Bri. If you had any idea of the things I've been planning to do to you over the past few months, you wouldn't even question it," I tell her.

Bri's eyes flare with hunger, and I scoop her off the counter bridal style. Nothing would make me happier than to have her legs wrapped around my waist and throw her up against the wall, but with two babies busting to get out of there, this is going to have to play out a little differently.

Her arms loop around my neck, and I take her up to our bedroom, being extra careful on the stairs, but fuck, it's hard, especially when those skilled lips come down on my neck. Reaching the bedroom, I lower her to her feet, desperate to have my wicked way with her, but in reality, I'm going to take my time to savor every moment of it and worship her body just as she deserves.

Bri reaches for my shirt and pulls it straight over my head, running her greedy fingers down my chest and abs, claiming every inch of me as though she's been dying for this very moment.

"Fuck, I've missed that," I tell her, goosebumps rising everywhere she touches me.

Unable to wait another second, I rush into her, scooping her into my arms, right where she belongs. I carry her to the bed as her lips fuze with mine, and the second I lay her down, those green eyes meet mine, silently begging me to give her everything I've got.

I kiss her again, unable to physically pull myself away, but the promise of getting to taste her, getting to feel her again, has me moving down her body. Reaching under her, I unclasp her bra and she grabs the fabric, hastily pulling it off her arms and dumping it on the ground beside the bed. If there's always one thing I can count on with Bri, it's that when we fuck or do anything even remotely sexual, she has to be completely naked. She's always loved the freedom and vulnerability of completely sharing her body, and now isn't any different.

Hunger burns through me as I take her in. She's usually a small C, but over the past month, her breasts have swollen to a DD, and while I know she's uncomfortable, and at times, even in pain, I can't help but admire them. She's so full, so fucking gorgeous, and I can't wait to explore every inch of her changing body.

I work my way down her body, keeping to her side so I don't squish our babies. My fingers brush over her nipple, and I watch with desire as it pebbles beneath my touch. She groans and arches her back, needing so much more, and goddammit, I'm going to give it to her.

"Oh God, Carter," she whispers. "Please."

My mouth closes over her nipple, my tongue gently rolling over it, and the way her nails dig into my back only spurs me on. My fingers trail down her waist and cup her sweet pussy, and she instantly grinds against the heel of my palm, desperate for more. I feel her wetness through her thong, and I can't fucking wait to taste her again.

"Carter," she groans, ever so impatient.

A grin tears across my face, and I get to my feet before striding around to the end of the bed. Bri watches me, those wicked green eyes sparkling with a ferocious hunger, and I'm sure that if I don't hurry up and give her what she wants, she'll push me aside and do it herself.

Popping the button on my jeans, I let my pants clatter to the ground, my cock springing free. I take hold of it, slowly fisting it at the base before stroking up and down and watching how Bri follows my movements. Then stepping up to the very end of the bed, I grab her ankles and drag her right down until her ass is just about falling off the edge. Hooking my fingers into the waistband of her thong, I slowly drag it down her legs.

Bri groans and braces herself on her elbows, watching as I drop to my knees, then with every ounce of control I possess, I slowly take her creamy thighs and open her wide, which is exactly when that last bit of control ceases to exist.

I dive in, closing my mouth over her clit and listening to her low groan as it rumbles through her chest, filling the room with the sound of absolute satisfaction. I work her exactly the way she likes, my tongue flicking over her sweet clit as my fingers slide up beneath my chin and slowly push into her needy cunt.

"Oh shit, Carter," she gasps, her hand threading into my hair and gripping tight as my other hand clutches the base of my cock, desperately trying to keep myself from coming all over my bedroom floor.

She's so fucking delicious. I don't know how the hell I survived so long without her.

My fingers massage deep inside of her, and I don't know if it's because of the pregnancy or because she's just so wound up, but it only takes a minute before she's throwing her head back and coming hard on my fingers.

Her pussy spasms around me, convulsing and squeezing as she cries out my name, and I don't dare stop, greedily claiming every drop of her arousal until she finally comes down from her high and her body falls back to the mattress.

Despite my hunger, I pull back and give her a moment to catch her breath as I get to my feet and bring my fingers to my lips, sucking them dry. Her eyes flame, unable to look away, and as I grab my cock once again, she knows we're only just getting started.

Without taking her seductive gaze off me, she sits up on the end of the bed, leans forward, and takes my cock right into her warm mouth. Her tongue circles my tip and instantly sends a wave of overwhelming pleasure rocking through me.

Her hand curls around my base, and I groan as she takes me deeper, moving her hand up and down, matching her rhythm, but it's that tongue. Fuck, I've always loved her tongue.

She works me hard, sucking and taking me right to the back of her throat when it becomes too much, and fuck it, I'm not ready to finish this yet. Pulling back, I release myself from the confines of her skilled mouth, and she looks up at me with those big eyes, knowing exactly how she affects me. "What's wrong?"

"You know damn well what's wrong," I tell her. "Turn around, baby. I need to sink into that tight cunt."

Her eyes flutter as though I just whispered the sweetest little nothings in her ear, but fuck knows my girl loves a man with a filthy mouth.

Hungry for more, Bri braces against my chest as she gets to her knees on the bed, and as she turns around to offer me her back, I take her hips, my thumb stretching out to brush over her firm ass. Eager to feel me pushing inside her, Bri flattens her chest to the mattress, her knees wide and that sweet cunt fully on display, just waiting for me to take her.

She's so fucking beautiful like this.

I can't help but play.

Releasing her hip, my finger skims over her ass and right down the center. She gasps as I trail over her hole, her whole body jolting, and before she can even let out a deep, throaty groan, I push two thick fingers into her cunt.

Bri pushes back against me, needing more, and I don't fucking hesitate to take her deeper. "You like that, baby?" I rumble, gripping my cock and slowly stroking.

"Oh God, Carter," she pants. "So fucking good."

My fingers split inside her, massaging her walls, and as she clenches down around them, I have to keep myself from coming in my fucking hand. My thumb stretches down and rolls over her clit, and the way she fists her hands into the bedsheets only spurs me on.

I work her body, and when it becomes too fucking much, I move in right behind her, my cock pressing against her. "Fuck, baby. I can't wait," I tell her, my tip teasing her entrance. "I don't want to hurt you."

"You won't," she pants, trying to push back against me. "Just be gentle."

Taking her hips again, I slowly begin to push inside, and my eyes roll with undeniable pleasure. Bri groans with the most delicious sound I've ever heard. I take her slowly, rocking my hips and thrusting into her tight pussy as her walls clench around me. "Fuck, Bri. I've missed this."

"Fuck, Carter," she mutters. "More."

Picking up my pace, I give her what she needs as my tongue rolls over my lip, my balls tightening with the need to release. "Reach between your legs, baby. I wanna see you work that sweet clit."

There's no doubt about it, Brianna Lucas is stubborn as fuck. She doesn't let anyone tell her what to do, but when my cock is buried deep inside her and there's an offer like this on the table, she can't possibly resist.

The second her fingers skim over her clit, I feel everything clench and my eyes roll, the undeniable power of her pussy crippling me. I hang in there, clenching my jaw and fighting the need to come, determined to see this through, and thankfully, I don't have to wait long because Bri is right there with me.

My eyes lock onto her sweet cunt, watching the way my glistening cock moves in and out of her as her pants become more ragged and forceful. "Carter," she groans. "I'm gonna come."

Thank fuck.

"Give it to me, baby. Let me feel you squeezing my cock."

"Oh God," she cries, and as I thrust into her one more time, she comes undone. Her orgasm tears through her as her pussy convulses, squeezing me tight.

"Fuck, baby," I hiss through gritted teeth, her sweet pussy throwing me right over the fucking edge as I come right along with her. Hot spurts of cum shoot deep inside her, but I don't dare stop, watching as she rides out her high.

Her orgasm works through her, and I watch in awe as she clenches her eyes, her hand fisting tighter in the sheets as she groans low. Then finally, her body begins to relax, but I can't find it in me to pull back. "Holy shit," she breathes, rocking forward and gently lowering herself to her side, peering up at me with a satisfied smile. "You're too much for me."

A smirk pulls at my lips, and I shake my head as I kneel on the edge of the bed, leaning over to press a kiss to her lips. "If I'm too much for you, baby, find less. But we both know that nobody can fuck you like I do."

"God, I hate when you're right," she laughs, reaching up and cupping my face in her warm hands, a seriousness seeping into her blazing green eyes. "I love you so much, Carter Waters," she tells me. "I know this has all been really hard for you, but please know that you make me the happiest woman in the world, and I can't wait to become your wife."

Absolute joy rocks through my chest, and as I hold her stare, I utter the words that I will live by every day for the rest of my life. "I will never stop trying to make you the happiest woman in the world, Brianna Lucas. You're the best fucking thing that has ever happened to me, and I'm never gonna let you go. You and me, Bri. I love you more than life itself."

Her eyes soften, and just when I think she's about to say something equally as cheesy, that sparkle hits her eyes and she laughs. "Jesus Christ, laying it on a bit thick, don't you think?"

I shake my head and roll her onto her back before gripping her thighs and dragging her back to the edge of the bed as she laughs and tries to swat at my hand. "Oh baby, you wanna see what laying it on thick really means?" I tease. "Your wish is my fucking command."

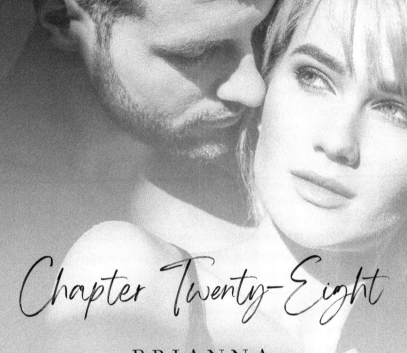

Chapter Twenty-Eight

BRIANNA

We pull up outside Sean's home, and I smile as I get out of Carter's truck, butterflies causing havoc in my stomach. I'm still living in a dream, hardly able to believe this is real, but the gorgeous rock on my finger would suggest otherwise.

I'm almost certain I went into shock when he got down on one knee and asked me to marry him. As much as I've always wanted to be his wife, I had come to terms with knowing that would never happen. I was content just being his. I'd put marriage right at the top of my *you fucking wish* list. But last night, he went and blew me the fuck away.

The fact he had the ring in his pocket for the past five months messes with my head. Why the hell did I not snoop around his place when I first moved in? I could have put all my doubts and fears to rest ages ago, but I respect his reasoning. He needed my trust, and he's right, a marriage without trust isn't a marriage at all. It never would have worked, and I would have hated going into something that was burdened by pain.

Ever since he found out about the pregnancy, he's been saying how he wanted to make this work, but the scars he left on my heart were telling me that he only wanted this for the twins, that he wanted to do what was right by them. It felt like he was punishing himself for knocking me up in the first place.

But now . . . I see I was wrong to doubt him. He truly does want this and has made my world complete by asking.

And then . . . he took me to bed, and it was everything . . . though slightly awkward with the size of my stomach. We had to be creative, but that's never held us back before. It was like coming home. I know we had that drunken night together, which obviously resulted in the invasion currently taking residence in my guts, but I feel like I haven't truly been with him that way since before the split. It was magical, and my heart has never been so full.

Swinging the door open, I try to hop out of the truck, but I'm stuck and have to call for Carter to come help. And I'm not surprised to find the stupid smirk across his face as he finds me half falling out the door. "What seems to be the problem?" he questions, knowing damn well that I'm stuck. Hell, I've been getting stuck everywhere lately.

"Shut up and help me out of here," I demand.

Carter chuckles, clearly thinking it's the funniest thing he's ever seen, and after a scathing glare, he hoists me safely out of his truck. Once I'm on my feet, Carter takes my hand and helps me up the stairs of Sean's huge home, his thumb rubbing back and forth across my knuckles and only making the butterflies worse.

Reaching the front door, Carter doesn't bother stopping to knock, though I'm not surprised. In the whole time I've known him, I've only ever seen him knock twice, and both times were when he was trying to break down my door. "Yo," Carter calls, as we welcome ourselves into the foyer. "Where is everyone?"

I hear Elle, Logan's fiancé, responding from somewhere within the enormous house. "We're all out back," she says.

We make our way through the house and find her in the kitchen, struggling to balance three plates, and Carter, being the perfect gentleman, swoops in and saves her, taking the plates off her hands.

"Thanks," she sighs in relief before leaning in and kissing him on the cheek. She moves on to me next and has to move around my side to get her arms around me. "How are you feeling?" she asks as we make our way outside.

"Exhausted," I tell her. "I can't wait to get these babies out of me. I swear, my whole body feels as though it's moments from giving out."

We step outside to find everyone sitting out on the grass with little Georgia, or Georgie, as she's been nicknamed, on a picnic rug, playing with all her toys. She's eight months old now and the light of my life. The little beauty is an absolute gift to this world, and I can't wait to watch her grow and develop into a beautiful young woman. Though I think watching her give her daddy hell over the next eighteen years is going to be the best part.

"Hey," Logan says as he notices us hovering around the back door. Everyone turns at his greeting and gets to their feet, and in no time, the whole Waters family is crowding around, giving hugs and kisses as they welcome us to the party.

"I'd love to stay here and chat all day, but my feet are killing me," I tell them. "I need to sit down." Carter hands the plates off to Jax and takes my hand to help me walk across the grass, and Cassie joins us on my other side, making sure I get there safely.

We eventually make it to the picnic rug where Georgie sits happily playing with her toys, and as I look at the ground, I realize getting down there is going to be a lot harder than I thought.

Well, shit.

I cringe as I attempt to bend a million different ways, going backward or forward and even trying the awkward side squat, but there's no way in hell this is going to happen. If I attempt again, I fear I might actually fall down and never get up again. "Hey, Logan," Carter calls to his brother, who's making out with Elle at the backdoor. "Bring a chair down for Bri."

Logan makes a show of saluting Carter, but he does as he's told, making sure to put a rush on it. Once the chair is firmly planted in the grass, I take a seat and feel a pain shooting through my back. "Ugh," I groan as the pain becomes worse. I wiggle around on the chair before reaching down and grabbing Carter's jacket that rests on the grass beside him. I shove it behind my back like a cushion, having to position it just right, and then finally, the pain begins to ease.

Thank God. I can't handle pain on top of everything else I've been feeling lately.

"How're my babies?" Cassie asks as she gets down on her knees beside me and places both hands on my ever-growing tummy.

"Good," I tell her with a smile as I dig through my handbag and pull out the latest ultrasound picture. "Here," I say, handing it over. "This was last week."

Elle peers over her shoulder as Cassie melts. "Wow, this one is sucking his thumb," she sighs, before talking directly to my stomach. "Can you guys hurry up and break out of there? Your aunty Cassie is dying to meet you."

I laugh as the babies react to her voice and start moving around, but it quickly becomes unbearable with how little space they have to move.

Carter picks up Georgie and gives her a tight snuggle, but she starts whining and gets thrust straight into my arms. "Hi, my sweet girl," I coo as I attempt to make her comfortable around my tummy. The whining stops almost immediately as she glances up at me with those big blue eyes that remind me so much of her mommy. A massive grin spreads over her face, which is quickly followed by the cheekiest little giggle that melts my heart. "Oh, you are just the sweetest thing," I tell her. "I bet you'll be breaking hearts all over the place when you grow up."

"Great," Sean mutters. "Just when I thought I had enough to

worry about, you had to go remind me about horny teenage boys."

I roll my eyes, but honestly, I doubt he'll have anything to worry about with all of her uncles around. It's going to take one hell of a brave boy to risk stealing Georgie's heart.

Sensing Carter's stare, I glance up to find him watching me in awe as I cradle his niece. He gives me a knowing smile as if clearly picturing our near future, and it's the best feeling in the world. My cheeks flush under his stare, and I have to look away, certain I'll explode if he doesn't kiss me soon.

Sean disappears and returns a moment later with stacks of food, and we all dig in as though we've never been fed in our lives. Carter sits in front of me, using my legs as a backrest as I run my fingernails through his hair, making him start to doze off like an old man needing his afternoon nap.

Georgie sits in the middle of the mat with all her aunties and uncles surrounding her, watching as Sean attempts to feed her. The baby mush is going everywhere except for her mouth, and after suffering through ten minutes of watching Sean drop mashed carrots all over Georgie's dress, Cassie's patience runs thin and she shoves Sean out of the way with a packet of wet wipes at the ready. After quickly cleaning her up, Cassie dives in with the spoon, proving once and for all that she really can do a better job.

Carter's hand comes up and takes hold of my hand that sits on his shoulder. He laces our fingers together before clearing his throat, demanding everyone's attention. "So, uhh . . . we have some news," he says.

They all look our way with curious glances and notice our hands in each other's grasp. "Oh, shit. You two finally worked things out," Jax smiles, quickly beaming at Cassie with a suspicious bounce of his brows, making me wonder if he's just won a bet.

Cass groans with disappointment. "I mean, I'm really fucking happy for you, but could you not have waited like . . . I don't know. Three more weeks? If you had any idea what I owe my husband now . . ."

"I don't wanna know," Carter mutters, glancing up at me with a knowing smile before turning back to everyone else. "And yeah, we are back together, but that's not quite the news we were wanting to share."

I watch as each of them glance at our hands before looking back at us with stumped looks on their faces. "Then what the hell is it?" Logan asks as he pushes Elle up off his lap. "Something about the babies?"

A laugh rumbles through my chest, and unable to resist another second, I hold up my left hand and turn it around so they can all see the big fucking rock that sits perfectly upon my ring finger. "We're engaged," I beam.

"HOLY FUCKING SHIT," Cassie squeals, throwing herself to her feet and scaring the shit out of Georgie in the process. Cass swoops down, scoops her into her arms, and before she can even take a breath, a loud sob tears from the back of her throat, her bottom lip wobbling uncontrollably. "I'm just," *sob*, "so," *snot*, "freaking happy for you."

She makes her way toward us, tears streaming down her face as Jax shakes his head at his wife's performance. Logan though, he gapes at

Carter like he must be possessed by some kind of alien life form, but Sean just grins, almost as though he knew it all along.

Carter gets up and helps pull me to my feet just in time for Cass to barrel into me. She wraps her arms around me, and we give Georgie a best friend sandwich as tears and snot start going everywhere. "Tell me this isn't a joke? Did he really ask?"

"Yeah," I tell her, a wide smile on my face as Elle crashes into us, joining in on the love. "He did. We're going to be a real family."

"I'm so happy for you," Cassie says as the boys start whooping and cheering for Carter as they crack open their celebratory beers.

Jax steps in beside me and awkwardly tries to hug me around his wife and Elle. "Congratulations," he says, pure happiness shining in his eyes.

I smile up at him when another shooting pain blasts through my back. "Ahh, fuck," I wince. "That was a bad one."

"What's wrong?" Cass asks, bracing her hands against my shoulders and shoving me back to see my face.

"It's nothing," I say, pushing out of their arms and searching for my chair behind me. "I just need to sit down."

Jax helps me get back into my chair, and I shuffle Carter's jacket behind my back again to help ease the pain, and like clockwork, it begins to fade away.

"I must admit," Cass says as everyone starts to calm down and take their seats on the picnic mat again. "I'm kinda shocked. After everything, I thought I was going to have to torture him before he'd finally find the balls to pop the question."

"You and me both," I tell her as Carter rolls his eyes, clearly not approving of our conversation. "But apparently, my ass is just too good to pass up."

"Got that right," Carter grunts before reaching up with an orange juice in his hand.

I bend to take it from him, and the subtle movement has another pain shooting through my back. "Fuck me," I mutter, starting to get frustrated with this bullshit. "This shit just won't give in."

Carter glances up at me, his brows furrowed. "Are you okay?" he asks, placing a calming hand on my thigh and giving a gentle squeeze.

"Yeah," I say, trying to breathe through the pain. "I just keep getting this awful pain in my back. I think the babies are using my kidneys for target practice or something. Either way, it fucking hurts."

"What?" Carter grunts in concern. "Why didn't you tell me you were having pains?"

"Because it's nothing," I say. "And it's not like you can do anything to take the pain away. You would have just sat there looking at me with this helpless, lost puppy dog stare like you're doing right now. I didn't want you worrying."

Carter scoffs, rolling his eyes. "It's not nothing," he says. "You could be going into labor."

I shake my head, secretly loving how concerned he is. "Nah, I don't think so. I'd know if it was labor. Besides, it's just random back pain, not contractions. Not to mention, I'm only eight months. It's too early."

"Are you sure?" he pushes, giving me a hard stare.

"Positive."

"Hmmm, I don't know," Elle says with a cringe. "I'm pretty sure back pain is a sign of labor."

The next few minutes are spent in a massive group debate over the topic of labor pains, but it's cut short when the pain shoots through my back again, making me groan as it starts getting so much worse. "That's it. I'm checking Dr. Google," Cassie declares, having enough of the back and forth.

We sit in silence, watching as she searches with Jax peering over her shoulder. Her eyes roam all over her phone as she skims through the information, her finger working overtime on the scroll. The silence kills me, and Carter takes hold of my hands, realizing the unknown is making me nervous.

"Okay," she says, looking up at me as calm as a cucumber. "You're having contractions. It's time to go to the hospital."

"What?" I grunt, my eyes widening like saucers. "Are you shitting me?"

"Fuck," Carter grunts, flying to his feet and frantically looking around for his things.

The picnic lunch goes into a flurry of movement. People shuffle around, grabbing their phones and wallets off the ground, discussing who's going in what car, and before I know it, they're all rushing to the house, leaving me sitting in the damn chair I can't get out of. "Hey, fuckers," I call to their backs. "You guys aren't having any babies without me."

"Fuck," Carter grunts again, rushing back to me and helping me out of the chair.

"I'm not ready for this," I tell him as we make our way back up to the house.

"You're so ready for this," he tells me, the confidence in his eyes blowing me the fuck away. "You're going to be an amazing mother."

"Of course I'm going to be an amazing mother," I grunt. "What I mean is that I'm not ready to push these babies out. I'm fucking terrified. After Sara—"

He wraps his arm around me as we make our way back through the house. "You're going to do great, and if you can't handle it, there's always drugs to cheer you up. We've spoken to the doctors about your fears of having a C-section, and they're on board. What happened to Sara isn't going to happen to you. There's no doubt that this is going to be awful. It's going to hurt and you're going to hate it, and there will come a point where you're going to want to give up, but I know you, Bri. You're going to push through the pain, and at the end of the day, you're going to have two beautiful little babies in your arms, sucking the life out of your perfect fucking tits."

"Fuck, Carter," I groan. "You were so close to making me feel better."

He chuckles as he helps me up into his truck, pausing to press a kiss to my lips. "Call it like it see it, babe," he grins.

Carter closes my door and hurries around to the driver's side, giving me the cheesiest fucking grin I've ever seen before finally kicking over the engine. Jax and Cassie climb into the backseat just in time for Carter to hit the gas.

Glancing out the window, I watch Sean buckling Georgie into his truck as Elle and Logan get in with him, and I realize that this is going to bring up a lot of memories for Sean that I don't know if he's ready to deal with just yet.

It's only a short ten-minute drive to the hospital, but every passing second only has my nerves getting that much worse. This must honestly be the scariest shit in the world. I mean, how the hell are these babies going to squeeze out of my vagina? It's going to fucking hurt. What the hell was I thinking?

My breathing becomes erratic and Carter reaches across the console to take my hand. "Calm down," he soothes. "You're going to be okay. I've got you."

I look over at him with wide eyes. "I don't want to shit on the bed."

"What?" he grunts, having to take his eyes off the road for just a moment to gape at me.

"A lady at work," I start, trying to slow my breathing, "she told me a friend of hers was sick and when it came time to push, she shit all over the nurses and doctor. Practically redecorated the whole birthing suite with explosive diarrhea."

"Fuck," he laughs. "That's not going to happen to you."

"You don't know that," I say, focusing my gaze out the windshield. I sit in silence the rest of the way, trying to calm myself when horror slams through my chest. "Oh, shit," I panic, turning my horrified stare on my fiancé as he comes to a stop outside the hospital. "You need to call Bobby."

"Don't worry, babe. It's handled," he says, nodding to Jax in the backseat who pulls out his phone.

Sean's truck pulls up in the space beside us, and as Carter makes his way around to help me out, Logan beats him to the punch and helps me to my feet. I'm just about to thank him when I look up at the hospital in fear—the same fear that flashes in Sean's eyes. "This is it," I tell Carter as he presses his hand to my lower back, leading me toward the door. "We're going to have some babies."

"Fuck yeah, we are," he says, not even a hint of nervousness. "Let's do this shit."

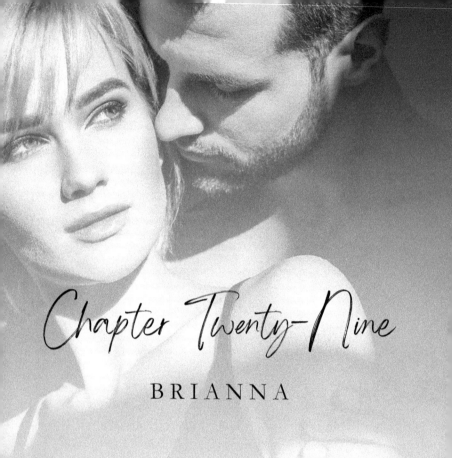

Chapter Twenty-Nine

BRIANNA

I step into the birthing suite with Carter at my side and take a look around, trying my best not to panic. A bed takes up the center of the room with a shitload of machines connected to it. A table is off to the side, stacked with all sorts of medical equipment, and a big ass tub sits in the corner of the room, which I'm assuming is used for water births.

It hits me that this is truly happening. In the next few hours, I'll be pushing two babies out of my lady taco and tearing my vag to shreds.

Fuck me. What was I thinking? I like my vag the way it is, and hell, I know Carter does too.

Walking deeper into the room, my fingers graze over the bed I'll be calling home for the next day or two as the rest of our family follows in. I find the dressing gown on the bed and pick it up before silently making my way into the connecting bathroom. I start getting dressed while listening to everyone making themselves comfortable in the room, not surprised when I hear Carter tell Logan to get the fuck off my bed and find his own damn chair.

As I take in my gown through the shitty bathroom mirror with my ass hanging out the back, I can't help but wonder if I really want everyone here for this, but the moment I start to reconsider, I realize I wouldn't want it any other way. Sure, it might be a little awkward at times, but these guys are my family, and I love them. Besides, their endless banter is sure to keep me distracted through the pain, and I'm pretty certain they'll all head out when it's time to push. And if they don't—shit. I really hope I don't poop on the bed.

Realizing I'm about to lose every ounce of dignity I possess, I strut out of the bathroom in my hospital gown, not bothering to cover up my ass. I start to climb up into my bed when Carter's concerned tone rumbles through the room. "You good, bro?"

I look over to find his heavy gaze locked on Sean, and it hits me—this could be the same room Sara was in during her labor. A heaviness fills my veins, realizing just how hard this must be for him. Hell, it's hard for us all, but Sean . . . fuck.

Sean cuddles Georgie into his chest and gives Carter an encouraging smile, one that doesn't reach his eyes. "I'm good," he mutters. "This is a happy day."

I give him a nod, wishing I could cross the room and give him a big hug, but that's so much harder than it sounds. So, I indicate to Cassie to do it for me and she immediately makes a move, giving her eldest brother all her love.

A midwife who looks to be my age comes striding in and has to pause as she takes in the crowd surrounding my bed. Her concerned gaze flashes to me, quickly scanning over me and making sure I'm in one piece before a breathtaking smile spreads over her face, making me pause. This woman is stunning. I think I have a bit of a lady crush. "Hi, Brianna, I'm Gigi. I'll be your midwife today," she says. "Now, you believe you're in labor?"

"Yes," I say before launching into the whole back pain debacle.

"Okay," she smiles. "That sounds about right, but I'll need to examine you to confirm you're actually in labor. Do you need the room to be vacated or are you good to go?"

Glancing at the group around me and knowing they're not about to go anywhere, I smile up at Gigi. "I'm good. No one but this asshole is gonna look," I say, hooking my thumb toward Carter.

Gigi follows my gaze to Carter and gives him a polite smile. "The babies' father, I take it?"

He nods and I smile wide. "Yep. My fiancé," I add, just because I will never tire of saying it.

"Excellent," Gigi smiles.

She walks around the bed and steps into my side before getting started on my examination. Both me and the babies are connected to heart rate monitors and a blood pressure cuff is strapped around my arm. She gets started on the physical part of the examination, and just like that, Sean, Logan, and Jax awkwardly glance away. Fingers go places I wasn't quite prepared for, and soon enough, Gigi confirms that I'm in labor and gets a round of applause and hollered whoops from every person in the room.

"Well, this is going to be a fun day," she murmurs to me as she goes about jotting down my information on my chart. She gets me set up before draping a blanket over me and making sure I'm comfortable.

The contractions continue and steadily get worse, but so far so good. They haven't been too bad, and I was right in having everyone here. They keep me distracted from the pain, though I'm not sure if it's them actually keeping me distracted or the fact they're grilling Carter on details about when he bought my ring and why the fuck it took him so long to ask.

Gigi comes and goes, checking the machines and examining me to keep track of how I'm progressing, which only makes me realize just how long we're going to be here.

Everyone starts growing tired, but they are wide awake when a lady starts screaming down the hall. "Holy shit," Jax grunts with wide eyes, looking at Cass. "You're never having babies, not if it's that bad."

"Shut up," she laughs. "She's the rare breed of superwoman who likes to forgo the drugs. Me, I'm no hero. I'll be having all the drugs."

I roll my eyes as another contraction comes on, and I start wondering about those drugs she mentioned. The pain gets worse, and I clutch Carter's hand, cringing and clenching my jaw. "Shit, this hurts," I say as Carter's other hand gently rubs up and down my thigh.

"Do you want me to get the midwife?" he questions.

"No, not yet," I say. "I can handle it a little longer."

Carter has been trying to convince me to use the gas or to consider an epidural for the past hour. He absolutely hates seeing me in pain, and so far, I've shaken off his comments, but Cassie's words hit me. Am I trying to be a hero? No one is going to judge me for getting something to ease the pain.

When the next contraction comes on, I give in. I'm definitely no hero. "Okay," I say, trying to breathe through the pain. "Get me the gas."

"Thank fuck," Carter says, relief flashing in his dark eyes as he presses the call button for the midwife.

Gigi comes in and gets shit sorted, and within seconds, I'm sucking the gas harder than I've ever sucked Carter. And like clockwork, my pain begins to ease. "Fuck me, this is good," I tell him.

"I bet," he says as Gigi notices Georgie fast asleep in her daddy's arms. She lets out an awed sigh, taken by the sight, just like the rest of us. "Oh my God, isn't she beautiful," Gigi tells him. Sean gives her a tight smile, still not quite coping despite putting on a brave face.

With that, Gigi scurries out of the room and appears moments later with a baby crib and a blanket, offering them to Sean to put Georgie down. "Thanks," he murmurs, giving her a real smile and making a rosy blush spread across her cheeks.

I can't help but grin watching the exchange because, girl . . . same. There's just something about these Waters boys that has every woman falling to their knees.

Gigi hightails it out of the room, and I get into a great routine of sucking back the gas with each contraction until I start feeling a little light-headed. Hell, I'm feeling a little high too. "You have to try this," I say with a sloppy grin, glancing at Carter, who watches me in amusement.

His brows furrow, looking a little closer. "Fuck. You're high."

"Am not," I laugh.

"Riiiiight."

I scoff, smirking at my fiancé. "Chicken."

Logan flies up off his chair, his hand already stretched out toward me. "I'll give it a try." He gives me a dorky grin, all but running across the room to get to the gas. I gingerly hand it over as Sean groans and lets him know that he's being an idiot.

Not giving a single fuck, Logan takes a hit of the gas, sucking that thing better than I do. Logan takes a few more hits before that dorky grin returns. "Holy fuck," he laughs. "This shit is good."

Logan turns to Jax and holds it out, tempting him to get in on the action, and Jax being Jax simply can't help himself. He shoos Cassie off his lap in his rush to get to the gas, and before I know it, both Jax and Logan are giggling like a bunch of school girls, more than high.

FOMO kicks in, and Cassie and Carter get in on the action, and between the four of them, I have more than enough entertainment to get through the next few hours.

Logan gets up and crosses to the supply closet before yanking open the door and pulling out a spare pillow. With a smile, he struts back across the room, only he doesn't go back to his seat, he stops at the bathtub, drops the pillow, and climbs right in. He gets himself comfortable and grins up at Jax before patting the space beside him. "Wanna cuddle?" he questions, raising his brows.

"Do I ever," Jax beams, practically launching himself over the edge and snuggling in beside him, looking like a teenage girl who just had the quarterback ask her to prom. They get cozy in the bath and share a pillow while playing games on their phones, making Sean roll his eyes as Cassie discreetly takes pictures and posts them to the private Colorado Thunder chat.

Carter gets jealous and climbs into the bed beside me, still holding my hand through the contractions. I instinctively snuggle into his chest and feel a million times better, despite being in the worst pain known to womankind.

The door flies open and in walks one of the biggest idiots I know. "I hope you're not having these babies without me," Bobby says as he struts in like he owns the place.

A beaming smile tears across my face. I was starting to worry that he'd miss all the action. "Ahh, if it isn't my wombmate," I laugh as he walks over to me and gives me a great big hug, holding me much longer than necessary.

Bobby takes a look around the room, taking in the boys in the bath and the goofy as fuck look on Carter's face. "Shit, you guys look fucking cooked."

"That would be because they are," I say, holding up the gas.

"Well, shit," Bobby grins, looking as though his day just got a shitload better. "I hope you saved some of that for me."

Without even a moment of hesitation, Bobby sucks on the gas and the boys and Cass instantly start another round of uncontrollable laughter, offering up the best kind of entertainment.

Twenty minutes later, Gigi comes in and takes one look at the three boys in the bathtub. She laughs to herself before letting them in on the secret. "I had a woman in there last night," she says. "Redecorated the whole thing with baby guts and shit. Took hours to scrub the stench out of it."

Gigi comes to examine me as the boys scramble out of the bath, yanking each other out of the way to be the first one out while Jax turns green and bolts for the bathroom. The boys start giggling again, and it takes two seconds for Gigi to realize they're high on gas. Thankfully she ignores it since they aren't disturbing any of the other patients, only me—not that I'm complaining about it.

Gigi starts examining me, all but shoving her whole fist up my hooch and having a good feel around. "Are you jealous?" I ask Carter, grunting with pain.

"Uhhh, usually I'd say yeah," he grunts, his lips twisting in disgust, "but that's kinda gross."

Trying to figure out what the hell we're talking about, Bobby looks my way and accidentally gets an eye full of me being fisted. "AHH, FUCK. MY EYES!"

A booming laugh tears from my chest, shaking my whole body and forcing Gigi to evacuate from my guts. "You know she can't have sex for like six weeks," Cassie says from across the room, adding her two cents.

Carter's face pales as he turns to his sister. "What?" he grunts, making me realize I never let him in on that particular secret.

He doesn't get a response as Gigi finishes my exam and gives me a bright smile. "Alright, Brianna. You're at eight centimeters, so it shouldn't be too long now. I'd say maybe another hour or two and you'll be holding your babies."

Carter squeezes my hand and presses a kiss to my sweaty forehead. "You're nearly there, babe."

"I know," I smile. "I can't wait."

Gigi smiles and leaves the room, but returns moments later with two baby cribs that she lines up against the wall. "Wow, shit's getting real," I murmur to Carter, keeping my eyes locked on the cribs that will hold my twins.

"Sure is," he says.

The next hour and a half is the longest hour and a half known to man.

Gigi comes back in and confirms I'm at ten centimeters, and with that, kicks everyone out of my room and boots Carter off my bed. He does as he's told as the room fills with a shitload of midwives, twice as usual to look after each of the babies.

Gigi pages Dr. Thompson, who shows up moments later and tells me it's just about time to get this show on the road.

Nerves filter through me, and my stomach does somersaults. I'm positive that I really am going to shit the bed. Carter grabs a cold wash cloth and pats down my face. "You're so fucking strong, baby," he says. "You've got this."

Dr. Thompson says it's time to put my legs up in the stirrups, and I grab the little gas sucky thing and jam it in my mouth, biting down on it, knowing I'm going to be needing it more than ever. My legs go up and I concentrate on Dr. Thompson, not wanting to miss a thing.

"Alright, Brianna," she says as Carter clutches my hand. "On your next contraction, I want you to push. I'll count to ten, you'll take a breath, and we'll go again. Understood?"

I nod again, my whole body shaking. I can do this.

I just have to do a little pushing, rip my body in half, and I'll be rewarded with two beautiful little babies.

I. Can. Do. This.

Feeling the contraction coming on, I take a deep breath and meet Carter's stare.

This is it.

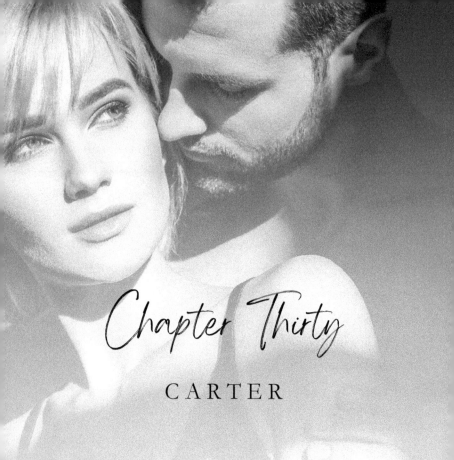

Chapter Thirty

CARTER

Holy shit. I'm about to pass out.

This is all happening way too fast. Brianna's legs are in the stirrups, and the doctor stands at the end of the bed, ready to catch our babies like Bri's a fucking quarterback shooting them out. The midwives flurry around the room, preparing everything, while I cling to Bri's hand to keep her calm.

Dr. Thompson casts a serious look at Brianna. "On your next contraction, I want you to push. I'll count to ten, you'll take a breath, and we'll go again. Understood?"

Ahhh, fuck. Fuck. Fuck.

Don't pass out. I'll never fucking live it down.

Bri squeezes my hand, and I realize this it is, the contraction is on its way. In just a few minutes, I'll have two babies in my care. Shit. I hope I don't fuck them up. Sean seems to be able to do it, and if he can, then surely I can too. Right?

My girl looks up at me in fear, and I give her an encouraging smile, knowing she's got this. She's the most incredible woman I know.

"Okay, Brianna. It's time. Let's go," Dr. Thompson says. "Push."

Taking a deep breath, Bri pushes with everything she has, squeezing my hand so fucking hard, I think it might be broken. Her beautiful eyes disappear behind clenched lids, listening to Dr. Thompson as she counts down from ten, coaching her through it.

"Fuck," Bri grunts, tears of agony spilling down her flushed cheeks as she's allowed a quick moment to catch her breath.

"Good job, Brianna," Dr. Thompson says. "Let's go again. Another push."

Her chest heaves, but being the strong woman I know she is, she keeps it up. She squeezes my hand harder, and I find myself mentally pushing with her. "Come on, baby. You're a fucking rockstar. You're doing great."

"SHUT UP!" she growls mid-push.

Gigi takes over the countdown and the contraction finishes, giving Bri a small break to catch her breath. I scramble, not knowing how to help her, so I stay in my zone, pressing the cool cloth to her forehead and trying to mop up her tears.

She looks up at me, and the agony in her stare cuts me to shreds.

"I can't do this, Carter," she says, shaking her head as more tears fall. "It hurts too much. I can't."

"You can," I insist, using a firmer tone, knowing how she needs it. "Think of those babies. You're at the finish line, Bri, and then you get to hold your children. You're right there. You've got this."

"The head is ready to come through, Brianna. Another push on the next contraction should have the head out, but I'm going to need a big one," Dr. Thompson instructs. "Once you get past this, the hard part is done."

Curiosity gets the best of me, and I inch down the side of the bed, peering over the stirrups, and what I see . . . fuck. I'll never be the same. My eyes widen, and I feel the color drain from my face. "Goddamn, babe," I say, giving Bri's hand a gentle squeeze.

Yep, I'm definitely gonna pass out.

Giving birth is the most natural thing a human body can do, and yet it's fucking gross. I know it's my baby down there, but fuck. I need to build Bri a fucking castle after this. Shit, no. That's not enough. Does she need an island? What about a whole fucking country?

"Carterrrrrr," Bri groans. "Don't look."

I get back to my position beside her and lean down to her face, a smirk pulling at the corner of my lips as I gently kiss her forehead. "You want me to take a photo, don't you?"

She meets my gaze, her eyes sparkling. "Yeah, kinda."

"You filthy little animal, you!"

Bri laughs and breathes heavily again, feeling another contraction coming on. "I saw his head, baby," I tell her, saying the one thing I know will give her the motivation to tear her body apart. "He has dark hair, just like me."

"Really?" she questions, those tears still swelling in her eyes.

"Yeah, babe. He's ready to come out."

Bri's bottom lip wobbles, and I know she'd rather be doing anything else than going through this pain, but she nods at the doctor and searches for my hand. I grab hold of it and she squeezes tight as one of the midwives gets in on the action with my phone, recording every moment for Bri to watch back, hopefully as a reminder when she starts wanting more.

"The contraction is coming," she tells the doctor.

"Right, let's do this, Brianna," she encourages. "Big push. Let's get his head out."

Bri takes a massive breath and pushes with all she's got, her face turning a brilliant shade of red. I can see the pain written all over her, and I know she is dying to scream, but she's holding it in, pushing through the pain.

Gigi continues counting, and the speed at which she counts makes me want to shove her out of the way and take over. Can't she see my woman is in pain? Count faster.

Bri lets out an agonized grunt, and I realize this is it, the head is coming. "Good job, Brianna," Dr. Thompson encourages over Gigi's counting. "You're doing it. Keep it going. You're nearly there."

Bri screams, and then suddenly she stops, letting out a loud gasp. "You did it, Brianna," Dr. Thompson says. "You can stop there. Take a breath. You got the head out. You got through the hardest part."

"Really?" she questions, breathless, her gaze flicking to mine, and fuck it, I have to have another look.

Getting my ass straight to the end of the bed, I drop my gaze between my girl's legs and feel my fucking heart explode in my chest. "Holy fuck," I breathe as I see my child looking up at me with those big blue eyes. "That's crazy."

His little head is poking out of Brianna's pussy. He's all squishy and covered in gunk, but it's the most incredible thing I've ever seen. That's my child, my whole fucking heart right there between my future wife's legs, and I realize without a fucking doubt that I would walk through the darkest pits of hell for this sweet, innocent baby. Hell, I'd give my life for theirs.

I've never seen anything so precious in my life. "Babe," I whisper, meeting Bri's exhausted gaze over her protruding bump, my eyes stinging with tears. "He's beautiful."

"Of course, he is," she says, the most breathtaking smile spreading across her face.

The doctor goes about checking that the cord isn't wrapped around the baby's neck, and as I step back into Brianna's side and collect her hand in mine, I drop a lingering kiss to her warm lips, tasting her spilled tears. "You are the most incredible woman I've ever met," I tell her.

Brianna smiles up at me as Dr. Thompson tells her it's time to push the rest of him out. As the contraction comes on, Bri pushes, and before we know it, our child is placed on Brianna's chest, his soft cries filling the delivery room. "Congratulations," Dr. Thompson beams. "You were right. It's a boy."

Tears stream down Brianna's face as she cradles our son in her arms, and I press a kiss to her forehead, looking down at the beautiful creature we've created. Nurses shuffle in with blankets and begin wiping him down, but she doesn't dare hand him over.

"Welcome to the world, my little man," Brianna soothes before glancing up at me, her eyes so filled with love, making me truly understand the extent of my mistake in ever telling her I didn't want this, because now that he's here and in her arms, I could never go back or deny the unconditional love I have for this sweet little boy. "You were right. It was worth every bit of the pain."

"I always knew it would be," I tell her, brushing my fingers over her forehead and pushing her hair back, knowing we're only halfway through.

"Do they have names yet?" Gigi asks as she admires our son.

"Yeah," Brianna smiles before glancing up at Dr. Thompson. "Do you know if this was the baby on the left or right side?"

"I believe this little handsome guy was the one jammed under your ribs on the left," Dr. Thompson says, a fond smile on her face as she starts checking over Bri and preparing her for baby number two.

Bri smiles the most beautiful smile I've ever seen. "Then this little man is Nate," she says.

"I love it," Gigi says. "What about baby number two?"

"Parker," Bri says.

"Perfect," I whisper.

"Okay, Brianna," the doctor says. "Can we hand little Nate off to Gigi? It's time to meet Parker now."

Unable to really move, Gigi comes forward and scoops Nate off her chest and takes him over to the crib where a nurse goes about cleaning him off properly and getting a diaper and onesie onto his cold little body.

Brianna squeezes my hand, and I realize that it's time. The contraction is coming on and along with that comes the pushing. I can't even begin to understand the amount of pain Bri must be in, and the fact she's had to do it twice goes to show just how fucking incredible she is.

All I know is that I'll spend the rest of my life making it up to her.

Bri pushes with everything she's got, squeezing my hand, and just like Nate, Parker is safely delivered into the world. When he's on Brianna's chest, the tears instantly start again, overwhelming joy taking grip of both of us and refusing to release us, but I never want it to. I could live in this bliss for the rest of my life.

Parker is whisked off and cleaned up by the nurses, and I watch as little tags are placed around their ankles so we can tell them apart. I find myself constantly hovering over them, making sure they're safe as the nurses rush around the room cleaning up after one hell of a messy delivery.

Once Brianna has properly caught her breath, I help rid her of her bloody gown and she somehow finds the strength to put herself through a quick shower before coming back, feeling refreshed.

Brianna lays down in the clean bed and indicates for me to bring our babies over, and I do just that, more than happy to sit here with them for the rest of our days.

Gigi comes in and tells us it's time to feed, which is a whole new experience, and I gape at our sons the whole time, not understanding how they can so easily know exactly what to do. But what can I say? My sons are geniuses. I passed on only the best genes.

Once she's finished feeding them, I roll both the cribs over to her bed and put them side by side, so Brianna can watch over them. "They're beautiful," she says, taking them in, both fast asleep after the exhausting day they've had.

She pats the bed beside her, and I squish in, being careful not to bump her as her body attempts to recover from the traumatic events it's just been through. She curls into my arms, and we spend the next twenty minutes basking in the undeniable joy of finally being a family of four, when she simply can't resist anymore and begs me to hand them over.

"Nate or Parker?" I ask, peering down at them.

Bri looks up at me with a smile and a sparkle in her exhausted eyes. "Both," she beams.

What my girl wants, my girl gets!

Carefully getting out of bed, I pull the babies from their cribs one by one, doing my best not to wake them in the process. I fail miserably and end up waking them both, but they're so exhausted that Bri's able to put them straight back to sleep like some kind of baby whisperer.

Bri looks down at the twins with such love in her eyes that I find myself wondering how I could have been so stupid to not want this. "Do you want to bring everyone in?" she asks, refusing to look up from our babies.

A proud smile rips across my face. Introducing my sons to my family is honestly the next best thing.

I've never been so proud as I strut out of the room to find them sitting on the ground in the hallway making complete menaces of themselves. They look up the second they see me, each one of them with wide eyes, except Sean, who looks completely miserable, this whole day bringing up all of that pain again. "Do you guys feel like meeting some babies?" I ask.

Cassie and Bobby practically fly off the floor and crash into the room, each of them fighting to get through the door first. The others follow me in, and I'm not surprised when Cassie doesn't make it to the bed. Getting one glance at the twins in Bri's arms, she stops in the middle of the room, drops to her knees, and starts uncontrollably sobbing on the ground, needing Jax to swoop in and save her.

"Oh my God," Cassie sobs as she takes it all in. And hell, I can't blame her. It truly is a beautiful sight. "Can . . . can I hold them?"

"Of course," Brianna smiles, indicating with a nod of her head to come on over and squish in on the bed. Cass scurries across the room and scoots in beside Bri before taking Parker in her arms, and like clockwork, she begins sobbing all over again.

Bobby walks around the other side of the bed and leans down to press a kiss to Bri's forehead as he gazes at the sweet babies. "You did good, sis," he murmurs before stealing Nate out of Brianna's other arm.

Bobby walks around and stands by Cassie's side on the edge of the bed so the twins can be together, and like that, everybody comes in to say hello. Sean holds Georgie tightly and she peers down at Nate like he's the most angelic creature she's ever seen before, squealing when she realizes there are two of them.

Congratulations and love are thrown around the room, and I find myself basking in it, so fucking proud of what Bri and I have created, deep down knowing that we had to go through the pain to make it to where we are today.

"Looks like we've got the next generation of Waters NHL players right here," Bobby says, making both Logan and Jax thoroughly agree. "They're going to be great additions to the New York Titans," Bobby grins.

"The fuck?" Logan grunts. "They'll be signing with the Colorado Storm."

On and on it goes . . .

As Bri begins to yawn, everyone starts dawdling out so she can rest, and once the room is clear, I'm finally able to climb in next to Bri and wrap her in my arms. "Bobby was right, you did good, babe," I tell her as my eyes remain locked on our twins.

"*We* did good," she corrects.

I look down at her and press my lips against hers. "I can't wait to make an honest woman out of you," I tell her as my fingers run through her hair, so unbelievably in love with this woman. "I love you, Brianna Lucas. I didn't realize it was possible, but you've just made my world so much bigger."

The softest smile comes over her beautiful face as she tilts her chin up to kiss me, and I give her exactly what she needs as I hold her gently.

Bri pulls back with another yawn, and I run my fingers through her hair. "Why don't you rest, babe? You've had a massive day."

"But the babies . . ." she says, looking at them in concern.

"I've got it, babe. I'll wake you if they need you. They're safe with me," I tell her, fully prepared to watch over my children. With me around, no harm or foul will ever come their way, Brianna included.

Bri nods, and I continue running my fingers through her hair, watching as she begins to settle into an exhausted sleep, forever safe in my arms. Then glancing around the room at my sleeping family, I know, this is exactly where we were always meant to be.

Fear tore us apart, and fate brought us back together, delivering to us the greatest blessing life could ever bring, and I know with everything that I am, I will never let them go.

Epilogue

CARTER

12 MONTHS LATER

I stand by the altar on my parents' estate with my brothers and sons right by my side. Logan, Sean, Jax, and Bobby stand beside me—Logan holding Nate as Sean struggles to keep Parker from trying to race off to chase the ducks that take up residence in the lake behind the property. It's been a year since the boys were born, and to say they've been a handful is an understatement.

It's been fucking crazy, but I wouldn't have it any other way.

They drive me insane—but in the best way. When I promised Bri that I wanted to be a family, I don't think I considered just how much work a baby would be, let alone two of them. They've kept Brianna and me on our toes, and it's been the most exhausting yet thrilling ride of our lives.

Brianna and I hadn't even left the hospital parking lot before we got into our first fight, which centered around the fucking car seats. She was convinced they weren't installed correctly, but I know damn well I did it right. She even had me call a professional to come and check them before she allowed the boys to ride in them. And sure enough, the guy came and confirmed that they were the best installed car seats he'd ever seen. But where's the surprise there? I'm a fucking legend like that.

To this day, she still won't accept that I was right, but I wouldn't expect anything else from her. It's one of the many reasons I'm standing here today, desperate to make her my wife.

Glancing at my boys tucked safely in my brothers' arms, I give them a wide grin. They look like the next generation of heartbreakers in their little suits, and it reminds me of me and my brothers growing up. Hell, they look just like us, too. They both give me wide, toothy smiles, and my world lights up, somehow even more in love with these little monsters than ever before.

"Are you ready for this?" Logan asks.

"Hell, yeah," I grin. If anything, I've been standing here way too long. I've already had to wait a year for her to marry me and want nothing more than to get this show on the road. Though, it wouldn't be Brianna if she weren't late to her own fucking wedding.

The guests pour in, all wanting to take their sweet time, and I resist the urge to tell them to sit their asses down and get these nuptials underway.

I wait the longest half an hour of my life, and all it manages to do is remind me that my parents aren't here. I'm the last of the Waters siblings to get married, and they've missed all of them. I know they're here in spirit, looking down on us, but to be honest, they're probably just checking in to make sure we don't trash the property during the after-party.

When the soft music begins to flow through the garden, the guests finally take their seats, and before I know it, it's go time.

My heart melts the second little Georgie starts making her way down the aisle. She's the best flower girl I've ever seen, even though at eighteen months old, she's still a little wobbly. She tips out all the rose petals at the top of the aisle before her eyes land on her daddy and she takes off like a rocket to get to him. Oh well, she did her best.

Georgie refuses to stand on the girls' side, so Sean passes Parker to Jax so that he can scoop up his little girl.

The music continues, and Bri's bridesmaids come down next. Elle struts down the aisle with tears in her eyes looking stunning as usual, though more so with her tiny little four-month baby bump, making Logan drool beside me.

Cassie follows up the bridesmaids as the matron of honor, looking absolutely gorgeous in her bridesmaid dress and eight-month baby bump, though to be completely honest, she looks about ready to explode. Cass makes flirty glances at Jax, and I have to cut that shit down before they end up screwing behind the altar.

The music changes and my breath catches in my throat.

This is it. The moment I've been waiting for.

Brianna appears at the end of the aisle, her arm linked through her father's and taking my fucking breath away. Her silk wedding gown wraps around her the same way I wish to be, showing off her intoxicating curves. But it's the neckline that gets me. Her dark hair is up in some twisty bun thing, showing off her neck, making me jealous that all the men sitting among the guests can see what's mine.

I hear Bobby suck in a breath as he takes in his twin sister looking like an absolute goddess. I want to turn to him to see his face, but I don't dare take my eyes off her. I'd be a fool to miss even a second of this. I'm sure the videographer will get it, though even then, my eyes will still be on my girl.

The veil covers her face, but I can still make out her eyes through the sheer material, and the second her gaze falls on mine, her whole face lights up with undeniable happiness that blows me the fuck away.

She's beautiful.

Nate notices his mommy at the end of the aisle and squeals in delight, making me jealous that I can't do the same thing. Parker quickly joins in with his brother, and before I know it, so does Georgie, the three of them like a fucking wolf pack who always have each others' backs.

Brianna starts her march down the aisle, and I can't tear my eyes off her, my future walking toward me step by fucking step. Damn. I just want her to run so I can catch her in my arms and never let her go.

Being back together has been everything I needed and more. Every touch, every look, every damn moment has made me so incredibly blessed to have her back in my life.

Bri finally makes it to the end of the aisle, and her father reluctantly hands her over. He still isn't too thrilled about the whole breakup and knocking up his daughter thing. He loves the boys, maybe more than he loves Brianna, but that doesn't change the fact that I hurt his little girl. I don't blame him. I still hate myself for putting her through that.

I take her hands in mine, but I can't wait any longer to see her face, desperate to see the way her blazing green eyes light up with happiness. Stepping into her, I raise the veil over her head, and the second that gorgeous face comes into view, she fixes me with a beaming smile and my heart fucking explodes right here at the top of the aisle.

My hand slides up behind her neck and I pull her to me, my lips crashing down on hers as I kiss her with everything I've got, silently promising to live every day with her like it would be my last.

Laughter erupts among our guests, but I ignore them, insisting on taking my time and enjoying the beautiful woman in my arms. Besides, it's our wedding, and we should be able to indulge in every last second of it.

Logan clears his throat beside me. "I think this is supposed to come after the vows," he says, amusement in his tone as little Georgie is heard groaning in disgust at our display of affection.

Reluctantly, I pull away, but I don't dare release the woman in my arms. Instead, I drop my forehead to hers, breathing her in. "You look fucking radiant," I murmur for only her to hear.

Bri beams up at me, her eyes filled with undeniable love. "And you look like the rest of my life," she tells me, raw honesty in her sweet tone.

Fucking hell. The way this woman just knows how to work me. Every word out of her mouth only has me falling in love with her more.

I press my lips back to hers, a new hunger blasting through me, and I kiss her until she laughs, forcing me to cut off our kiss. "Can we get married now?" she questions.

"Fuck, yeah."

Over My Dead Body

Sheridan Anne

Thanks for reading

If you enjoyed reading this book as much as I enjoyed writing it, please consider leaving an Amazon review to let me know.

For more information on the Denver Royalty series, find me on Facebook –

www.facebook.com/sheridansbookishbabes

Stalk me

Join me online with the rest of the stalkers!!
I swear, I don't bite. Not unless you say please!

Facebook Reader Group
www.facebook.com/SheridansBookishBabes

Facebook Page
www.facebook.com/sheridan.anne.author1

Instagram
www.instagram.com/Sheridan.Anne.Author

TikTok
www.tiktok.com/@Sheridan.Anne.Author

Subscribe to my Newsletter
https://landing.mailerlite.com/webforms/landing/a8q0y0

More by Sheridan Anne

www.amazon.com/Sheridan-Anne/e/B079TLXN6K

DARK CONTEMPORARY ROMANCE - M/F

Broken Hill High | Haven Falls | Broken Hill Boys | Aston Creek High | Rejects Paradise | Bradford Bastard

DARK CONTEMPORARY ROMANCE - REVERSE HAREM

Boys of Winter | Depraved Sinners | Empire

NEW ADULT SPORTS ROMANCE

Kings of Denver | Denver Royalty | Rebels Advocate

CONTEMPORARY ROMANCE (standalones)

Play With Fire | Until Autumn (Happily Eva Alpha World)

PARANORMAL ROMANCE

Slayer Academy [Pen name - Cassidy Summers]

Ingram Content Group UK Ltd.
Milton Keynes UK
UKHW040807240723
425668UK00003B/202